THE WAGER AND THE WEDDING

The De Veres, Book 5

Leslie Vollard

ARE YOU SIGNED UP FOR DRAGONBLADE'S BLOG?

You'll get the latest news and information on exclusive giveaways, exclusive excerpts, coming releases, sales, free books, cover reveals and more.

Check out our complete list of authors, too!

No spam, no junk. That's a promise!

Sign Up Here

www.dragonbladepublishing.com

Dearest Reader;

Thank you for your support of a small press. At Dragonblade Publishing, we strive to bring you the highest quality Historical Romance from some of the best authors in the business. Without your support, there is no 'us', so we sincerely hope you adore these stories and find some new favorite authors along the way.

Happy Reading!

CEO, Dragonblade Publishing

Additional Dragonblade books by Author Leslie Vollard

The De Veres Series
The Skull and the Lute (Book 1)
The Sword and the Damsel (Book 2)
The Broken and the Bold (Book 3)
The Monk and the Maiden (Book 4)
The Wager and the Wedding (Book 5)

CHAPTER ONE

Northumberland, 1153 A.D.

MOTHER WAS SMILING, and that was never a good sign. Isabella put down her armful of scrolls on her mother's angled desk and turned to leave quickly, fearing what that smile might mean. If she had to guess, it had something to do with the baron who had arrived the previous night, talking to her father about marriage, but she prayed she was wrong. While she hadn't seen the man, she'd overheard enough to make her worry.

Clutching her heavy green wool shawl around her shoulders, she reached for the door.

"Not so fast, Little Bird," her mother said from her bed.

God's teeth, she hated that nickname! It was ridiculous, especially now that she was significantly taller than her mother. There was nothing little about her.

"Come help me up," her mother ordered.

Isabella seethed inwardly as she made her way to her mother's side and helped her rise, pull on a brown wool robe over her cream linen shift, and seat herself at her desk.

"Stoke the fire. There's a draft in here."

Icy February winds rattled the shutters, and her mother's room was so cold, Isabella could see her breath. Bamburgh Castle certainly wasn't designed for the comfort of its residents. It might be good for fending off Vikings and Scots, but wind was another matter. How she missed the moderate climate of her native

Bordeaux!

Grudgingly, Isabella added a log to the fire and nudged it a few times with a poker. It rankled how her mother had always treated her daughters like servants. At least Isabella had the strength to stand up to it, unlike her little sister, Adelaide.

"Comb my hair and tell me the news," the countess ordered as she began to peruse the scrolls with brisk efficiency.

Isabella bristled at the command.

"Shouldn't your lady's maid do this?" Really, her mother was pushing too far. Isabella wasn't the biddable girl from five years ago that her mother had sent away to court.

"You'll do as you're told, girl," her mother snapped, slapping her hand down on the desk. "I swear, you are just as ill-mannered as you were the day that I sent you off to Queen Eleanor to be her lady-in-waiting. Shall I write to her and tell her how disobedient and ungrateful you've become?"

If there was anyone Isabella did not want to cross, it was Her Grace, Eleanor of Aquitaine, no longer queen of France but soon to be queen of England, she hoped. Isabella had been with the duchess through every agonizing moment of her annulment with King Louis, the kidnapping attempts that followed, and her hasty marriage to Henry, Duke of Normandy. And then, with no explanation, Isabella had been sent away.

Biting her tongue with difficulty, Isabella slid off the ribbon that held her mother's gray-streaked chestnut locks in a simple braid, picked up the tortoise shell comb, and began pulling it through the silken skein. She still remembered how to read her mother's moods like a Book of Hours. That smile spelled danger. Would her mother give anything away about the strange man as Isabella gave her morning update?

She almost missed serving Queen Eleanor. It should have been a relief for Isabella to return to her family after all that had transpired, but she had only traded one ruthless matriarch for another. Though they looked entirely different, her mother petite and dark-haired and Lady Eleanor a voluptuous redhead, they had the same cold eyes.

What had she done to anger Her Grace? The thought gnawed at her. There had to be some explanation.

"A man named Lord Martin arrived last night," Isabella said, combing out the tangles none too gently. She paused to see if her mother would mention the man's marriage intentions, but she remained silent. "I overheard him telling Father that Henry is back in England attempting to relieve the siege at Wallingford by besieging King Stephen's castle at Malmesbury. The king is livid, but his barons don't want outright battle with Henry, especially not in the middle of winter. It's only a matter of time before King Stephen falls and Henry takes the throne."

Her mother's smile broadened. "Good. Very good. Our efforts on Henry's behalf are coming to fruition. Your father isn't much use for anything except hacking people apart in battle, but his guests do bring the most delicious tidbits our way. You have been very useful to me, do you know that, Little Bird?"

"Please don't call me that." The urge to yank her mother's hair became almost intolerable.

"Such a shame you're so tall and awkward," her mother continued, setting aside the scrolls and turning to look at Isabella. "If only you were prettier, you might have found a decent husband by now. At least you've learned your lessons at court well. You never did miss a thing when I sent you out to spy for me, and I see nothing has changed."

Isabella had hated doing her mother's dirty work as a girl, but she'd never been given much choice. And her mother wasn't wrong. She was good at what she did. At least it kept her mother's attention away from Adelaide, who had been frail and sickly ever since a fever when she was a baby.

It had broken Isabella's heart upon her return to see how pale and thin her sister was, like a plant deprived of sunlight. Guilt flooded Isabella every time she thought of the years she'd spent away, unable to give her sister the love and support she needed to thrive.

"It's such a shame I must give you up," her mother said, almost as an afterthought.

All the air left Isabella's lungs in a rush as if she'd received a blow. The last time her mother made a pronouncement like that, Isabella had been thirteen, and they had still been living near Bordeaux. Her mother sent her off to King Louis and Queen Eleanor's court. Five years passed with barely a word from her family until her father inherited the Bamburgh earldom from a distant cousin and she was abruptly sent away from Her Grace to her new home. And now she was being exiled again?

Her thoughts immediately went to Adelaide. Isabella had hoped to find a way to get her sister safely away from this poisonous place before she was forced to go away again.

"What do you mean you have to 'give me up'?" she asked carefully.

There was a knock on the door, and her mother's grin widened. "Oh good. Adelaide is here too. Come in, Little Mouse!"

Adelaide peeked into the room. Isabella's heart squeezed painfully at the sight of her fourteen-year-old sister, thin as a reed, her wispy, sable hair in a careless braid down her back. She shuffled into the room and took a place beside Isabella, eyes on the floor.

"I'm glad you're both here because this concerns both of you," her mother said, looking between them. Isabella met her gaze steadily. She would not show weakness in front of this woman. "Lady Eleanor, in her infinite wisdom, has selected a husband for you, Isabella, and she has requested that Adelaide join her in Normandy, taking your place."

Panic gripped Isabella. She was braced for the news about a prospective husband, but Adelaide's summons to Normandy was a complete surprise. Isabella flicked her gaze toward her sister just in time to see Adelaide's back go rigid. Her sister's breathing rasped as she stared fixedly at the floor, eyes wide.

"What do you mean?" Isabella only barely managed to keep her voice even as she tried to match her mother's cold nonchalance. The countess didn't take kindly to displays of emotion.

"The man you overheard talking to your father last night? That was the Martin de Vere, Baron of Winchelsea. He arrived yesterday, bearing a signed and sealed letter from Lady Eleanor with her instructions. She wishes you to marry him."

The news descended on Isabella with the force of a headsman's axe. It was all she could do to remain standing, even though she was expecting such a blow. Adelaide's eyes met hers for a split second, offering sympathy before she hurriedly looked back at the floor.

"Speechless with gratitude, I see."

Truly, there were no words.

"Little Mouse, get out my brown wool gown with the gold-trimmed sleeves." Adelaide hurried to the chest with her mother's dresses and laid out the requested gown, then squeezed herself into a corner of the room as if trying to disappear.

"Little Bird, finish my hair then return to your chambers and put on your best gown. You marry at noon."

Noon? Of this very day? She needed more time to undo this, but it seemed her mother and her monarch had already thought of that.

"I'm not marrying Lord Martin, and Adelaide is absolutely not going to Normandy." Lady Eleanor and her mother had out-maneuvered her quite neatly, but they both underestimated her if they thought she would accept this unchallenged.

"Don't be ridiculous, girl. Your future queen has asked you to do your duty. I know you know better than to risk Lady Eleanor's wrath."

It was true. Isabella had seen what happened to women who tried to cross the once and future queen. She still remembered when Lady Collette was caught spreading the rumor that Queen Eleanor had slept with her uncle. Her Majesty retaliated by producing a fabricated marriage certificate as proof that Lady Collette had secretly married a goatherd before she wedded Lord Etienne. The queen sent it to the Pope, and Lady Collette's marriage was annulled, leaving the unlucky lady utterly humiliated and in poverty. Perhaps Isabella should count herself lucky that she was only being married off to a baron.

"There must be a way to undo this. What if I propose a better match that is more advantageous to Lady Eleanor and bring Adelaide with me?" It was worth a try. At least it would buy some time.

Her mother laughed. "You presume to know better than Her Grace? Her orders were quite clear. I have her letter right here. And frankly, you should be grateful. Men don't like tall women. As for your sister, she'll do as she's told, just as she always has. She'll travel with you as far as Winchelsea, and then you will put her on a ship to France."

Adelaide turned a wide-eyed, panicked gaze on Isabella, who tried to convey as much silent reassurance as she could manage.

But Isabella herself was anything but calm. Adelaide would never survive the journey, let alone serving the Duchess of Normandy. There had to be a way to save her sister. But a mere baron would be of no help when it came to defying Lady Eleanor, especially if he came to Bamburgh Castle at the duchess's bidding. Isabella needed to marry someone powerful who could stand his ground.

Her mother pulled a scroll of parchment from her desk drawer and handed it to Isabella. "See for yourself if you don't believe me."

Taking the document, Isabella fought the urge to throw it into the fire. But destroying it wouldn't change its contents. Her and Adelaide's futures were laid out in plain Latin, and there was no mistaking the signature at the end. Adelaide scurried to her side and peeked at it with her. What were they going to do now?

"Seethe all you like, but finish brushing my hair while you do it," her mother ordered.

"No. I'm not your lady's maid." Isabella was altogether too angry to keep doing her mother's bidding.

The countess grabbed her hand, digging in her nails. "You'll do as you're told, Little Bird."

Lips pursed, Isabella relented, soothing the skin where her mother had left red marks. Her fingers went through the motions without any input from her mind, which spun frantically seeking a loophole. All the while, she kept casting glances at Adelaide, who had somehow grown even more pale than her natural state.

"I'm finished," Isabella said as she jabbed the final hairpin in place with a little bit too much force.

"Ouch!" Her mother gave her a dirty look and adjusted the pin. "Impudent girl. I can see your temper is as fierce as it always was. I can only hope your husband knows how to tame you. Lord knows I've failed. You are dismissed. And you too, Little Mouse."

With a perfunctory curtsy, Isabella turned to go, putting a protective arm around her sister and leading her out.

"Little Bird," her mother said in a sing-song voice just as they reached the door, forcing them to pause. "Don't think you can get out of this. I can practically see the wheels turning in that devious mind of yours. The duchess has declared you will marry, and you shall. She needs someone she can trust in Winchelsea. It's an important port, only a stone's throw from Hastings, and the baron has sway with the Cinque Ports."

While the Cinque Ports were a critical link to the continent and had high strategic importance, marrying a complete stranger of low rank from a town she'd never heard of solved none of her problems and left Adelaide at Lady Eleanor's mercy.

"It is wise of her to take steps to ensure her control over the Cinque Ports," Isabella said in as even a voice as she could manage, knowing she'd gone too far by jabbing that pin. "And I am always happy to serve Her Grace in any way I can. But why now? Truly, she honors us too much with her thoughtfulness."

The countess shook her head and smiled. "You read her letter. It says she likes you and thinks he'll be a good match for you."

Isabella didn't believe that for a moment. Lady Eleanor never did anything out of the kindness of her heart. "A good match,"

Isabella answered, meeting her mother's cold gaze. "You must be joking."

"Do you doubt the word of your mother and your rightful queen?"

The countess smiled deviously. Once upon a time, Isabella had lived for that smile. It meant she was going to have a chance to prove herself. But that was back when she was foolish enough to believe anything would earn her mother's respect. Over the years, she had learned better.

"Very good," her mother said, mistaking her silence for acquiescence. "I'm glad we understand each other. I would hate to think you would displease me by refusing the generous gift Lady Eleanor is offering. Now go get dressed and pack up your things, both of you. You leave for Winchelsea tomorrow morning."

Unable to form words, Isabella turned her back and reached for the door, clutching Adelaide's hand.

"Goodbye. I'll see you in the chapel in a few hours," her mother said, waving them out.

Isabella stormed through the door without replying, pushing Adelaide ahead of her, and slammed it behind them.

For a moment, the urge to cry almost overtook her, but she caught herself just in time. Clenching her fists, she led Adelaide down the echoing halls of the castle to the tiny, windowless chamber they shared and closed the door.

"Are you all right?" Isabella asked as soon as they were alone.

"I will be. It's not as if we have a choice." Adelaide sat down on her narrow bed and rested her head in her hands.

"There is always a choice. I'll find a way out of this for us."

Rummaging through her trunk of gowns, Isabella considered their options. Could they run? No, that would be foolish. Women couldn't travel alone through the countryside without risking life and limb, especially not in the midst of a civil war. And where would they go?

Perhaps she could convince Lord Martin not to marry her. If only she could get the man alone for a few minutes before the ceremony, she could try to convince him she was an unmarriage-able shrew. Lord knew her parents already thought her one. But would that buy her enough time to come up with a real plan? It was worth a try. She had to do *something*.

Reaching into her trunk, she pulled out the gown folded in the bottom. As she shook it out, a tear dripped down her cheek. Truth be told, Isabella sewed this dress with the intention of being married in it, but the wedding she dreamed of was so very different. She would walk down the aisle of Westminster Abbey to wed a powerful earl with her family and Lady Eleanor, now queen of England, looking on. She would be able to look with equanimity at her parents, knowing it would be the last time she or Adelaide had to see them. After years of faithful service, she had earned her rightful place by the side of a man of high position.

In her daydreams, the man she married would offer her free-dom and respect, never making demands and giving her a free hand to manage the household. He would appreciate her mind, be able to match wits with her but never demand to win for the sake of winning. Alas, such a man did not exist outside of fairytales and troubadours' songs.

In real life, the most she could hope for was to marry for power and influence and make the best of things. After watching her parents' marriage and Lady Eleanor's disastrous match with King Louis VII, she knew better than to expect anything but misery from the institution, so she might as well have power and wealth to compensate so that she could have some modicum of comfort and independence. This baron from Winchelsea could offer neither, so she had to find a way out.

Drying her tears and stiffening her spine, she pulled on the heavy velvet gown with sleeves that dripped to the floor. She pinned up her hair in neat side buns and donned a jeweled crespinette that fit her like a crown with circles of gold netting covering the buns.

"Leave it to me," Isabella said, patting her skirt. "Meet me in the solar after the church bell rings for Terce, and I'll let you know the plan."

Adelaide nodded and started packing up her things.

There was no need for Isabella to pack. All her worldly belongings were already folded away in her chest, as she had only just arrived.

Squaring her shoulders and opening the door, she set out to see if she could convince her future husband to call it off before the church bells struck noon.

Chapter Two

MARTIN NEEDED AN intelligent wife. That was his one request during his brief audience with the Duchess of Normandy when he'd paid her a visit in the fall.

He went seeking an arranged marriage. Though he was still grieving the loss of his father, he knew his duty to his people as a newly-minted baron. It had not escaped his notice that he was the only Cinque Ports baron that lacked a bride, and he knew the Duke of Normandy needed loyalty from the ports if he was to succeed in his bid to become king of England. Thanks to his father's efforts, Martin had strong ties with the other barons, and they were sickened at the civil war that had reigned since King Stephen had taken the throne. Martin was their representative, testing the waters to see how the prospective king might view the ports.

Which was why he was currently dressed in his finest cotte, breaking his fast in the great hall of Ferdinand de Martillac, the new earl of Bamburgh, attempting to tamp down his nerves about meeting his bride. What would she think of him? He wasn't some handsome paragon. He was the sort of man women looked at and decided they wanted to be friends with—middling height, middling looks, middling social standing. As the daughter of an earl, she'd probably be disappointed to find herself marrying a baron. Fortunately, he had more wit than the average man. If she could look past the surface, perhaps he could win her over.

The morning meal was an informal affair with members of the earl's household and some of his higher-ranking soldiers wandering in and out at their leisure. The hall's rough stone walls were unadorned, the family having just taken possession of the castle the previous month. But despite its spare décor, the space still had a rugged grandeur. It was at least twice the size of his great hall back in Winchelsea.

Martin sat at the head table beside the earl, forcing himself to pick at the food before him to stay calm. There was no going back now. Lady Eleanor's letter had been delivered, and the wheels were turning. He would be a married man by sunset, whether he was ready or not.

He'd even shaved off his moustache for the occasion. His upper lip felt naked without it, but he knew his bride wouldn't appreciate such an unfashionable affectation. He wasn't what most women would consider a prize in terms of looks, and he didn't want to make it worse.

"I hear you have been quite successful with shipping investments," Lord Ferdinand said, taking a bite of fresh-baked bread with a slice of hard cheese on top, a few crumbs falling down the front of his heavy wool surcotte.

"I have been very fortunate, my lord, and I take an active interest in my investments. Like my father, I take to sea as often as I can manage. I know every port from Ribe in the north to Malta in the south, and I've journeyed as far as Venice in my travels. But since my father's passing, I have been unable to travel much. Pressing matters at home in Winchelsea have prevented me. That is one of several reasons I asked Lady Eleanor to find me a wife. I need someone who can manage my interests on land when I take to sea."

Lord Ferdinand washed down his bread with a swig of ale. "If you manage to win Isabella over, which I assure you will not be an easy task, I think you'll find her quite capable of managing in your absence. Perhaps a little bit too capable. Don't let her get too comfortable, or she'll try to start managing you as well. Believe me. I speak from experience."

Good. Martin liked a woman who could hold her own. "Your daughter manages here?"

His lordship waved his hand dismissively. "Not Isabella. My wife. But the two of them are far too alike—peas in a pod, as they say." He took another drink. "I'm the earl. You'd think this household would answer to me, but everyone knows who truly holds the power. God, how I wish I were back on campaign with the Duke of Normandy. Unfortunately, His Grace wants me here. Says he needs an ally in the north. So I'm stuck in this drafty castle with my loving wife, dancing like a marionette to her tune, God help me. Watch yourself, or you'll go the same way. Mark my words."

Martin bit back a smile. This all sounded very promising. He wasn't afraid of a little challenge. On the contrary, he relished the thought. Other men might fear such a wife, but Martin had learned a great deal from his parents' happy marriage. "Thank you for the advice, my lord. I will be wary."

And he would. But he liked a woman with a mind of her own. How could he not with a mother like his? Lady Aveline was his father's partner, his equal, guiding Winchelsea with firm conviction while he sailed far and wide, establishing trade partnerships that had turned around the town's fortunes. If she hadn't lost most of her vision after the same fever that took his father, Martin would have happily left her in charge for years to come. She was the one who had advised him to seek out the duchess and ask for a bride after his father passed. Constant civil war had taken too much of a toll, and she believed Henry could bring peace as king.

"I'm headed out for a ride," Lord Ferdinand said, rising from his place. "Care to join me? The weather is godawful, but I can't stay cooped up in this place another minute."

Martin glanced at the tall, narrow windows of the hall. Snow swirled down in the whistling wind. "No, thank you, my lord. I must write a letter to Lady Eleanor to let her know I have arrived according to plan."

"As you wish." The earl turned, clapping twice. A servant hurried over. "Malcolm, bring parchment, a quill, and ink for our guest."

Malcolm bowed and hurried off to find the necessary implements.

"I shall see you at the chapel at noon, Lord Martin. Enjoy your last few hours as a free man."

With that, the earl swept out of the room.

Martin finished his breakfast, feeling considerably better after that conversation. What would his bride be like? How would he win her over?

He wasn't tall and handsome like his little brother, Lance. But what he lacked in looks, he'd always made up for with cleverness and wicked humor. It wasn't easy wooing women with Lance around, but he'd had some occasional success. He knew how to weave words to great effect.

Lady Eleanor had warned him that Isabella had a sharp wit. Nothing would please him more than to win a woman who knew how to stand her ground. Like the Roman dictator, Fabius, he would goad her to engage with him and retreat to leave her wanting more. It had worked for him before, and he hoped it would work here.

One way or another, he would win her over. He had a great deal of affection to give and would do his best to be a good husband to his bride. She might never love him the way his mother loved his father, but he could offer her a good life.

His thoughts were interrupted by the return of Malcolm with the writing implements he'd requested. He turned his attention to the task at hand and was halfway through composing a missive when an arrestingly beautiful young woman entered the hall and fixed her piercing gaze on him.

The woman's dark eyes threatened to bore a hole in him as she strode toward him in a blue velvet gown that hugged the curves of her statuesque figure. Her dark hair was pinned up beneath some sort of headdress. He was no expert in women's fashions, but he thought the regal attire suited her perfectly.

She stopped by his side without saying a word, merely taking in every detail with a haughty, disapproving glare. By God, she was magnificent! Was it possible this vision in blue was his bride?

"My lady," he said, standing and pulling out her chair for her, noticing as he did, that she was several inches taller than he. "Allow me to introduce myself. My name is Martin. I'm the Baron of Winchelsea. I arrived last night and don't know anyone here besides the earl. Would I be correct in assuming you are one of his daughters?"

She sat down and unsheathed her eating dagger, keeping it in her grasp rather than laying it on the table. "I know who you are and why you are here. I wanted to speak with you before this travesty of a wedding takes place," she said in a low voice, then glanced around to check that no one overheard.

So it was to be war. He stifled a smile. "I take it you are Lady Isabella?"

"Yes," she said, looking him up and down with a threatening squeeze of her knife. "There's been a terrible mistake. I'm sorry you came all this way for nothing."

Her frosty expression might have put another man off, but it lit a flame within him. "Oh? Do tell."

"Lady Eleanor must have been thinking of Isabella of Dover. It's not the first time the two of us have been confused."

Martin nodded gravely. "Do you mean the baroness Isabella who is married to my friend Herbert?"

Isabella pursed her lips until they turned white. "I see you know the family."

"Quite well, and Herbert was in excellent health when I saw him last month. His wife was certainly not a widow seeking a second marriage. Are you going to bring up Isabella of Boggy Bottom next? I hear she is quite a catch."

"Are you mocking me, my lord?" she asked, eyes narrowing.

"I would never mock my bride-to-be." He held her gaze steadily, enjoying the way her irritation made her flush pink. Why did he find headstrong women so irresistible?

"You wouldn't want to marry me. I would make your life miserable."

"Is that so?" he asked, thoughtfully. "And here I'd heard such wonderful things about you. Why, your father was just telling me how delightful you are."

Her grip on her eating dagger tightened until her knuckles were white. "Then you are hard of hearing, my lord."

Martin would have been rubbing his hands together in glee if it wouldn't have given away his game. The first arrows had been unleashed. *Let the battle begin.*

"Not in the least. He praised your virtue, your beauty, and your intelligence. How could I not wish to wed you?" Her cheeks grew redder with each word of praise. By God, she was lovely when she was riled up.

"If you believed that, then you have as much wit as this chair I sit on."

Some demon possessed him to say, "If I am a chair, then come sit on my lap."

She gave him a scornful look. "Don't get your hopes up."

"Too late, my lady. My hopes grow with every word from your sweet lips." *And every lash of your sharp tongue.*

"Then you are a fool. I am not for you, Little Baron."

He grinned. "Little Baron? Is that the best you can come up with?"

"You wish for worse? I assure you, my lord, I can sting you where it hurts. Don't tempt me."

He sat back and crossed his arms. "Do your worst, honeybee. Let's hear it."

"You asked for it, you walnut-sized nitwit," she said, shaking her head.

"Do you insult my height or my length, my lady? You must be more specific."

Her ears flamed red as she took his meaning. "Ugh. Cease talking. More of your conversation would infect my brain."

"What can I say? I am infectious." He was enjoying this far too much.

"Truly, you are a disease, my lord. You make me sick."

"Lovesick already? I had no idea I was so potent."

"I told you to cease talking, you toad. Your croaking offends my ears."

"In faith, my lady, I am disappointed. Surely you can find some more interesting way to insult me." With Lance as his brother, he'd already had a lifetime of unflattering comparisons to thicken his hide. Her barbs couldn't pierce his good humor.

"You are too far beneath my notice, and I can't be bothered," she said, turning her attention to her bread and cheese and taking a large bite.

Martin considered her in silence for a long moment. "Do you know," he said at last, "I think you're putting on an act. Your heart doesn't seem to be in this. Are you pretending to be a shrew to put me off marriage?"

She choked on her bread and had to wash it down with a generous swallow of ale. Clearly, he'd hit close to the mark. Time to retreat and lure her in.

"I see," he said, softening. Poor thing. He'd had several months to get used to the idea of matrimony, whereas she only just learned of the match. "What can I do to put your mind at ease? I promise to take things slowly. I insisted on forgoing the bedding ceremony when I arranged things with your father for the wedding. I know it will take time for you to get used to the idea of being my bride, and I swear to you I will do everything in my power to be a patient and good husband to you."

His bride sighed and closed her eyes. "You aren't the right man, and this isn't the right time."

Words of truth at last. "If that's the case, what do you propose we do?"

She must see how impossible it would be to defy Lady Eleanor in this matter.

"I don't know," she said softly, her shoulders sagging. "Did you know it's my birthday today? What a way to celebrate turning eighteen."

"I'm sorry. This must all be something of a shock to you." He reached out and put a hand over hers, squeezing gently, then withdrawing quickly at her venomous look. Her skin was so soft and warm beneath his. The brief contact made him long for more, but clearly, she wouldn't welcome it. Yet.

She met his gaze, fierce eyes gleaming with unshed tears, and his heart melted. He had to win her favor if it was the last thing he did.

"I have a proposal," he said, folding his hands together to keep from reaching out and stroking her cheek. "We must go through with the wedding. Lady Eleanor has made her wishes known, and your parents want the match. We could hardly defy them in their own castle. But there's no reason we must consummate it. Give me…let's say…the time it takes us to travel to Winchelsea to win you over. If by the end of our journey you still feel I am the wrong man at the wrong time, we can have the marriage annulled. I have no desire for an unwilling wife. All I ask is that you keep an open mind and let me woo you for the duration of our voyage."

She blinked. "I know I cannot defy Lady Eleanor, especially not while I'm under my parents' roof. I accept your offer on one condition."

A little flame of hope sprang up in Martin's breast at her words. "Yes, my lady?"

"Let my sister, Adelaide, stay with me at Winchelsea while I find a new husband. She is supposed to continue to Normandy to enter the duchess's service as soon as we arrive, but I wish to delay her journey until my future is settled."

It would be tricky keeping Lady Adelaide in defiance of Her Grace's wishes, but he supposed he could figure out a way to explain a minor delay. If it helped him win Isabella over, it would be worth it.

"As long as it's a brief stay, it would be my pleasure. I don't wish to risk Lady Eleanor's ire, but I doubt she'll notice a few extra weeks."

Isabella narrowed her eyes and pursed her lips, and she looked at him in silence.

"Are we agreed then?" he asked tentatively.

"We are, my lord," she said at last.

Wonderful news! In just a few hours, he would wed this lovely, intelligent woman, and he had weeks at sea to convince her to stay. That should be more than enough time to win her over. The Fabian strategy was working.

"You are grinning too much, my lord. Don't get your hopes up. I am not the wife for you." She stood, gave him a little nod, and swept out of the hall.

We shall see, my lady. We shall see.

CHAPTER THREE

PERHAPS NOT ALL hope was lost, Isabella thought as she made her way to the solar. The soft padding of her feet in her pointy-toed, leather-soled pigaches echoed in the bare stone corridors of Bamburgh Castle. At least she would be heading south soon. Not as far south as she would like. Winchelsea was still a long way from her childhood home in Bordeaux. But the weather would be milder.

And maybe Lord Martin was someone she could work with. Not that she could trust him an inch. After all, he was Lady Eleanor's man. He was also deeply irritating, the preening fool. But the deal he struck indicated he might be malleable, persuadable. If she could only convince him to annul the wedding, perhaps she could salvage this terrible situation. She just needed to keep up her shrew act long enough to convince him to give her up.

As she entered the solar, she was relieved to find it empty. She needed a moment to herself. All she wanted was to sit at the loom and mull things over as her fingers went through the motions of weaving in different colored threads. It was easier to think when her hands were occupied. Something about the rhythm of tapestry weaving seemed to clear her mind and help her puzzle out the thorniest problems.

This room had received more attention than the rest of the castle as the family settled in. Tapestries depicting the Crusades hung on the walls. Her father was quite proud to have gone on crusade with King Louis and Queen Eleanor back in 1147. His armor stood vigil at one end of the room, a lurking presence that never ceased to make Isabella feel uneasy. The swords of defeated enemies hung on hooks above the hearth at the other side of the room.

The scene emerging on the loom was of yet another battle. Her mother's bloodthirsty nature played out in handicrafts. Isabella was quite certain her mother's disdain for her father was born of jealousy. Why should he get to ride out into battle when she was forced to stay at home and sew?

Settling on a wooden stool, Isabella began to weave. And plot.

Several weeks' journey wasn't very long for her to figure out her future or to rescue Adelaide, but she was certain she could play the shrew sufficiently well to put Lord Martin off. Not that the act was too far from the truth. The man was insufferable, and she had no desire whatsoever to find herself tied to him for life.

Once she was rid of him, should she marry an English earl or a Norman count? Either would suit her purpose, though she needed someone with enough distance from the duke and duchess to defy them and keep Adelaide. As she mentally listed her marriage prospects and weighed their relative advantages, her fingers flew across the strings of the loom.

How would she gain their attention? Lady Eleanor might be able to send a missive to the man she wanted to marry and have him come running, but Isabella didn't have the richest province in France to entice her prospective groom. She would have to find some other means of convincing them to come to her aid, especially since, to all outward appearances, she would already be wed.

Looking down at her work, she realized she'd woven a strand of green where she needed to weave white, and she went back and fixed it before settling back into the rhythm of the loom.

Who should she choose? The Earl of York, the Earl of Norfolk, and the Earl of Chester were the three most promising candidates for husband that came to mind. Each one offered a different strategic advantage. All three were currently unmarried. The Earl of York was a supporter of King Stephen's. He would certainly be willing to defy the Duke and Duchess of Normandy, but would he even consider Isabella a prospect after her time with Lady Eleanor? The Earl of Norfolk, on the other hand, remained neutral, courting both sides in the war but aligning himself with neither. The Earl of Chester was a Norman by birth and a longtime supporter of Henry's claim, but he thought Lady Eleanor wielded too much influence over her husband. He might be willing to take her down a peg by defying her, though it was risky.

Finishing a row, she checked the pattern that was emerging and checked her thread supplies. She was going to need more brown for this next row. There were a lot of horses to depict. Reaching into a wide basket on the floor beside her, she pulled out another roll of brown and began her weaving again.

Of the three, the Earl of Norfolk seemed the most likely candidate. She'd met him several times, even flirted with him once at a saint's day festival. He'd gone as far as kissing her, though she had escaped before things went any further. He had a reputation for ruthlessness and ambition that she thought she could work to her favor. She cared far less about what kind of husband he would be than about his ability to protect her and Adelaide. His persistent neutrality in the face of civil war gave her confidence that he would think nothing of defying Lady Eleanor's demand for Adelaide.

Her thoughts were interrupted by the opening of the door. Adelaide entered, carrying a lute, and her red-rimmed eyes told Isabella she'd been crying.

"Do you have a plan yet?" Adelaide asked, loosening the thick shawl around her shoulders.

"I have the start of a plan. The less you know the better, at least until we set sail," she answered carefully. "Otherwise,

Mother might try to pry it out of you. You've never been good at keeping secrets. Your face gives everything away."

Adelaide nodded and sniffed. "I know. I'm sorry."

"Don't be. You are honest and innocent, and I pray that never changes." Isabella dropped her hands from the loom and reached out to squeeze her sister's arm.

"Have you met your husband yet?" Adelaide asked, blinking back a new round of tears.

"Yes," Isabella answered with a frown. "I met Lord Martin this morning."

Adelaide put down the lute, leaning it against the wall, and pulled a high-backed chair over beside her sister, putting a gentle hand on Isabella's that almost broke her. "What's he like?"

Isabella closed her eyes and pulled away, willing herself to stay calm. It was too much that her sister was worrying about her when she should be worrying about herself. And what could she possibly reveal about Lord Martin without offending her sister's ears?

The man was a coxcomb and not to be trusted. She didn't like the mischievous twinkle in his chestnut eyes or the way his dark brows arched in amusement. But when his red lips curved into that arrogant smile of his, something within her seized up. It must have been from revulsion. That was the only reasonable explanation.

Why did Lady Eleanor pair her with someone so unsuitable? This eager popinjay was not someone Isabella could tolerate, regardless of his sharp wit or his generous offer. It must be a punishment of some sort from Her Grace.

"He's an ass," she blurted, then covered her mouth.

And he didn't care a whit when she insulted him, which was strangely alluring. *No, no.* It wouldn't do to start thinking of Lord Martin as alluring in any way.

Adelaide cracked a smile at her slip. "That's all you have to say about him? That's rather uncreative, coming from you."

No, she could say a great deal more, but it was easier to fixate on that than on his enervating appeal, which she had no desire to acknowledge aloud.

"He's an irritatingly optimistic baron from a town of no importance with an exasperating sense of humor. And if Lady Eleanor sent him, he is not to be trusted. My bridegroom is merely the final insult in this steaming heap of humiliation."

Her sister's smile broadened. "You protest too much. I'm starting to think you like him."

"What? No. Impossible. How could I like a man whose attentions are intended to mortify me? If there was any justice in the world, Lady Eleanor would have recognized my worth and matched me with a husband suitable to my rank and years of loyal service. But no. She's discarding me like yesterday's table scraps, despite my efforts in her name."

Unable to sit still, Isabella stood and started pacing. "Didn't I help her collect the dirty details she needed to persuade King Louis to annul their marriage? Didn't I risk life and limb fleeing with her to Aquitaine as kidnappers pursued her? Didn't I braid flowers into her hair the day she married the Duke of Normandy in secret? In what way have I failed her to deserve such a fate?"

Adelaide shrugged in sympathy. "Have you considered the possibility that this isn't a punishment? Perhaps Lady Eleanor thought you and he would suit. And maybe she thinks you'll be safer in the days to come if you're with a backwater baron than with one of her prominent vassals. There is a war on, after all."

Isabella squeezed her eyes shut and clenched her fists. "Have you ever known Lady Eleanor to do something kind and considerate? You know the woman has no heart. If only I were more like her."

If only Isabella could quash all her inconvenient emotions and follow Lady Eleanor's example! With her cold, calculating mind, she'd find a way out of this fix in no time.

"I only know what you tell me about her," Adelaide answered. "You make her sound just like Mother." She picked up her lute and started tuning it.

Isabella shook her head. "Mother is merely mean. Lady Eleanor is diabolical. And why shouldn't she be? Look where it's gotten her. She was queen of France, and any day now, she's going to be queen of England."

"Yes, but she doesn't sound like a very happy person." Adelaide plucked a few tentative chords.

"Nobody's happy in this world. The best we can hope for is to marry a man of position who protects us and our loved ones from harm."

Adelaide gave her a level look. "Now *you* sound like Mother."

That stung, but she could hardly tell Adelaide her true motivation. It wouldn't do to burden her narrow shoulders with the weight of it. "I'm sorry. It seems I've grown cynical over the years. You shouldn't listen to a word I say, sweeting. You're far too good for this world."

Her sister put down her lute and came over to Isabella, opening her arms for a hug.

It was embarrassing how badly Isabella needed that hug. Surrendering her dignity, she stood up and embraced her sister. Adelaide felt so small and fragile in her arms. Isabella was almost afraid she was going to break her.

"I'm so sorry this is happening," Adelaide murmured in her ear.

Something inside Isabella broke at those words, and she began sobbing uncontrollably against her sister's boney shoulder.

"There, there," Adelaide said in a soothing singsong. "It's going to be all right. You are strong and clever, and underneath all your prickliness and sharp wit, I know you have a loving heart. Together, we'll find a way through this."

Isabella sniffed. "You overestimate me. The truth is, I'm just like Mother. She and Lady Eleanor have made sure to purge any tender sentiments I might have possessed. I'm as heartless as they are."

Tears ran down her cheeks, and despite her protestations, she must have had a heart because it was breaking at her sister's kindness.

"Hush." Adelaide murmured a steady stream of empty reassurances as the storm blew itself out.

After several long minutes, Isabella was able to take deep breaths and compose herself. Thank God no one had come in to witness this pathetic display. She untangled herself from her sister's arms and went to a side table with a water pitcher and basin. Pouring water, she splashed some on her face. The cool, refreshing drops cleared the last of the distress, and steely resolve replaced the aching vulnerability she'd felt in her sister's arms.

"I'm better now," Isabella said, as she returned to her stool by the loom. "I can face this. I'm sorry for losing control like that."

"Don't be."

The sympathetic look on her sister's face almost sent her over the edge again, so she turned to look at her father's armor. That was what she needed—a metal suit to shield her from harm.

"Play me a song of war," Isabella said without meeting her sister's gaze. "No love songs today. We need to prepare for battle."

A moment later, Adelaide began strumming swift, martial chords and started singing their father's favorite song about King Arthur at the Battle of Camlann in her quivery soprano.

Isabella began weaving again, taking heart from the lyrics about bravery and sacrifice, as King Arthur triumphed over Mordred. Fortunately, there wasn't time for Adelaide to sing all the way to the tragic end where King Arthur perished after his victory. Sure enough, as Adelaide reached the climactic moment, the door to the solar opened, and a servant walked in.

Adelaide stopped playing, and their mother's lady's maid entered and said, "The countess requires your presence in the chapel, Lady Isabella."

"I wish Crispin was here," Adelaide said dismally. "He'd put a stop to all this."

Isabella shook her head sadly. "We probably won't ever see our brother again. If he survives this war, Father will surely bring him back here, and we'll be at the other end of the country." The three of them had been inseparable as children. Crispin had always been his sisters' greatest defender, but he was a knight in the service of the Duke of Normandy now. There was no way to enlist his help in their current troubles.

"My lady?" her mother's maid inquired.

This was it. There was no avoiding this wedding. She could only pray that her new husband stuck to his end of the bargain and that she had a chance to execute her plan. What she would do if she ended up stuck with the obnoxious baron for the rest of her life, she had no idea.

"I'm coming. Let's get this over with, shall we?"

Taking her sister's arm, she swallowed her anxiety and mentally donned her armor, ready to face battle. She would marry with her head held high, come what may. And then, the real work would begin.

Chapter Four

M ARTIN STOOD BESIDE the priest as his bride approached on her father's arm, a portrait of fearsome resolve. Her back was straight as a sword, and she held her head high, as she faced her fate. It would be the triumph of a lifetime to win her over, and Martin had never relished a challenge more.

It was a small wedding, carried out in the castle's chapel with a minimum of fanfare. Candles flickered and guttered with drafts of cold air that seeped in despite the stained-glass windows and thick stone walls that kept out the worst of the howling wind. Attendees were mostly members of Lord Ferdinand's household. The earl and countess were dressed in velvet and fur, while the rest of the small smattering of guests clutched their woolens tight against the cold. Most wore dark colors, making somber shadows in the pews. The only splash of color was Isabella in her rich blue gown.

As they spoke their sacred vows before those assembled, his heart was fit to burst with anticipation. He had a worthy adversary at last, and her surrender would be so sweet. He wouldn't defeat her by trying to tame her. *Oh no.* What a shame it would be to see his lioness declawed. He wanted her in all her razor-sharp glory, an equal in all things, knowing she had met her match.

She bristled as he slid the beautifully crafted ring that he had purchased onto her finger. It held a large, beautiful sapphire and had cost a princely sum that, fortunately, he could afford. It was worth it to see the lovely hand of his bride adorned with such a jewel, even if she was glaring at him in a way that could give a man frostbite.

When the priest pronounced them man and wife, she was clenching her jaw so hard that her cheek bulged. And when the priest said it was time to kiss the bride, he approached her with all the caution he would use with an angry bear. A light peck on the cheek was all he dared, and even that was risky. From her rigid stance, pursed lips, and narrowed eyes, he was certain she would have liked to take his head off for it. He was lucky she didn't use her clenched fists to knock him out for his audacity.

As they left the chapel and made their way to the great hall, Isabella rested her hand lightly on his arm, as if trying to maintain as little contact as possible. The silence between them grew into a tangible thing, and he'd had enough of it. It was time to goad his gorgeous termagant into speech.

"My lady, I cannot believe my good fortune to have such a proud and lovely wife. Your beauty is beyond compare, and your wit is sharp as a poignard. I am smitten."

As he expected, her fingers tightened on his arm, and she dug her nails in hard. "Save your breath, fool. Your honeyed words are wasted on me."

It was a good thing she had no idea that the little shock of pain created a very different sensation in another part of his body. "Not wasted, I think, because now you are speaking to me. If we are to spend the rest of our lives together, I would prefer not to do so in silence."

"This wedding is a sham," she whispered so that no one else could hear. "If you attempt to change the terms of our agreement, I'll make you regret it."

He smiled. "Ah, but we need everyone here to believe it is real," he murmured. "Should a doting husband not be trying to win over his new wife with sweet words?"

She made a frustrated noise in her throat.

At least he was provoking a reaction from her. If she lacked any interest in him, she would have simply ignored him, but even her silences were pointed. He had her full attention, and he intended to use it.

"I have grand plans for our wedding night," he said, knowing full well he was stoking her fury.

She turned such a delightful shade of red as she turned on him and yanked him close. "Have you forgotten your promise so soon?" she grumbled in a low voice.

"Careful, wife. Your parents are watching."

She glanced at her mother who was indeed directing a disapproving look her way. Isabella turned back to him with an entirely false, ingratiating smile.

"And no, I have not forgotten my promise at all," he said quietly with a bland smile. "Have you forgotten yours? You promised to let me woo you. I won't lay a finger on you without your leave, I swear, but I do plan to make my case. And you *did* say you would hear me out."

Her sharp exhale at his words was all the acquiescence he was likely to get. Fortunately, these were only the opening strikes and parries in their tender war.

"I will find a way to win your heart," he said as they stepped into the relative warmth of the great hall and made their way to the head table. "Every castle has a weakness. Every armor has a chink."

"In faith, you are unbearable," she said as he led her to her place at the table, pulling out her tall-backed chair for her, and took a seat beside her.

"I would never ask you to bear me. Horses are made to bear, and you, my lady, are above such menial labor." He winked at her, and the ice that was in her gaze turned to pure fire.

"Very true, my lord, and above you too."

That sent his mind to dangerous places. "I would very much like you above me while I bear you. Perhaps you would like a true wedding night after all?"

"You are an ass."

"Then ride me."

"Never. You are not a worthy mount."

"Certainly not. I am a wicked beast." The thoughts running through his mind with each lash of her tongue were getting worse and worse. The mental picture of her atop him, taking her pleasure, was too much to bear. Fortunately, they were seated, or he might have embarrassed himself. "Tame me, Isabella. Take me in hand and show me the error of my ways."

The effect of his words on her was no less profound. She was a glorious bonfire before him—flushed, dark eyes sparkling, lips parted as her tongue darted out to lick them. She might be spitting mad, but there was something more there, he would swear it. Despite herself, she was responding to him.

"I'll do no such thing. Your wit is too dull. I could not teach you," she said, and turned away to grab her goblet, hand shaking just a touch as she drank deeply.

He watched the column of her throat work with intense interest, wishing he could kiss and nibble his way up her neck and nip on her ear. "And yet sharp enough to score a hit. You're blushing, my lady."

"You are mistaken. It is merely the red light of the fire." She fanned herself with her hand. "Is it warm in here?"

They were interrupted by Lord Ferdinand. "I hope my daughter is behaving herself," he said, taking a seat beside Martin at the center of the table. "I did warn you she can be willful at times." He cast a warning glance at his daughter, who composed her face into a careful blank. "You wouldn't want us to report back to Lady Eleanor that you're defying her will, would you?"

"I obey Her Grace in all things," she said, looking for all the world like a demure and obedient daughter.

What a pity! He much preferred her fiery side. It was a waste to hide such a magnificent flame beneath a bushel of obedience. "She is everything I hoped for in a wife and more."

"Well, best of luck to you, lad. Don't let looks deceive you. She may appear sweet and innocent right now." Indeed, she was a portrait of a demure damsel beside him. "But she has studied the art of subtle machination at court, and I dare say you've already discovered her temper. She has learned at the knees of the two most devious women I know, my wife and my queen. Don't say I didn't give you fair warning."

"Don't listen to my husband," said Isabella's mother with a withering glance at Lord Ferdinand. "Isabella knows where her duty lies and the consequences of disobedience. She wouldn't dare step out of line and disappoint Her Grace."

Before Martin could respond, servants arrived, spooning pottage into bread trenchers. It was a hearty meal, if not particularly elegant. There was nothing to suggest this was a wedding feast as opposed to an everyday dinner.

His poor wife. What must it have been like to grow up in such a cold, uncaring family? They were the opposite of his own. His mother and father had doted on him and his siblings and raised them with the utmost care. Had she ever experienced the warmth of love and acceptance? He suspected not from what he observed. No wonder she was so prickly and hostile.

He turned to find her deep in whispered conversation with a thin, frail young woman who he presumed to be her sister. Their murmurs were warm and animated. Perhaps there was some love after all. It seemed she and her sister were close. He ate his lackluster pottage and let her chatter with her sister, uninterrupted. It warmed his heart to see her happy. He could only pray that he too could earn her trust and her smiles in time.

The meal concluded quickly with his new wife ignoring him completely. He didn't mind. He could hardly begrudge her some moments of love and comfort with her sister, who she clearly doted on.

"Lord Ferdinand, you must toast the newlyweds," the lady of the castle said to her husband, disdain dripping from every word. "Go on, you hapless meat sack," she murmured in a low voice just loud enough for Martin to hear. "Do your duty, or do I have to prod you with my eating dagger?"

Casting a resentful glance at his wife, Lord Ferdinand rose and raised his goblet. Clearing his throat, he said, "To the happy couple, blessings and happiness and whatever else it is I'm supposed to say."

A few of the earl's men at other tables raised their glasses uncertainly. Lord Ferdinand shrugged and sat back down, draining his cup and pouring himself another, which he also drained.

"You bloody idiot," his wife murmured as he drank. "I ask you to do a simple thing, and even that you bungle. What a useless bag of guts you are."

"If you'll pardon me, I have some things to attend to," Lord Ferdinand said, rising abruptly.

"Good riddance," said Martin's new mother-in-law a little too loudly before draining her goblet of honey wine.

What a family! No wonder Isabella was prickly and defensive, with parents like this. He couldn't get her away fast enough.

"Lord Martin, I'd like a word," Lord Ferdinand said beckoning Martin to follow him.

Reluctantly, Martin rose and bowed to Isabella before he turned to follow the earl out of the hall into the dimly lit corridor. "What did you wish to discuss, my lord?" The sooner he could return to his bride, the better.

"By marrying my family, you are allying yourself to the Duke of Normandy's cause, even if we're all technically still vassals of King Stephen. Is Winchelsea ready to take up arms in this fight?"

All Martin wanted was an end to the violence that had ravaged the English countryside for far too long. It had become clear that King Stephen was far too weak to win against Henry, so there was only one path forward that Martin could see. If he and the other Cinque Port barons threw their weight in with Henry, perhaps it would be enough to end this godawful mess.

"We are, my lord, and the other Cinque Port barons are with

me." Martin had given clear instructions to his knights and men-at-arms before he left to see Lady Eleanor in the fall. They were prepared for battle, and they had what they needed to survive a siege for at least six months, if it came to that, which he prayed it never did.

"Good. Very good," Lord Ferdinand said, clapping Martin on the shoulder. "Well, you'd best get back in there. Your bride awaits her wedding night. Don't let her eat you alive."

"I think I can handle myself, my lord. I plan to take my time and win her over." He only had a fortnight, give or take, but if in that time he had not succeeded, he would do as she asked and let her choose a husband more to her liking.

Lord Ferdinand grunted. "Good luck with that."

Martin smiled tightly. "Thank you, my lord."

"And with that, I bid you good night."

Martin bowed and made his way back into the great hall.

He returned to the table to find that the countess had slipped into his chair and had her talons dug into Isabella's arm. "…and I expect blood on the sheets in the morning. If you don't consummate this marriage, I'll tell the duchess and let her deal with you," the countess said in a carrying whisper.

"My lady," Martin said, quietly interrupting. "Your daughter and I will become acquainted in our own good time. She's no longer your concern, and how we spend our wedding night is none of your business."

His mother-in-law turned the full force of her poisonous gaze on him. If looks could kill, he'd be pinned to the wall with a sword through his heart. Fortunately, he didn't give a fig what this woman thought. He and Isabella were boarding his ship and sailing for Winchelsea in the morning, and good riddance.

He turned to his wife, who blinked at him as if seeing him for the first time. Perhaps no one had even spoken to her mother that way, at least in her presence. "Isabella, I believe it is time for us to retire," he said, offering a hand to help her rise. Fortunately, his bride appeared as anxious to escape as he was. She stood and took his arm without complaint.

"Goodnight, Adelaide," she said, ignoring her mother completely.

"By your leave, my lady," he said to the countess, nodding his head and offering a cold smile. He didn't wait for her response before leading Isabella from the great hall and through the corridors to the guest room where he was staying.

"Thank you," she murmured almost too quietly to hear once they were out of earshot.

"What was that?" he asked, not quite believing the sweet words that reached his ears.

"I said 'thank you' for rescuing me from Mother. Don't make me repeat it again, or I'll truss you up like wild boar and roast you on a spit."

He nodded gravely, tamping down his delight at this small triumph. He'd chipped a tiny hole in her defensive wall, and with time and luck he would open a gap wide enough for him to climb through.

CHAPTER FIVE

T HE DOOR OF their marital bedchamber thudded closed, and Lord Martin locked the latch. Every hair on Isabella's head stood on end. She was trapped in a bedroom with a stranger she disliked and didn't trust, one who had made no secret of wanting to bed her. All that stood between him and claiming his husbandly rights was a flimsy promise. It was a relief not to have been subjected to a bedding ceremony with the whole household looking on, but that small kindness was no guarantee that he would stay on good behavior.

Her trunk sat beside the door, a sign that she could not seek refuge in her old room, no matter how terrified she might be.

Her temporary husband might have rescued her from her mother moments ago, but that was very little to go on. Was he a man of his word? If not, she was doomed. While she might be a few inches taller than him, it hadn't escaped her notice that he was well-muscled beneath his silver-embroidered black-woolen cotte. If it came to a fight, she wasn't sure she was strong enough to fend him off.

She cast her gaze about for something she could use as a weapon if worse came to worst. As her eye came to rest on a poker, as he opened his travel chest and reached into it. Heaven only knew what ominous item he might be getting in order to subdue her. Did he have rope in there? Did he plan to tie her up?

Because she would fight him with everything she had.

She hardly breathed as he pulled out…

A diminutive, stringed instrument. A citole.

Oh, thank God!

"Do you mind if I sing you a song?" Martin sat on a stool, plucking the citole with surprising skill. His fingers flew as he cradled the instrument in his arms. Her sister would be impressed.

"I'd rather listen to the braying of a donkey, but if you must." As long as his hands were on the citole, they weren't on her.

He winked at her and started to sing.

"A new song I shall make for thee
Before the cold wind freezes me.
My lady puts me to the test
To make sure that I love her best.
No matter what harsh words she speaks
I know I am the man she seeks."

Much to her annoyance, he had a nice tenor. Under other circumstances, she might have enjoyed his song. "The lyrics remind me of something I heard in Bordeaux."

He continued to strum as he answered, "I'm not surprised. This is a rough translation of something Lady Eleanor's grandfather composed."

She swallowed and stared. "You know troubadour songs from Aquitaine?"

"Lady Eleanor mentioned how you loved songs from your homeland. I tried to learn a few before I set sail."

That was surprisingly thoughtful of him. One of the few things Isabella missed about Lady Eleanor's court was the music. Her Grace was a great patroness of the arts. Her own grandfather *had* composed troubadour lyrics once upon a time. There was always some minstrel strumming away, singing of impossible love. It was a glorious escape from the cold and cynical calculation that consumed her days.

Isabella might not like the fellow making the music, but the song warmed her heart ever so slightly. "You may continue, if you wish. Don't let me stop you."

"I'm hers. Her words set me aflame.
In charters she wrote down my name.
I swear to you I am not drunk.
She's virtuous as any monk.
Without her, life is meaningless.
I hunger so for her caress."

There was nowhere for her to sit except the hulking, cano-pied bed, since he occupied the only other seat. Cautiously, she settled on the edge, making sure she was closer to the poker than he was. Perhaps she wouldn't need it after all, but it never hurt to be careful.

It was unfair the effect the music had on her. The soft pluck-ing of strings lulled her into a false sense of safety. So far, this all seemed tame enough. There was nothing to fear in a little music.

She wondered what her true wedding night would be like. Her mother hadn't told her anything except that there would be blood. She was vaguely aware that one generally took off one's clothes, but beyond that, it was a mystery. Even with a man she had chosen, a wedding night was something to be feared.

Perhaps, she thought dismally, this was the best wedding night she would ever have. A man with a pleasant voice singing her love songs was certainly preferable to any alternative she could think of.

The song finished, and she tensed, bracing herself for what-ever was to come next.

"My lady," he said, putting down the citole without breaking his gaze. "I know it is too much to ask."

"Then you had best keep your mouth shut," she snapped, but curiosity consumed her about what he was going to say.

"And yet I will speak," he said gently. "Would you permit me to comb your hair?"

His words surprised her so much that her jaw dropped. He wanted to comb her hair? She'd never heard of a man asking such a thing. Had he gone mad?

And yet the thought of him touching her head as gently and deftly as he'd pluck those strings was more appealing than she wanted to admit. Though it could also be a prelude to things she didn't want to contemplate.

"Only if you hand me the poker so that I can stab you if you do something I don't like," she said at last, certain he wouldn't agree to any such condition.

He chuckled. "I wondered why you kept glancing at it. You do not need a weapon to defend against me, but if it makes you feel better, then here." The provoking man took the poker and knelt like a knight presenting his sword to his liege. "Your poker, my lady. I have no doubt you would make good use of it if I broke my word."

She let out a long breath as her hand closed around it. The knot in her chest loosened ever so slightly as she clasped the rough iron. "If you insist on humiliating yourself and playing lady's maid, the comb is in my trunk. It should be on the top."

Martin rummaged in her trunk and returned with the comb. Kicking off his shoes, he climbed onto the bed behind her. Every muscle in her body tensed as he reached out to remove her crespinette and pluck out the hairpins that held her side buns in place. His fingers brushed her ear, making her jump. If he touched her anywhere improper, she would jab his eye out.

"Be at ease, my lady," he crooned as he pulled out the remaining hairpins. Her hair fell down in two thick braids, and he leaned to the side to set the pins on the bedside table. Moments later, he was behind her again, not touching her back but so close she could feel the heat radiating from him.

As the wind howled outside, she gripped her poker, instincts warring within her. Part of her longed to run away as fast as she could. But another part of her longed to curl into that warmth. It was so cold here at Bamburgh and so rare that she ever managed to thaw out completely. Did she dare get closer to take the edge off her chill? She still had a weapon to defend herself with. Fortunately, good sense prevailed, and she stiffened her back. "Hurry and be done with it before I change my mind."

He chuckled as he picked up a braid and began combing it out. "My little sister, Eglantine, taught me how to braid," he said as the comb slid through her hair, teasing apart any tangles so gently that she didn't feel anything beyond a soft tug. "You'd think my brother, Lance, would have been the one to order us all around, given his size, but my sister ruled my childhood with an iron fist."

The comb grazed Isabella's scalp, sending tingles down her spine. Against her will, she found she rather liked the sensation. It took more effort than she expected to remain impervious to all outward appearances. "I didn't know you had a sister, or a brother, for that matter," she said, making conversation to fend off the heavy languor that was descending on her at his touch. She couldn't afford to let her guard down, even for a moment.

"Oh yes," he said. "You'll meet them both when we get to Winchelsea. They'll absolutely adore you."

As he continued his work, some rebellious part of her wanted to arch into his hand like a cat seeking pets. What dark, nefarious magic was this? "Adore me?" she asked, struggling to keep the thread of the conversation. "No one adores me."

"No? Not even your sister?"

Her heart squeezed at the mention of Adelaide. "She's too tenderhearted for her own good. Our parents have never been…" She ought not to complete that sentence while under this roof, if she knew what was good for her. "Well, you've met them."

"No need to explain." Setting down the comb, he traced his fingers lightly through her hair, sending irritatingly pleasant shivers down her neck.

"We only ever had each other. And our brother, Crispin. But

we haven't seen him for many years."

He began to massage her scalp, and her breathing hitched as the day's tensions melted away beneath his skillful touch. Coxcomb that he was, his fingers were doing a marvelous job of putting her at ease.

"I've always looked out for them, and they've always looked out for me, at least when we've been together. Leaving them was the hardest part of going off to serve Queen Eleanor at King Louis's court. My brother was sent out to foster around the same time I was sent away. Poor Adelaide was all alone for years. How she survived and stayed the sweet young woman she is, I don't know."

He pressed his thumbs at the base of her skull, and she couldn't stop herself from moaning aloud. "By all the saints, that feels heavenly. Where did you learn to do this?"

"My mother's healer," he said, his thumbs making gentle rounds as they pressed. "She has terrible headaches from time to time, and this helps alleviate them. You seemed tense. I thought this might help you relax."

Her shoulders tensed. "So that I'll let my guard down and you can have your way with me?"

"Never," he said firmly, his fingers tracing down her neck and kneading her shoulders. She should have stopped him, or at least objected, but she didn't. "I swear to you, Isabella, I will never lay a hand on you without your leave."

As if to demonstrate, he lifted his hands away from her shoulders.

"No, please. Don't stop what you were just doing." The sweet ache his clever hands released was too much to bear. She needed his touch to soothe it away, even if it left her boneless and lethargic. Her grip on the poker had loosened considerably, though she had no intention of letting it go.

Martin pressed his thumbs into a mass of muscle between her shoulders, and she gasped. "Yes, please, that." She couldn't form a sentence.

He chuckled softly. "Someday, I'll make you say that in our marriage bed."

His words made her bristle, but whatever magic he was working with his fingers immediately smoothed the tension away.

"We are in our marriage bed," she observed in a breathy voice she hardly recognized as her own.

"Not in the way I mean." His lips were so close to her ear, they could have brushed it. Why was she disappointed that they didn't? Whatever battle he was waging, she was clearly losing.

"And what way do you mean?" She probably shouldn't pursue this line of questioning, but curiosity was too deep. And her mind was addled by the steady rhythm of his hands on her back.

"Is it possible that no one explained this to you?"

Her head began to loll as his hand continued their magic work.

"My mother said there would be blood, but not why or from where."

Hence the poker.

"I see. Do you remember the part of our vows where we said, 'With my body, I thee worship'?"

His thumbs dug into a mass of muscle at the base of her spine, and she couldn't help but let out a low, "*Mmm.*"

"Well," he continued, "a good man will do exactly that. He would worship every inch of his woman's body with hands and lips and tongue until she cries cry out with pleasure."

Something inside her clenched at his words. Heat pooled between her legs in a way she hadn't experienced before. Why there, she wondered?

"Only when the honey of bliss overflows and you are aching to be filled, will he cover you with his body, resting between your legs, sliding his hardened cock inside you and then moving within you until he spills his seed in your womb."

She could hardly breathe. So that's why that part of her had grown warm? Even more so *that* was the mystery of the bedchamber about which everyone was so tight-lipped. Her body knew, even if she didn't.

While she'd never seen a naked man, she had seen little boys and knew that they were shaped differently from girls. The thought of a man's…thing…growing hard and moving inside her sounded thoroughly absurd, and yet the way he said it made her want to experience it for herself.

Except for one thing.

"And what about the blood? Mother said there would be blood." She tightened her grip around the poker.

He continued to press and knead her back, soothing away the sudden tension. "When a woman welcomes a man inside her for the first time, there is often some pain and bleeding. But if a man has properly prepared her, it should be no more than a passing pinch."

"And if he hasn't?"

His fingers gripped her tightly for a moment before letting go and returning to their rhythmic movement. "There are many men who fail to live up to their marital duty and think only of taking their pleasure, never of giving it in return. I pray that you never find out what that feels like. But with me as your husband, you would be perfectly safe."

"But you will no longer be my husband once we arrive in Winchelsea." God willing. She had to find a way out of this.

His fingers paused. "We shall see." He combed his fingers through her hair and began to braid it back up again. "But for now, I think it is time for you to sleep. It has been a long day."

"It has," she said, stifling a yawn. Having her entire life turned upside down had drained her of the will to fight anymore, at least for tonight.

He tied off her braid with the piece of ribbon that had originally held it bound, then slid off the bed and went to face the corner of the room.

"You can change out of your gown," he said without turning. "You have my word I will not look."

Warily, she put down the poker on the bed and took off her gown, leaving her in her linen shift. She folded the dress and put it away in her trunk, then retrieved her weapon and climbed beneath the covers, hugging the rough metal against her. "Where will you sleep?"

If he answered, "the bed," she would run him through on the spot.

"I think I'll settle on this stool and lean against the wall."

Wise man. It sounded terribly uncomfortable, but that was hardly her problem. It was bad enough she would be forced to endure an entire night with him in the same bedchamber.

Hugging the poker close, she closed her eyes. "Don't try anything or I'll run you through," she said through a yawn.

"I know you will. Sleep well, and dream of me."

And God help her, she did.

CHAPTER SIX

MARTIN WOKE BEFORE dawn with a crick in his neck and frozen toes. He could not wait to leave Northumberland. Winchelsea wasn't exactly warm this time of year, but it wasn't nearly as icy as these northern reaches.

Shivering, he stole a glance at his sleeping bride and smiled. He'd made progress in his campaign to win her over. The night before had been quite successful as far as he was concerned. There was still a considerable distance to go, but with dedicated effort, he could get her to lower her defenses bit by bit and let him in.

If it was too cold for him in this room, it was certainly too cold for her, even if she was under the covers. Aching, he got up and threw more wood on the embers of the previous night's fire until it grew to a merry flame.

Isabella stirred in her sleep. She looked so sweet and vulnerable resting there, poker clutched close like a child's favorite toy.

He had best sit back down and pretend to sleep. It wouldn't do for her to wake and find him staring at her. It would have confirmed all her worst suspicions about him.

Settling back on his stool, he closed his eyes and then opened them a crack when she stirred again. Through lowered lashes, he watched as she climbed out of bed, cast a wary glance at him, and then stretched.

The pale light of dawn streaked through chinks in the shutters, making her shift nearly transparent in places. Her ample breasts came to pert points where her nipples, hardened from the cold, tented the thin fabric. The curve of her buttocks made him want to weep.

God in heaven, what have I done to deserve such sweet torture?

She lowered her arms and padded over to her chest, pulling out a serviceable green wool gown, putting it on, and tightening the laces on the sides. Then she pulled on thick, black, woolen stockings and tied the garters, in the process exposing tantalizing glimpses of her bare thighs.

Thank God his voluminous surcotte hid his reaction or she might use that poker on him yet.

Then she unraveled last night's braid, combed her hair out, and began winding it into side buns. The visceral memory of touching that lustrous skein almost undid him. It had been so soft beneath his fingers, and he had breathed deeply the light herbal scent from her bath oils. How he would love to bury his face in its silken warmth!

Instead, he sat still as could be, struggling to keep his breathing deep and even so that she wouldn't suspect the extent to which she affected him.

She walked over to him with poker raised and prodded his shoulder with the point. "My lord, it is time to get up."

That's *my* Isabella, he thought as he feigned being startled awake.

"My lady, I am at your mercy."

"And don't forget it." She narrowed her eyes and pressed to punctuate her point.

"How could I forget when you are standing over me like Cupid, ready to pierce me with love's dart? I had no idea you were so desperate for me, my lady. I am yours for the taking."

She gave him a withering look and lowered the poker. "Must you speak such nonsense so early in the morning? Your tiresome wit makes my head ache."

He smiled. "And your fearsome wit makes my heart ache. You are magnificent. I could sing your praises all day long."

"I would rather listen to bleating sheep."

"Then let me join your flock, my shepherdess. You have hooked me with your crook."

She cocked her head. "No, I think I'll throw you to the wolves. You are too troublesome, and I do not care what befalls you." The teasing look on her face said otherwise.

He laughed. "Are you so heartless, my lady?"

"Oh yes," she said, setting down the poker and stepping toward him. "It is pointless to woo me, my lord. You cannot win my heart when I do not have one." She held out her hand as she stood over him. "And now it is time for us to depart. The sooner we leave, the better."

He took her hand and stood, delighted that she had reached out to touch him voluntarily. It was a small victory, but a victory, nonetheless. Lifting her hand to his lips, he kissed her fingers. "On that we agree, beloved."

She pulled her hand away swiftly. "Don't call me that."

"Then what shall I call you?"

"Isabella."

Another victory! She was allowing him to use her name. "Then let us prepare for our departure, Isabella." He stood, his body aching from the awkward night atop a stool, not to mention the tightness of his braies. At least on the journey back to Winchelsea, he would be able to sleep in a hammock with the rest of his crew, away from temptation. He would leave the captain's cabin to her and her sister, of course. "I need to wash and change my clothes before we depart. Since you are already dressed, perhaps you would like to break your fast before we leave and check that your sister is prepared to depart."

She looked him up and down, and he prayed that his state of arousal wasn't obvious to her, not that she would know what it meant. Still, after last night's talk about marital relations, he certainly didn't want that. At long last, she shrugged. "Meet me in the great hall once you have dressed, and don't tarry. I wish to be gone from this place as soon as we can manage."

"As you wish, my lady." He swept into a deep bow.

With an eyeroll, she left the room.

As soon as she was gone, he stripped off the heavy wedding cotte and pulled off his shirt, walking over to the water pitcher and basin. A layer of ice had formed at the top of the pitcher, and he cracked it with his hand before pouring frigid water over his head. The combination of the water and the chill air on his chest did what he had hoped, and his arousal abated at last. Then he got out the sharp blade he used for shaving and removed the prickling hairs on his chin, leaving his upper lip alone. By the time he got back to Winchelsea, he would have his full mustache back, thank God.

He dressed hurriedly, donning a plain, linen undershirt and the practical, dark-blue wool cotte he wore for sailing. Then he packed his few belongings into his sea chest and flagged down a servant in the hallway to request that his chest and hers be taken down to his ship and that his crew be notified of their imminent departure.

That taken care of, he headed to the great hall for a quick bite before they set sail. Isabella was sitting with Adelaide in deep conversation. The earl sat alone, and the countess was nowhere to be seen.

"Come join me, my lord," the earl said, beckoning.

Martin would rather not have, but he had little choice in the matter. Besides, if he was to leave Isabella free to annul the wedding, he needed to plant the seed that they had not yet consummated. He'd already concocted an excuse to give the earl and countess.

"You're still in one piece, so I take it the wedding night was a success?" his father-in-law asked, winking.

Ugh. What a way to treat his daughter. "It was, my lord. I didn't touch her, and she didn't kill me. I would call that a resounding success under the circumstances."

The earl frowned. "You didn't consummate? What are you playing at, man?"

"My family is very traditional, and they would prefer that we consummate upon reaching Winchelsea. They want to be fully assured of my bride's virtue and that there is no risk to the succession." Fortunately, the earl had no way of knowing how far that was from the truth.

Lord Ferdinand nodded. "I see. Very wise. And it gives you time to tame your tempestuous bride so that she's obedient when the time comes."

"Indeed," Martin said with a thin smile. God's bones, what a terrible father. Not that what he said was so very different from what most fathers would say. Martin was fully aware he'd had unusual parents. Still, hearing her father talk of taming her made his skin crawl.

To avoid further conversation, Martin turned his attention to the food before him, taking a large bite of bread and chasing it down with a swig of ale. He could do with a bit of fortification before taking to sea in this frigid clime.

As soon as he had eaten his fill, he stood. "My lord, I'm afraid we must be going. Thank you for the hospitality of your hall. We must take our leave."

The earl stood and clapped him on the shoulder with manly bonhomie. "Best of luck to you. I've had my men load her dowry onto your ship. Feel free to check it and let me know if anything is amiss."

The dowry was the last thing on his mind. Winchelsea was prosperous. What it needed was an intelligent baroness who could manage things while he sailed the seas to keep it that way. "Thank you, my lord. I'm sure everything is in order. Isabella," he said, turning to his bride, "it is time for us to depart."

She turned from her conversation with her sister and nodded. "Very well, my lord."

Isabella and Adelaide stood and pulled thick shawls around their shoulders. Just as they were about to take their leave, their mother came sweeping in, descending on Isabella like a hawk on its prey. She dug a talon into Isabella's shoulder.

"There was no blood on the sheets this morning. Have you shamed me, you worthless strumpet?" she hissed in her daughter's ear just loud enough for Martin to overhear.

"No, my lady," he said in a low, cold voice as he reached for Isabella. "We did not consummate the marriage last night. My family wishes for us to do so in Winchelsea. Isabella," he said, pulling her up and away from her mother, "are you ready to leave?"

"Yes, thank you. Goodbye, Mother. Goodbye, Father," she said, curtsying stiffly. Adelaide followed suit. It was more than those two wretches deserved, the way they treated their daughters. Isabella turned her back on them and linked arms with him and Adelaide, practically propelling them from the hall. "Let us be gone from this place," she murmured to Martin as soon as they were out of earshot of her parents.

He led her out to the courtyard where horses were waiting for them, and they rode in silence down to the dock where his ship was moored, buffeted by freezing wind.

The Wind Song looked slate gray in the morning light against a sea the color of pewter. The colorful shields adorning the forecastle were mere shadows as milky wisps of fog curled around them. Its single mast pointed skyward, crossed by an enormous spar and crowned by the crow's nest, nearly lost in the clouds. Martin could barely make out Will up there, awaiting orders to climb out onto the spar to unfurl the enormous rectangular sail stitched with the de Vere coat of arms. Poor Will must have been freezing. The sooner they set sail, the sooner the gangly youth could climb back down to the deck and warm himself.

Martin led Isabella and Adelaide up the wooden planks serving as a ramp, careful to ensure they kept their balance. Isabella ascended without difficulty and had no trouble keeping her balance on the swaying deck, even though Adelaide leaned on her at every step.

"You've traveled by ship before?" he asked.

"Many times," Isabella answered, looking warily at the crew.

"Do you get seasick?" Martin had been worried about this. Traveling by sea was far safer than by land, given the anarchy that prevailed, but not everyone found it comfortable.

"Never," she answered proudly.

He couldn't help but smile. *Good.* His wife should be able to tolerate life on board a ship, after all he spent more time at sea than not. While he intended for her to stay home and tend to the town's needs, it would have been nice to bring her along from time to time.

"And how about you, Adelaide?" he asked, turning his attention to her sister. "Have you been on a ship before?"

Adelaide smiled shyly. "Only the ship that brought us to Bamburgh Castle."

"Then this will be an adventure for you," he said with a grin. "If there is anything at all you need during this journey, you have only to ask."

"Thank you, my lord." Adelaide looked all around, wide-eyed and wondering as she clutched her sister's arm. It was certainly easier to charm her than Isabella. Perhaps if he could win Adelaide over to his cause, it would help him with his bride. He would have to work on charming the girl.

"Let me show you to your cabin." He helped them down the hatch to the lower deck where cargo was stored and the crew's hammocks hung, swaying with the ocean waves. A few strategically placed lanterns provided meager light as he guided her to the stern of the ship where he opened a door for her. "This is where you will sleep for the duration of the journey. Normally, this is my cabin, but I will sleep with my men so that you two can have it to yourselves."

He led them into the compact space, sparsely furnished with a built-in bed with a straw pallet on it and a small, round table with two chairs. Their chests had been stowed here. There was little room for anything else. It was as generously proportioned of a captain's cabin as he had ever seen, but life on board a ship was a far cry from the vastness of Bamburgh Castle.

"This will be adequate," Isabella said, looking around the small space in the lantern light. "We shall stay here and warm ourselves for a bit while you make preparations to depart."

"As you wish." He bowed. If you need anything at all, you have only to come find me."

"I'm certain we can manage quite well without any assistance from you, my lord."

He smiled. "If you'll excuse me, then, I have a ship to prepare for departure and a campaign of seduction to plan."

"Do your worst, Little Baron. Your meager charms are insufficient to overcome my dislike, no matter how many honeyed words you serve up."

His grin grew wider. "I disagree. You're enjoying my efforts to woo you, despite your protestations to the contrary. Your eyes give you away every time. They flame and spark with interest, even as you lash me with your barbed tongue. But I will respect your wishes and give you some time to settle in and collect yourself."

He turned away without giving her a chance to retort, and left, closing the door behind him.

Everything was proceeding according to plan, he thought as he ascended to the deck and sought out his first mate, Halfred. The wizened old man had served his father before him, but he was still hard as iron. Martin found Halfred up on the aftercastle, directing the crew as they lashed everything down and prepared to set sail. The old man's only concession to the cold was that his shirt sleeves were rolled down rather than up to the elbows as was his usual habit.

"My lord, are you ready to set sail?" Halfred asked, bowing his head.

"As soon as you are, Halfred. I'm more than ready to see the last of this place." Martin looked forward to seeing it disappear behind them on the horizon, hopefully never to be seen again.

"Aye, my lord. And the ladies are comfortable below?"

"As comfortable as I can make them." There was little he could to do improve the accommodations. A ship was a ship, and there wasn't room for much in the way of creature comforts, but Isabella seemed to take it all in stride, which was a blessed relief. Adelaide seemed delighted by the novelty of it all.

"Very good, my lord. My felicitations on your marriage, by the way. She's quite a beauty."

"She is indeed, and I'll thank you to see to it that the men don't bother her or her sister." Not that he thought his crew would dare, but it needed saying, nonetheless.

"They wouldn't dream of it my lord."

Martin nodded his approval. "Let us depart."

Halfred shouted orders to the crew to cast off. Will climbed out on the spar and unfurled the sail before shimmying down to the deck. Christopher, a hearty sailor his own age, signaled the earl's men to remove the planks used for boarding and to unlash the ropes that tied *The Wind Song* to the dock. Good old Ulf was at the tiller, his long golden beard blowing in the wind.

To his surprise, Isabella and Adelaide emerged from the hatch, thick, wooled shawls pulled tightly around their shoulders. Martin hurried over. "Is there anything that you need, my sweet?"

Isabella furrowed her brow at the endearment but let it pass without comment. "No, thank you. We only wished to watch that awful place disappear behind us once and for all."

"I can't say I blame you for that." He offered his arm and led her to the railing. "You should have a good view from here. I must review the charts with Ulf, if you'll excuse me."

Isabella reached out and touched his hand to stay him. "Thank you for taking us away. We both hated it there." It clearly cost her to express her appreciation.

"I can see why," he said, warming at her kind words despite the icy wind. Perhaps he was making more progress than he thought. But he wouldn't push his luck. It was time to retreat. "If there is nothing else, I must take my leave."

He kissed Isabella's gloved hand, and she didn't shrink away. As he headed toward Ulf, he smiled to himself. She would be his before they landed at Winchelsea, he was certain. He looked up and saw gathering clouds in the gray sky, which immediately dampened his mood. Perhaps it would not be smooth sailing after all.

CHAPTER SEVEN

T HE MAN RAN a tight ship, Isabella thought to herself as she stood in the shelter of the forecastle watching the sailors go about their business. The wind was vicious, but she couldn't bring herself to go below where there was nothing to do but wait. She sent Adelaide back down to the cabin to keep warm. It wouldn't do for her to risk her health, despite her obvious curiosity about everything happening around her. But there was a great deal Isabella needed to think through, and it was easier to keep a clear head out in the open than down in the dim cabin with her sister where the walls seemed to close in around them.

But as she tried to focus her mind on her future and how she would keep Adelaide out of Lady Eleanor's clutches, she couldn't help watching as everyone on the ship went about their business. They moved with the ease and familiarity of an experienced crew, and she could swear it made Martin's effortless air of command make him seem several inches taller. He was in his element, and she couldn't help but be impressed by his skill and authority. It was a very different side of him than she had seen to date.

But she couldn't let herself get distracted from the task ahead. She had one husband to get rid of and another husband to convince to marry her. Perhaps she could get Martin to stop at Yarmouth on the way south. That was part of the Earl of Norfolk's territory, and she was certain she could find a way to make contact. She'd met Lord Christopher, the local baron, on several occasions, and she was certain he would pass along a message to his liege lord. Maybe she could even aggravate Martin so much that he would leave her behind in Yarmouth. But what was the best way to irritate her husband? He seemed to be so much better at irritating her than the other way around.

She fixed her gaze on the horizon and opened her ears, listening for any tidbit from his men that might help her. Listening without appearing to do so was a longtime habit, honed over years with her mother, followed by years at court. She had an instinct for picking out the most useful pieces of information from an ocean of irrelevant blather. It was like fishing with a net. Irrelevant words streamed through, but the important ones were trapped until she could examine their meaning at length. That was the true art—crafting conclusions from the flotsam and jetsam.

Focusing in on two men swabbing the deck of the forecastle, she overheard, "Thank God we're headed home. It's colder than a witch's titty up here. I can't wait to get home to my Flora and sit in front of a roaring fire with a tankard of ale. She'll warm me up good and proper, if you know what I mean."

"Aye," said the other man. "I wouldn't mind a bit of female companionship myself. I tried to find a willing wench up at the castle, but they were all gave me the cold shoulder."

"It's because you stink like week-old fish, you manky bilge rat."

Nothing useful to be learned there. Isabella turned her attention to three men gathered on the forecastle, looking over a chart, glancing at them only briefly before directing her gaze out to sea once again.

"I still think we should sail straight to Winchelsea without stopping," said the first man.

"But his lordship wants fresh food for the ladies," said a second man. "You know how picky females can be. Can't exactly feed them salt pork and hard biscuits."

Now, *that* was promising. Perhaps she could get him to stop at Yarmouth by demanding particular foodstuffs.

"I'm with Ned," said the third man. "The sooner we get to Winchelsea, the better. It's bad luck having women on board a ship."

Even better. She could definitely make something of their superstition about women and ships.

Unfortunately, at that moment, it began to drizzle, forcing Isabella belowdecks. As she entered the cabin, she saw her sister sitting on the bed, arms wrapped around her knees. Her face was pale and sweaty.

"I don't feel so good," Adelaide said, then clamped her hand over her mouth and convulsed.

"Come," Isabella said, holding out her hand. "You need some fresh air, even if it is raining up there."

She pulled her sister briskly out the door and up the stairs to the deck, getting her to the rail just in time for Adelaide to vomit over the side. *Oh dear.* This was going to be a very long journey if Adelaide couldn't tolerate being on a ship. Isabella rubbed her lower back and made soothing sounds as her sister retched again.

Martin came running over. "Seasickness?" he asked Isabella. Adelaide wasn't in any state to answer for herself.

Isabella nodded.

"I have ginger biscuits that will help calm her belly, and I have a sleeping draught that can help her sleep off the worst of it."

Did she dare entrust her sister's health to this man?

But then, what choice did she have?

"I appreciate anything you can do to ease her suffering."

Their gazes connected for a moment, and all she saw was kindness and concern. Gone was the pompous coxcomb who had sparred with her nearly every time they spoke. Who was Lord Martin really, underneath all the bluster? Most men she'd known did not improve on acquaintance, but perhaps this one was different.

She shook herself and looked up at the dismal sky, not wanting to pursue that line of thought. He was still sent by Lady Eleanor and therefore not to be trusted.

Martin followed her gaze. "Yes, I wish I could do something about the weather, but alas, that is not within my control. Blue skies are rare as rubies this far north at this time of the year. I'm afraid we're in for rough weather and choppy seas these next few days."

He turned back to look at her as Adelaide retched once again. "I'll go get those biscuits and the sleeping draught and meet you in the cabin."

As soon as Adelaide's stomach was empty, Isabella helped her back down belowdecks. She didn't like how cold and clammy Adelaide's hand felt on hers, or the way her sister was shivering. Isabella could only pray that their brief foray into the elements didn't bring on something far worse than a little seasickness.

In the cabin, Isabella helped her sister onto the bed. Martin returned and knocked on the door, then opened it, holding out a carved, wooden cup with a dram of the sleeping draught.

"Thank you," Adelaide murmured before swallowing it down.

Martin handed her a small, hard biscuit, and she took it with a tenuous smile.

"You are too kind, my lord." Adelaide took a few tentative nibbles. "*Mmm.* You're right. That does help."

He gave her a gentle smile. "That's good, my lady."

Isabella's heart melted a bit at the sight of Martin's kindness to her beloved sister. She couldn't afford to like this man, but she had to admit, grudgingly, that sometimes he wasn't terrible.

"I'll leave you two alone to dry off and rest," he said, bowing. And then he was gone.

Adelaide took off her shoes and slid beneath the thick wool covers on the bed after finishing off the last of the biscuit, and Isabella sat down beside her.

"I like Lord Martin," Adelaide said, peering up with her big brown eyes. "He's kind. I'm glad you married someone with a good heart."

Clearing her throat, Isabella tucked her sister in. "Well, don't get too attached." She smoothed stray hairs out of Adelaide's face.

"What do you mean?" Adelaide started to sit up, brow furrowed and face full of concern.

Isabella pressed her gently back down. Should she tell her sister of her plans? It would be hard to hide in such close quarters. Perhaps it was time to be honest. "I don't plan to stay married to him."

She explained about the deal she'd struck with Martin, and her sister's frown grew deeper.

"But why would you leave a good man? I don't understand." Adelaide reached out for Isabella's hand with an imploring look.

"He's not a good man. His head is as swollen as an overfilled wineskin. Besides, I need to marry someone who is willing and able to defy Lady Eleanor so that I can keep you with me. There is no way I'm letting that harpy have you."

"But maybe Lord Martin can—"

"He won't," Isabella said firmly. "Lady Eleanor sent him, remember? We can't trust him. And you should hear the way he talks to me. Please believe me when I say that the baron is not the solution to our problems."

Adelaide frowned and retreated beneath the covers. "If you're certain you've thought this through—"

"I have." *Well, maybe not entirely.* Certain details were still fuzzy. Isabella needed time to think.

Adelaide covered her mouth as an enormous yawn overtook her. At least the sleeping draught was working quickly. Perhaps then Isabella might have some time to truly plot out her future.

As her sister dozed off, Isabella kicked off her shoes and settled back against the headboard. At last, she had some peace and quiet to consider her options. She began a mental list of possible ways to approach Lord James of Norfolk. For hours, she was absorbed in her planning, so it startled her when there was a knock on the door.

With a silent curse, she got up and went to the door. She didn't want to wake her sister.

Opening it, she saw Martin. *Of course.*

"How was your day, my lady? It looks like I interrupted you in the midst of deep thought."

She slipped out the door and let it close behind her to leave Adelaide in peace.

"I was planning. I think I'll marry the Earl of Norfolk once our marriage is annulled. He always liked me." There was no reason to keep her intentions a secret. It wasn't as if Martin was truly her husband.

A muscle in Martin's jaw bulged momentarily before he schooled his face into nonchalance. Was he bothered by this news? If so, it served him right for thinking this marriage was anything other than a pretense.

"That oaf?" Martin asked lightly. "He knows how to handle a lance on the tourney grounds. I'll give him that. But don't expect him to be a good and faithful husband to you. From what I've seen, he dips his wick in any passing strumpet that shows him a bit of leg. And he has a reputation for being cruel and ambitious. Is that truly what you want?"

Isabella was well aware of the earl's reputation and habits. "Why would I care what he does and with whom if I'm the countess of all of Norfolk?" It wasn't entirely true that she didn't care, but her life with her mother and Lady Eleanor had taught her to prize practicality above sentiment under all circumstances. The earl served her purposes, and that was all that mattered.

Martin looked at her long and hard, unnerving her completely. Then he shrugged. "Suit yourself. How is Lady Adelaide?"

"Mercifully asleep. The sleeping draught was quite effective." She gritted her teeth, then mumbled, "You have my thanks."

He beamed and winked, the scoundrel.

"I am very glad to hear she is resting peacefully. The seasickness should only last a day or two, and then she'll adjust. In the meantime, there are plenty of ginger biscuits. Might I trouble you to bring me my citole?" He gestured at the door. "It's in my cabin, and I don't want to disturb her."

Isabella ducked into the cabin, found the instrument, came back out, and handed it to him gingerly.

"Here's your little lute," she said, hoping to annoy him.

He grimaced for a moment before composing himself. Good, she'd scored a hit. It wouldn't do for him to think she was softening toward him. The sooner he concluded she had no heart to give, the better off everyone would be. She was on a mission and didn't want the distraction of his courtship.

"I was hoping you would join me for dinner and let me play you a few more tunes from Aquitaine," he said, strumming the instrument a few times and tuning the strings.

His proposal sounded rather tempting, which was dangerous. "I would rather hear a dog howl at the moon than listen to another one of your love songs."

Chuckling, he leaned close, his lips nearly brushing against her ear and whispered, "Woof."

Her breath caught and her pulse spiked, as tingles ran through her body. "Don't taunt me, you cur."

"Then don't bait me, you temptress. If I'm a dog, you'd best beware my bite." His teeth clicked shut right next to her ear, and she gasped. Why was she wondering what it might be like to have his teeth graze her earlobe? Worse yet, why did she want his lips to trail down her neck, for him to nibble on her shoulder and perhaps on places lower down?

He took a step back and gave her a look that was pure sin as his gaze lovingly caressed every curve, his lips twisted in wicked amusement. "Give in, Isabella. You know you want to."

"Give in to what?" Her voice was altogether too breathy.

"Everything. Let me worship you, my queen. Let me give you pleasure you've never dreamt of. Let me love every inch of you, goddess of my heart. Just say you'll be my wife in truth, and I'm yours."

All she could do was stare into those chestnut eyes flecked with amber and onyx. She was transfixed. Her heart was going to beat out of her chest if this went on much longer. Could he see what he was doing to her? Did he know?

"Or, if that's too much," he said, holding out a hand, "you could simply agree to join me for dinner."

"I suppose dinner would be acceptable," she said, resting her hand in his as if in a trance, but then she shook herself, forcing her mind back to reality. "The rest is never going to happen." She hoped he couldn't hear the regret in her voice.

This was no good. She had a plan, and she had to stick to it. Martin was a rogue who was under Eleanor's thumb, and she couldn't let herself forget that, not for one moment. There was too much at stake.

Martin only smiled. "Good. I've prepared a place for us to dine in the hold. I'll go ask Baldwin to set the table and bring the food, and I'll return for you in a trice, if you'll excuse me, my lady."

"You are excused." She wiggled her fingers dismissively, and he walked away chuckling, the bothersome lout. Ducking into the cabin to check on Adelaide one last time, she mentally braced herself for battle. By the time he knocked, she was ready for war, and come what may, she intended to win.

CHAPTER EIGHT

MARTIN GRINNED AS he reviewed his plan for the evening one last time. His campaign to pierce her defenses would begin even before they sat down to dine. It was clear that Isabella doted on her sister, and winning over Adelaide would go far toward softening her heart. While he'd been at Bamburgh Castle, he'd assigned his men the task of making friends with the servants and learning as much as they could about what the sisters liked.

He held a tray in his hand as he knocked on the cabin door. Given the state of Adelaide's stomach, he'd kept her meal simple—a bowl of hearty chicken broth, an apple, and a small dish of honeyed walnuts, which he happened to know Adelaide adored. There was a sprig of holly with bright red berries to decorate. But the real *pièce de resistance* was the scroll that lay on the side of the tray. He could hardly wait to see her open it.

When he knocked, Isabella opened the door, eyeing the tray with suspicion. "What is that?" she asked pointing her chin at the tray.

"Dinner for Adelaide," he answered. "Will you let me in?"

Isabella looked him up and down as if examining him for weapons, then grumbled as she opened the door.

"Oh dear," said Adelaide, as he carried over the tray. "Thank you for your kindness, but I don't think I could eat a thing."

Narrowing her eyes and giving him a withering look, Isabella took the tray and turned to her sister. "You must try, sweeting," she said in the softest, kindest voice he'd ever heard her use. "You must keep your strength up."

Adelaide bit her lip. "Perhaps I could stomach a few of those honeyed walnuts. Those are my favorite. How did you know?"

Martin leaned against the doorframe and smiled. "A lucky guess."

Straightening and turning abruptly, Isabella pinned him with a glare. "I know what you're up to and it won't work."

"I have no idea what you mean." He met her gaze with a smoldering one of his own. Oh, it was working. It was definitely working. And she didn't like it one bit. *Good.* He liked her riled up and feisty.

"Ooh, what's this?" Adelaide asked, unfurling the scroll. And then she gasped. "Oh my goodness, you brought me music! And not just any music, a *pastorela* by Cercamon! Where did you get this?"

He shrugged casually. "It's just something I picked up in Narbonne last year." More like something he'd hunted down over the course of multiple visits, spanning years. This was his favorite troubadour verse, and he simply had to hold the notes in his hand. He'd made a copy for himself, of course, but he was giving her the original. The man that sold it to him claimed it had been penned by the great Cercamon himself.

"This is too much," Adelaide said, clutching the parchment to her chest. "Did you know Cercamon is my favorite troubadour?"

He was starting to really like Adelaide. It was a shame he had to send her off to Lady Eleanor. Her company was delightful, and she certainly had a mellowing effect on her sister.

"I knew you were from Bordeaux and played the lute. I thought you might appreciate a little something from your homeland to distract you while you're feeling unwell." Her wide eyes gleamed with appreciation, and he knew he'd hit his mark. She would be an ally in his campaign to win Isabella, and even his warrior queen of a wife couldn't stand for long against a united front.

"Might I escort you to dinner?" he asked Isabella, holding out his arm.

Isabella pursed her lips and stalked toward him, then grasped his arm with fearsome strength.

"Enjoy your dinner," he said with a little bow to Adelaide before he opened the door for Isabella.

As soon as the door closed behind them, Isabella turned on him. "I won't let you use Adelaide as a pawn in your game."

"All I have done is offer her dinner and distraction. Any gracious host would have done as much." Never mind that he had put more thought into this evening's meal than he had about any other repast in his life. But it was worth it. *She* was worth it.

Isabella dug in her nails. "I'm watching you."

"Can't keep your eyes off me, eh?"

"Don't flatter yourself."

"I'd much rather flatter you. Come," he said, leading her to the hold where he'd set up an intimate grotto.

Guiding her through the door, he was rather proud of the effect he'd achieved. Pine boughs hung from the rafters as if they were under an enormous tree, their fresh scent mingling with the rich and decadent meal set on the table in the center. Panels of dark fabric hung down the sides of the space, covering the bulkheads, creating an intimate, velvety darkness. A metal lantern with tiny stars pierced through its sides hung above the table, creating the illusion of a starry night's sky as specks of light twinkled against the black. A single candle in a Venetian glass bowl provided a warm glow in the center of the table.

Her swift intake of breath was all the reward he needed for his efforts. She might deny it up and down, and almost certainly would, but she was impressed. He pulled out a chair for her, and she sat, eyes wide, taking in every detail.

With a smile of satisfaction, he sat down across from her and poured them each some wine, a special vintage made in her native Bordeaux. Then he began carving up roasted venison, serving the most choice cuts onto her plate and dolloping pepper sauce over them. The cook at Bamburgh had been with the family since Isabella's childhood and claimed it was her favorite meal.

Baldwin had really outdone himself replicating the recipe. They didn't usually have fresh meat on board, but one advantage of the frigid weather was that such delicacies could be stored without spoiling, at least for a little while. He would have to switch to fish before the end of their journey, but he would ply her with succulent roasts while he could.

Isabella licked her lips, even as her gaze turned wary. "Let's get this over with. I would like to return to my sister."

"As you wish, my queen. To your health," he said raising a glass and taking a sip. *Mmm.* This was an excellent vintage. He would have to make a point to order more.

"To a swift journey," she said, narrowing her eyes at him. "The sooner we can get off your little boat, the better."

His smile faltered. It was one thing for her to insult him, but *The Wind Song*? "This *ship* is as fine a vessel as any that sails the seven seas."

She shrugged. "It's adequate for a short journey, I suppose."

He shouldn't let her get to him. She was trying to goad him into biting back, and he couldn't allow her to win, but he couldn't help the twinge of irritation that her words provoked.

"Then it's fortunate we don't have far to go. But I've sailed to Venice and back in this ship. She is the finest in my fleet." He was glad none of his crew could hear them. They didn't take slights to *The Wind Song* lightly.

"A handful of fishing vessels and rowboats does not make a fleet."

He twitched, squeezing his hand into a fist beneath the table. *Take a deep breath, Martin. Let it pass.*

She carved off a piece of meat, staring him down in challenge. Piercing it with her eating dagger, she popped the bite into her mouth, and for a moment her expression changed to pure bliss.

Baldwin had done well indeed, though Martin found himself wishing that he, rather than his cook, had been the first to make her make that particular face. "You like the venison?"

She immediately schooled her expression back into stony disdain. "It's dry."

"If you say so." He took a bite himself, and truly, Baldwin had outdone himself. "And my fleet is made up of two knarrs, four hulks, and five cogs like this one." He should have left her insult unanswered, but it bothered him like a hangnail. He couldn't leave it alone.

"And I'm supposed to be impressed by that?"

He shrugged. "It's larger than average."

"Perhaps for a little baron from a small town."

"I assure you," he said, grinning, "there's nothing little about me, as you'll find out when you finally surrender to my seduction."

She choked on her wine. Swallowing it down with difficulty, she answered, "Then I'll live in eternal ignorance because I will never surrender." *Ha.* He was back on solid footing. He'd rocked her.

"We shall see." He winked at her, and she bristled beautifully—all haughty outrage and imperious disdain. A blush swept down from her cheeks to the tempting swell of her breasts. An answering burst of heat settled in his groin. Oh, the things he would do to her when he won this war! But these were barely the first skirmishes. He couldn't afford to get ahead of himself.

"I'm told you like to weave." It was time for him to retreat, draw her out. He had stoked her fury enough for one evening.

"I do," she answered stiffly between bites. It seemed his wife had a healthy appetite, no matter what she might have said about the food. His eyes were inexorably drawn to the sight of her full and luscious lips closing around the succulent venison at the tip of her eating dagger. She had no idea what she was doing to him just by sitting there and eating.

He turned his attention to his own food, shoving away the

mental pictures that were starting to play through his mind unbidden. "What do you weave?" he asked, hardly daring to look up.

"Tapestries, mostly," she said between bites. "It's very dull. I'm sure you don't want to hear about it."

"I do. Tell me." He leaned in and offered an inviting smile. "And have some of these roasted carrots in butter and sage. They're delicious," he said, spooning some onto her plate. Another favorite dish of hers.

She took a tentative bite then let out a barely audible, "*Mmm.*"

The look on her face was playing havoc with his self-control. What sweet torture it was to sit so close and yet be unable to touch her! But he had to keep his head. He was playing a long game, and it wouldn't do for him to get ahead of himself and scare her off.

"You like the carrots, then?"

"They're…acceptable."

He chuckled. "High praise. Don't worry. I won't let it go to Baldwin's head. But you were telling me about tapestries."

She stared at him for a long moment, then shrugged. "I like to keep my hands busy. The rhythm of it soothes me, helps me organize my thoughts. It requires just enough of my attention that it forces me to shut out the noise of the outside world. Weaving takes me out of myself and turns my endless nervous energy into something beautiful."

He smiled gently at her. "That's how I feel about playing the citole. There's something meditative and engrossing about plucking the strings in just the right way to make a lovely tune. My art is more ephemeral than yours, but we both like to create beauty with our hands. Something we have in common."

She raised an eyebrow at him. "So we do, I suppose. Not that it means anything."

But it did mean something. To her too, if his guess was correct. He'd worn her down from insults to mere wariness. It was progress.

"Would you mind if I play for you while you finish your meal?" he asked, reaching for his instrument.

"Do as you wish. I don't care," she answered, glancing up at him for a moment and then quickly averting her gaze. But in that fleeting glance he saw cautious hope. She wanted connection, needed it, if only she would let her defenses down long enough to let him in.

Isabella needed a friend in this world, he thought to himself as he began to strum a haunting tune he'd learned in Poitou. She was so busy trying to defend and protect Adelaide but who would defend and protect her? He would be at her service if only she would let him in. And someday she would, provided he bided his time and kept up a sustained campaign to slip behind her battlements and reach the loving heart that he knew beat within.

He glanced at her finishing her meal as he played away. Her beauty truly took his breath away, but it was her strength, intelligence, and loyalty that moved him. Could he truly win someone so magnificent? He talked a good game, but beneath his confident veneer, uncertainty pricked him.

He could very well lose this bet, and she would be lost to him forever, a prospect he could barely bring himself to contemplate. If that was truly what she wanted in the end, he would let her go, not because he didn't care but because he cared more than he should. There had been too much misery in her life, and he owed her the chance at happiness, even if it cost him his own.

But he planned to fight for her love with every weapon in his arsenal.

As he strummed the last notes of the song, their gazes met, and the wordless longing he saw in her eyes shook him to the core. He didn't move, terrified to break the moment. But she ended it with a blink. Immediately, her defenses were back up, and she refused to meet his gaze. "I should get back to my sister."

He bit back his disappointment. He could happily have played for her all night long.

"Of course, my lady," he said, setting his citole aside. "Let me escort you back to your cabin."

They traversed the short distance in silence, and he stopped at the door with a bow. "I bid you good night." Raising her hand to his lips, he brushed them softly with his lips.

He was delighted to hear a little gasp escape her. He'd made progress tonight, however miniscule. As far as he was concerned the evening had been a success.

"Good night, my lord." She turned and entered the cabin swiftly without looking at him.

As he stared at the closed door after it closed, he couldn't help worrying that his heart might be in very grave danger indeed.

CHAPTER NINE

ISABELLA WAS READY for battle as she strode out of the cabin and onto the deck the next morning. She'd let him weaken her defenses during dinner the previous night, and it wouldn't do to start getting sentimental over a baron who was manipulating her on behalf of Lady Eleanor. Everything depended on her keeping her head and remembering with whom she was dealing.

After breaking her fast with Adelaide, who was still looking decidedly green, she put on a red dress that displayed her figure to perfection. Most of the time, she tried to deflect attention so that she could listen unhindered and gather information, but this morning, she wanted to stand out.

Sailors were notoriously superstitious, and it was well-known that women were considered bad luck on a ship. It was time to stir up a bit of trouble—not enough to actually endanger the running of the ship, but enough to put Lord Martin on the defensive. If he was distracted placating his crew, he wouldn't have time to ply her with food and wine in the evening, lulling her into complacency with his citole. And maybe she could create enough of a stir to make him want to be rid of her entirely.

Her gaze snagged on Martin, standing on the forecastle, deep in conversation with two of his men. An unwanted burst of pleasure shot through her at the recollection of the previous night's dinner. A mental image of Martin's smoldering look as he plucked his citole with mesmerizing skill and dexterity made her bite her lip before she schooled her face back into a mask of haughtiness. She could not afford to speculate about what it might be like to have those skillful hands touching her, making good on his promise to worship every inch of her body.

Remember Lady Eleanor. You'll be her marionette forever if you give in.

Walking to the rail, she took deep, calming breaths, grateful for the brisk breeze that cooled her unwanted ardor. She had a job to do and a husband to lose. It was time to set to work.

Casting her gaze about and listening carefully, she looked for the man who had spoken about women being bad luck on a ship. The day before, she'd purposefully directed her gaze out to sea, so she wasn't sure what the man looked like, but she was certain she would recognize his voice.

Snippets of conversations wafted by as she cast a wide net.

"We're making good speed. Eight knots…"

"…and there's this place in Calais where the ladies all…"

"Swab that deck like you mean it, you wart on the arse of a…"

"Where did you want this barrel of ale?"

"Your left elbow is dipping when you thrust…"

Ah, *there* was the one she wanted. She turned her gaze toward a small group of half a dozen men on the starboard side near the aftercastle that appeared to be going through swordsmanship drill. Their leader was a great slab of a man demonstrating each move with his wooden practice sword, each stroke swift and sure. Clearly, he needed no steel to disembowel a man. His nose had been broken several times over, and his grizzled brown beard was flecked with white.

She sauntered over to the group, drawing every eye, one by one, until they were all gaping at her as she leaned against the rail beside them. "Good morning, boys," she said with a little wave. "Don't mind me. I just want to watch. Carry on."

The leader turned his thunderous gaze on her. "My lady, you

should be resting belowdecks." He hitched his head sideways in a none-too-subtle command.

"But I was bored," she pouted. "Can't I watch, even for a little bit? It's like being at a tournament. It's ever so much more interesting than my sewing. Please?"

She batted her eyelashes, then glanced at the other sailors. "I'm sure the men don't mind. Do you?"

Casting coy glances around, she smiled inwardly as they started to preen and posture before her.

"C'mon Osric. It can't do any harm to let the lady watch," a youth with a few scraggly chin hairs wheedled.

"You heard the lady. She's bored," said a tall, skinny man missing his two front teeth.

Osric grumbled as others joined the chorus.

It was a bit dangerous to attract the interest of so many of the crew's men this way but so was staying married to Lord Martin.

"All right, all right. You can stay," the big man said, cutting them off and turning to her. "I would ask that you stay silent and don't interfere, my lady." It clearly cost him to make the request politely.

"I wouldn't dream of interfering, my good man," she said with a triumphant smile.

As she settled back against the rail, every eye was on her and not a one on Osric. She ignored the rapid beating of her heart at being the center of their collective attention, and she beamed at them all.

"Pay attention, you limey boneheads. Eyes forward."

They all snapped to attention, guilty looks on more than one face. Her plan was working.

"Now raise your swords."

As one, they raised their wooden practice blades and began to drill. Only half of their attention was on their efforts, though. They kept stealing covert glances at her as they tried to show off. *Good*. That was exactly what she wanted.

When she was certain she had the attention of at least three of them, she drew a handkerchief from her sleeve and faked a violent, high-pitched sneeze. Scraggly-beard and Skinny-no-teeth tripped over each other and landed in a heap on the deck.

"Oh, dear me, what bad luck! Are you all right?" she asked, all innocent concern as she rushed to them.

Osric glared down at the scene, looking like a cauldron about to boil over.

"Are you hurt?" she asked the two men, bending down over them. "Such a shame I only have one handkerchief to bind your injuries. How ever shall I choose between you?"

Both men's eyes widened, and they began scrambling over each other. "It hurts here, my lady," said the youth, pointing to his knee.

"I can barely move my arm, my lady," said the other, eyes brimming with hope.

"What terrible luck that you should both be hurt while I'm looking on," she exclaimed, determined to rub it in and play her part to the hilt. Half-measures would not get her and her sister thrown off the ship. She tried to channel the manipulative, flirtatious energy of one of the ladies of the French court. They were masters at this sort of thing. "You were both so valiant with those big, heavy swords. I don't know how to decide, but I must."

"I'm suffering so! Please help me, my lady," the youth plead-ed with an exaggerated moan.

"I pick…" She closed her eyes and moved her finger back and forth between them. "You."

She pointed to Skinny-no-teeth. Scraggly-beard turned bright red and looked like he planned to knock a few more teeth out of his crewmate's mouth at the earliest opportunity. Kneeling down, she made a production of tying her handkerchief around the skinny man's arm.

The men all around were looking daggers at the man she was fussing over.

"Get up, you lazy—" Osric clamped his mouth shut to prevent whatever foul curse he was about to utter from leaving his mouth. "Up. All of you. Get back to work. Especially you," he ordered, pointing a thick, calloused finger at Skinny-no-teeth. "And, my lady, I will ask you once again to please leave us in peace."

Despite being delighted with the upset she'd caused, she was slightly worried about the edge in Osric's voice. But her ploy was working all too beautifully. Martin was sure to throw her off the ship in no time.

Indeed, the man himself came striding over. An unwanted sense of relief crept over her at his presence. He would keep his men in line in case any took this game a bit too seriously. It was a delicate line to walk—trying to get sent away but not putting herself in danger. But given the risks in every direction, she had to gamble on getting it right.

"What's going on here?" Martin demanded, staring down Osric despite the fact that he was at least a foot shorter than his crewmember.

The giant ham hock of a man quailed before Martin's disapproving gaze.

"She's stirring up trouble, my lord," Osric grumbled. "Tell her to go below and keep to herself. It's bad luck to have her mixing with the men."

Martin turned his gaze on her and cocked his head, a knowing smile curling his lips. *Damn the man.* "Were you stirring up trouble, Isabella?"

Steeling herself, she looked him in the eyes with no remorse. "I don't know what he's talking about."

Her husband looked her up and down, taking in the red dress and the way it clung to her form. Anyone with eyes would know she had dressed for trouble, and her husband was no fool.

"Walk with me," he said, offering an arm, in a genteel voice that nonetheless brooked no dissent.

Reluctantly, she obeyed. *Out of the pot and into the cauldron.* Dangerous as the crew could be if they truly turned against her or took her flirtation too seriously, the man before her was the one whom she truly had to worry about.

He steered her up the steep stairs to the forecastle and brought her to the bow of the ship, out of earshot of the other men. He looked at her with eyes full of what appeared to be admiration, though she knew that couldn't be true. Could it? "I know what you're up to, and it won't work."

"Oh?" she said lightly, as if he was wrong and she was innocent of exactly what he accused her of being. Be like Adelaide, she told herself. Sweet. Innocent. Naïve, even. She made her eyes soft, cow-like, and blinked. "And what exactly is it that you think I'm doing?" Nothing at all…

"I think you're trying to get out of our bargain early. In fact, I think," he said, leaning close enough that his warm, sweetly-scented breath whispered against her cheek, "you're afraid you'll lose."

She was frozen to the spot, unable to pull away from the magnetic pull of his proximity. This was no good at all. "You're wrong," she said in a voice that was too husky for her liking. "I never lose. The sooner you give up and let me marry an earl, the better off we'll all be."

He responded with a voice more like a purr, soft and velvety. "Why would I give up when I'm so clearly winning? I can see your pulse fluttering in your neck, you know. Don't try to pretend I don't affect you. I love the way your voice turns sultry every time I get close, the way your cheeks flush, the way your gaze turns molten. You want me, Isabella."

Was it written so plainly on her face? "No, I don't," she said in a breathy voice. That wouldn't do. Clearing her throat, she tried again. Harder. Harsher. "No, I don't. I'll never surrender to your pathetic efforts to woo me. I'm far too clever to fall into your poorly made trap."

His face turned suddenly serious. "Not a trap, Isabella. An offer. I would never try to trammel your fierce spirit. I want to give you joy and love and freedom in a world that will try to put you in a cage."

Freedom! Ha! What honeyed nonsense he speaks. "There's no such thing as freedom. At best, we get to choose between cages, and frequently not even that. You're in a cage too, my lord. Don't pretend otherwise. Are you not trapped between a weak king and his ambitious rival? Is that not why you sought marriage to a stranger? You are a kept pet, and I fear your cage would not fit us both."

It was the most honest thing she'd said since boarding this vessel. Perhaps it was unwise to reveal so much, but the need to confide in someone, even her enemy, had become too overwhelming. She'd never felt as alone as she did aboard this ship. There would never be anyone to defend her but herself. She had to escape Martin's snare, and the pressure of trying to evade such a clever opponent was wearing her down.

Martin sighed and shook his head. "I am sorry you feel that way. I must work harder to convince you otherwise. Look around you. Do you see any bars here? Or warring factions for that matter? At sea, we are free of their shackles. Until we reach Winchelsea, we leave war behind. And I have done everything in my power to keep Winchelsea free of strife as well. Its walls are well-defended. Within them, we can live as we please."

It was a valiant effort, but he was only strengthening her point. "And would we not be trapped within the walls of Winchelsea? Is that not a cage in and of itself? And a rather small one at that…"

"And you think an earl would give you freedom I cannot?"

His words struck far too close to the heart of the matter. She had no assurance that the future she fought for was an improvement on the one she was trying to escape. But with Martin, it was certain that she would be eternally under her ladyship's thumb and would lose her sister. With an earl, there was a chance she might work things to her advantage. Of course, it could all go terribly wrong, but she wasn't going to dwell on that.

"I'm not a fool. I know there will never be any freedom for me. But if I must live in a cage, I would like for it to be one of my choosing. Married to an earl, my cage would be spacious enough that I might forget the bars. Whereas with you, I would be hobbled and cramped. I have no intention of becoming your pet, my lord." It was the most honest answer she could provide. She had no reason to expect anything but misery from marriage, and she had to grasp for what compensation she could for surrendering herself to such a miserable state.

Martin nodded slowly. "You've given me much to think about. I must find a way to convince you that marriage to me is not a trap."

Poor deluded little baron. Nothing you could possibly say will change my mind.

"Talk all you like. I care not. But know that no words will sway me, no matter how clever and witty they might be."

He smiled, the coxcomb. "We shall see, my lady." And then the man had the audacity to wink at her. What gall! "In the meantime, I must ask you to please leave my crew out of your machinations. Keeping order on a ship is a matter of life and death. If you and your sister wish to arrive safely at your destination, do not interfere."

That sounded ominous. What did he mean by that?

She stiffened. "Is that a threat?"

"No, Isabella. Merely the truth."

Looking at the frigid ocean around her, she couldn't help shivering at the thought of how fragile their vessel was and how easily they might all succumb to a watery death. "You have my word I will not interfere with your crew."

There were other ways to sway the baron. She would find a way to land in Norfolk one way or another.

"Thank you. And now I must return to my work. You are welcome to scheme all you want, by the way, as long as you confine your conniving to me. I welcome the challenge." He winked again and turned to go.

Isabella couldn't help but smile at his parting words. Martin de Vere had no idea who he was dealing with. She would win this war if it was the last thing she did.

CHAPTER TEN

ALL IN ALL, Martin was feeling rather pleased with his progress as he stood on the forecastle next to Ulf, looking out at the sea and basking in a rare patch of sunshine. An invigorating breeze filled the sails and cleared the last cobwebs of drowsiness from his head. The ship was making good time. The weather was holding. And Isabella's defenses were weakening by the day. He could only bless his good fortune and pray it lasted.

"Ulf, have you ever tried to win over a woman who was determined not to be won?"

His first mate laughed. "Before I met my Rosie, there was a woman named Emmeline who I took a fancy to. The problem was everyone else did too. She was a pretty little wench, daughter of the town cooper. When she passed by, every head turned, and she knew it. I didn't stand a chance. But I didn't know that at the time."

"What did you do?" Who knew what wisdom his bearded friend might have? Perhaps he could glean an idea or two.

Ulf shrugged. "The usual things—flowers, sweet treats, offering to do chores and run errands for her. She was happy to let me beg and scrape, but she never gave me a smile that was just for me. It took me a whole year of addle-headed nonsense before I came to my senses. The first time she ever seemed to notice me was when I stood up to her and refused to do her bidding. She wanted me to carry a bundle to her cousin in the next town, but it was raining, and the roads were muddy. I decided I'd had enough, and I said *no*."

"And how did she react to that?"

Martin tried to imagine saying *no* to Isabella. She might very well push him overboard.

"She stared at me, and for a moment, I thought she was going to unleash seven hells on my head, but then the strangest thing happened."

"What?" Now, he had to know.

"She smiled, and before I knew what was happening, the saucy little wench tried to kiss me. Unfortunately for her, I wasn't interested. It was the dullest kiss of my life. Learned my lesson that day good and proper."

Martin couldn't help but smile. Somehow, he didn't think kissing Isabella could ever be dull. Unlike Ulf, he knew he was in a merry war from the start, and their traded barbs only made him want her all the more.

"But I don't think you'll have that problem with Lady Isabella, my lord," Ulf said, as if reading his mind. "She's a vixen, no doubt about it. And she won't make it easy on you, but the way she looks at you when she thinks no one is looking... I'd say you've caught her fancy and then some."

It warmed the cockles of his heart to hear that. "A man can hope." A flash of blue caught his attention. "Ah, there she is now. I think I'll go try my luck."

He walked over to where she now rested against the rail beside her sister, wisps of raven hair escaping from the interwoven braids down her back. He breathed deep, reveling in the herbal scent of her mixed with the sea breeze. Trying Ulf's technique was a gamble, but he had to get through to her somehow. It was just crazy enough to work.

"Good afternoon, ladies." He doffed his cap and then continued on his way, not waiting for a response. Would she take the bait?

"Where do you think you're going?"

A bite. A little thrill of triumph ran through him. "I'm going about my business. Running a ship requires careful attention, so if you'll excuse me…"

Yet again, he made to leave.

"Does your cook have any pheasant?"

That brought him up short. Why in heaven's name was she asking about pheasant on board a ship? "I'm afraid not, my lady. We cannot keep fresh meat for long while we are at sea. We still have some of the venison we enjoyed last night if you are craving something other than fish."

She sighed dramatically. "What a shame! Pheasant is a particular favorite of ours, isn't it, Adelaide?"

Her sister frowned and opened her mouth, then closed it again. "Is it?"

"Of course, it is!" Isabella's overly bright smile failed to convince her little sister, whose brow furrowed more deeply with each word. "We simply adore pheasant. I don't know how we'll manage such a long sea journey without it. Oh, but perhaps we could stop along the way and get some."

Ah. The game she was playing became clear. "You wish for us to stop in port. To get pheasant. By any chance, would the port you wish to stop at be in Norfolk?"

Isabella narrowed her eyes. "And what if it was?"

Damn it all! He thought he was making progress. She was nothing if not stubborn and single-minded.

"Then I would tell you that we do not have plans to stop in Norfolk. It would lengthen our journey and, given the ongoing war, put us all at risk. We will not stop and endanger the crew for a mere craving, but I would be happy to introduce you to Baldwin so that you can plan your meals with the provisions we have at hand. Come. I'll show you to the galley."

He held out his arm, waiting for her to take it. Perhaps calling her bluff wasn't the wisest tactic at the moment, but her continued obsession with Norfolk annoyed him too deeply to think straight.

"Oh, but I wouldn't want to trouble him." She clasped her hands in front of her and averted her gaze.

He couldn't help but laugh out loud. "You were willing to divert my entire ship and put my crew in danger for a whim, and now you won't even talk to my cook? You must choose more subtle stratagems, my lady. Your motives are all too transparent."

She raised herself up to her full height and crossed her arms as she stared at him. "It was worth a try."

So brazen! She wasn't even bothering to pretend. He wasn't sure whether to be insulted or impressed. From the way his cock twitched, he rather thought the latter.

"No, it wasn't," Adelaide interjected. "We would never want to trouble you or your crew, my lord. You have been most kind to us."

Well, that was unexpected! Adelaide had certainly come around to his side. And what a pleasant surprise it was to see her standing up to her sister.

He bowed. "You, dear Lady Adelaide, are no trouble at all. Your sister, on the other hand…"

Isabella arched an eyebrow. The flash of defiance in her eyes set his heart ablaze.

"She is exactly the type of trouble I like. God help me."

For a glorious moment, Isabella smiled despite herself. Another chink in her castle wall. Before their journey was through, he would bring it all crumbling down. She tried to school her face back into a look of haughty disdain, but it was too late. In that moment, she had revealed herself.

"And you are the type of trouble I cannot afford, my lord." She turned away and looked out at sea.

A more honest answer than he expected. Somehow, he needed to convince her that he wasn't trying to trap her, that she was safe with him. "If only you would give me a chance to make my case—"

"Save your breath. There is nothing you can say to sway me."

"What offense have I committed that you are so adamant against me?" He hadn't intended to speak so plainly, but perhaps he might get an answer.

"*You*, my lord, are the offense. Is that not obvious?"

She certainly didn't pull her punches. Her bald attack made him chuckle. "And which part of me do you find most offensive?"

She crossed her arms and narrowed her eyes, perusing him. "It is difficult to choose. Your position is lowly. Your ship is small. Your person has all the appeal of a boiled potato. Your eyebrows are too thick. But of all your flawed parts, I must say your tongue causes me the most frequent offense."

"My *tongue*? I have much better uses for it, if you will but let me demonstrate." His imagination began to spiral with possibilities as he watched her reaction.

Her eyes widened, and something like interest sparked deep within them, but she quickly shuttered it. "Your conversation is as interesting as a boiled gruel. Please leave me in peace." Turning away from him, she looked out to sea once more.

Clearly, she had no interest in continuing the conversation. Very well, then. He'd won a small victory, and now he needed time to regroup and rethink his tactics. And he still hadn't fully given up on Ulf's advice. "Then if you'll excuse me, I have a ship to run."

Adelaide put her hand on his arm and waylaid him. "Please don't mind Isabella. You truly have been most kind to us. We appreciate your taking us away from Bamburgh and taking such good care of us on board your ship. My sister is grateful too, even if she doesn't show it."

What a dear Adelaide was! He smiled and patted her hand, ignoring Isabella's huff from the railing. "Have no fear. I know she's coming around, even if she doesn't want to admit it."

Isabella made a rumbling noise in her throat, and he thought it best to make a swift retreat. "If you'll excuse me."

As he headed to the forecastle, Isabella and Adelaide began arguing in low murmurs. About him, no doubt. The thought made him grin ear to ear.

"You look pleased with yourself, my lord," said Ulf, glancing away from the astrolabe he was studying. "Any luck wooing your bride?"

"Not to hear her tell it. But I do think I'm making progress, little by little." Looking out at the horizon, he was pleased to see that it looked like the weather was holding, at least for the time being.

"You have your father's optimism," Ulf said with a chuckle. "He married your mother sight unseen, you know, and they were one of the happiest couples I ever met."

The mention of his father gave his heart a pang. How he wished his father had lived long enough to meet Isabella! He would have charmed her immediately, just as he did everyone he met. That would have been something to see. No one could withstand Papa's buoyant cheer, gentle kindness, and penchant for mischief for long. Everyone fell under his spell eventually.

Many had commented on how alike Martin and his father were, at least in personality. His brother had gotten their father's looks.

Unfortunately, Martin had gotten his looks from his maternal grandfather, a man of middling looks and middling height who made up for those deficiencies with a superb intellect. Martin was grateful he'd inherited that in some measure as well. He needed some advantages to make up for his uninspiring outward appearance.

But Papa's unquenchable spirit lived on in him, and he planned to make the most of it as he wooed his reluctant bride.

"I've heard my parents' story many times—how he married the notoriously headstrong daughter of an earl to save his fiefdom from ruin after several years of poor harvests. How he brought her favorite flowers every morning and plied her with almond cakes until she succumbed to his charm. Mama always did have a sweet tooth."

"And your father took full advantage. Have you tried wooing

Isabella with food?"

Martin smiled ruefully. "She's demanding pheasant."

"At sea?" Clearly, Ulf agreed that the request was unreasonable.

"I know." Martin sighed. "It's a ploy to try to get us to stop in Norfolk."

"Why does she want to stop in Norfolk?"

Martin debated how much to reveal to his first mate. He trusted Ulf with his life, but this was a sensitive topic. The last thing he wanted was to sow doubt about his marriage to Isabella in the minds of his men. "She has a friend there who she wants to see, but I told her it was too dangerous."

The truth, if a bit hazy on the details. He didn't want the crew to know he had a potential rival for her hand. They were fiercely loyal, and he didn't want to sway them against Isabella any more than they already were.

"Agreed. The earl's allegiances are unclear. It's best not to risk it." Ulf clapped him on the shoulder. "You'll find a way to win her heart one way or another. There's too much of your father's spirit in you. Sooner or later, she's bound to fall. Besides, you're married. It's not as if she can go find someone else."

Ah. That was the crux of it. Time was short, and she had designs on that loathsome earl. He prayed he could win her before it was too late. Perhaps it had been foolhardy to make such a wager with her. She was far more effective at defending herself than he could ever have believed. Still, he was making progress, however slowly.

"She'll come around." Martin pretended more confidence than he felt. "She can't hold out forever." If only he had forever. He was certain he was cracking her shell, but their voyage seemed far too short to achieve his end.

He glanced back at where Isabella stood with Adelaide, still deep in discussion. Perhaps his friend's advice earlier about ignoring her might work. It was a risky gambit, but he had to try something new and keep her off balance. She was adapting to his tactics far too quickly.

"Bring me the charts. I want to check our progress," he said to Ulf. There was plenty of work to be done, and the common wisdom was that absence made the heart grow fonder. Perhaps he could make this work.

CHAPTER ELEVEN

How dare Martin ignore her! He'd left Isabella and Adelaide alone for dinner the previous night, Baldwin serving them in their room. He hadn't bothered to so much as say "hello" as she broke her fast in the morning, standing on deck, shivering in the frigid sea breeze. How was she supposed to convince him to stop in Norfolk if he refused to even speak to her?

Adelaide's continued seasickness was another worry. Isabella plied her with broth and ginger biscuits, then gave her a sleeping draft when her sister's stomach still threatened to rebel.

As Isabella paced the deck, the weight of her isolation came crashing down on her. There was no one she could turn to as the ship journeyed onward. If she didn't find a solution quickly, she was going to lose her sister. She was married to an irritating man who had no reason to release her aside from his word. At any moment, he could decide he wanted to keep her, and there was nothing she could do about it except try to convince him that they wouldn't suit. Except that everything she did to try to fend him off only seemed to fan the flames.

"You seem restless, my lady." The deep male voice nearly made her jump out of her skin. She turned around quickly to see Martin's first mate.

"Ulf, isn't it?"

"Aye, it is, my lady. His lordship sent me to see if there was anything we can do to make your journey more pleasant. A ship doesn't offer many opportunities for entertainment, but we aim to make you as comfortable as possible during our journey."

Isabella looked the large man up and down, deeply skeptical that he was capable of offering any diversion she would enjoy. But perhaps he could be useful.

"Tell me, good man, why his lordship couldn't come and inquire after me himself?"

It irked Isabella that he was sending an emissary rather than subjecting himself to her campaign of persuasion. But perhaps Ulf could be persuaded. What would make the first mate of a ship want to land when his captain and liege lord didn't?

"Running a ship and managing the men requires a great deal of attention. He is preoccupied at the moment, I'm afraid, and is likely to remain so all day." Ulf was putting on a good show, but he was clearly making excuses for his lord.

"And so he sends his first mate? Doesn't he need you too?"

"He can spare me for the moment." Ulf looked her in the eyes as if daring her to keep questioning him.

She was starting to rather like Ulf. He stood his ground, and clearly his loyalty to his lord ran deep. "Excellent. How long have you been his first mate?"

"Five years, my lady. It's been an honor serving him. I couldn't ask for a better captain. Or a better liege lord, though he's only been baron for a year now."

"So recent! I knew his father had passed, but the grief must be fresh." An unwelcome sliver of sympathy wormed its way into her heart. "Were they close?"

"Oh, aye. Lord Gilbert took his son everywhere, introducing him to life at sea and to his many friends at various ports of call. He was right proud of the way Lord Martin took to it. His other son, Lord Lance, never cared for it and has always preferred to stay on shore. The two brothers couldn't have been more different."

Isabella couldn't help but be intrigued by these insights into Martin's family, but she chided herself to focus. She shouldn't care what Martin's family was like, as she was unlikely ever to meet them. It was time to redirect the conversation. "I'm sure that you also have many friends at various ports of call. Which are your favorite ports along the English coast?"

"Aside from Winchelsea?"

She nodded.

"It's hard to choose. I do like the southern ports better than the northern ones, especially in winter. I spent my youth gadding about the Cinque Ports taking odd jobs on ships. I had an itch to explore, and what better way than at sea? But my heart belongs in Winchelsea."

That was all fine and good but of no help to her plans. "Tell me about the ports we're passing on our voyage. Surely some are better than others. If we were forced to stop along the way, where would you recommend?"

Ulf stroked his bread. "Hmm. It depends on why we had to stop. Different ports offer different advantages. Lord Martin knows the local lords in Scarborough, Skegness, Yarmouth, Ipswi—"

"Yarmouth! How interesting!" Yarmouth was exactly where she wanted to go. "Lord Christopher is the local baron, is he not?"

"Aye, my lady. It's a goodly port. Plenty of trade when there isn't a war on, and there's an excellent shipwright who knows his business when it comes to repairs."

That could be useful. "Is this ship in need of any repairs?" She wouldn't go so far as to sabotage anything, but if there was some maintenance that was needed, perhaps she could argue for a stop.

"Not at present, my lady. Have no fear. Everything is ship shape aboard *The Wind Song*."

How disappointing! "And what about—"

Her thought was interrupted by Martin clearing his throat behind her. *Good.* Exactly the man she wanted to see. She whipped around to find him holding a bundle of scrolls and an astrolabe. "A thousand pardons for my interruption, but I must borrow my first mate. Ulf, I need you to take a look at these charts with me. Come."

Curses! He wasn't here for her.

Ulf bowed his head. "Apologies, my lady. Duty calls."

"Will I see you later, Lord Martin?" she called after the retreating back of the bane of her existence. How was she supposed to convince him to stop in Yarmouth if he wouldn't take the time to speak to her?

He paused and turned. "I'm afraid navigation in this part of the sea requires careful attention. I'm likely to be occupied all day. Now if you'll excuse me."

He turned his back on her again, the scurvy knave!

"Will I see you for supper, at least?" What happened to the man who had all the time in the world to ask her about weaving and play his citole?

"Unlikely, my lady. As you can see, I am otherwise occupied. Now, if you'll please let me go about my business…"

She pursed her lips together and narrowed her eyes. He was playing a game with her. She was certain of it. "If you must."

The long-suffering smile he wore failed to hide the glint of mischief in his gaze.

Fine. If he was going to ignore her, she was going to ignore him right back, making sure he saw every moment of her complete inattention.

Catching the arm of the first passing sailor, she said, "Excuse me, my good man. Would you mind assisting me? I wish to ascend to the forecastle, but I'm afraid I may be unsteady on the ladder. Would you mind climbing up behind me to make sure I don't fall?"

The poor man turned bright red and made noncommittal noises.

"Excellent. Thank you so much for your assistance. What is your name?"

"Oh…*er*…*um*…Fergus, my lady." He looked a bit like her

brother, Crispin. They had the same dark hair and similar muscular build. He seemed exactly the sort of man who might make her temporary husband jealous.

"Thank you so much for agreeing to help me."

"I...*um*...I didn't—"

"Wonderful."

She headed over to the ladder to the forecastle, making a production of climbing up and then slipping intentionally so that Fergus had to catch her. He released her as soon as she was righted, as if she was made of hot coals.

"My lady, I don't think you should—"

"Nonsense. I'll be just fine."

She winked at him and started up the ladder again, glancing over her shoulder to make sure that Martin was watching. He was. At least for a moment. He quickly turned away and started speaking to Ulf, but she'd caught him. *Good.* This was working.

On the forecastle, she twirled around and breathed deeply. "I simply love it up here! Don't you?"

"I...if...if you'll excuse me, my lady."

Fergus fled. She'd pushed him too far. *Ah well.* There were other ways to irritate her pompous little baron.

She looked around and found a weapons chest. Smiling, she drew forth the smallest sword she could find and began going through the basic drills Crispin had taught her when they were children. Before her mother had caught her when she was ten and put an end to her secret sparring with Crispin, she had been rather good with a sword. Hopefully, the sight of her swinging a weapon about would catch his lordship's attention.

Sure enough, it did. Martin took several steps in her direction, then stopped and waylaid one of his men. Much to her disappointment, it was a minion and not the man himself who climbed the ladder.

"Excuse me, my lady, but I must insist you leave the weapons in the weapons chest."

Martin's emissary was a middle-aged man, this time with a

balding pate. He looked at her like a wayward child up to mischief. Which, she supposed, she was, at the moment.

"I assure you that I'm being perfectly safe. I merely need some exercise after being cooped up below decks for so long."

The man shook his head. "You may walk about the deck if you need to stretch your legs, but leave the weapons alone please, my lady." It clearly cost him to be polite about it.

"I'll stop if Lord Martin asks me to himself."

Let her so-called husband come up here to try to stop her. She'd had enough of the silent treatment and was growing desperate.

"Lord Martin is otherwise occupied, my lady. Please hand over the sword."

"I answer to my husband, not to you." She knew she wasn't making any friends amongst the crew with her behavior, but perhaps that would work in her favor. If they all wanted to get rid of her, perhaps they wouldn't mind dropping her off at Yarmouth.

The sailor stormed off and spoke to Martin.

With a smirk, she took a few more experimental swings with the blade. It felt rather good in her hands. Perhaps she should learn swordsmanship in truth. It was a rare skill for a lady but not unheard of. After all, hadn't Lady Eleanor herself been armed when she went on crusade?

"Give me the sword, Isabella." Martin had climbed onto the forecastle and now held out his hand.

Triumph! She had his attention, at last.

She narrowed her eyes. "Ask nicely."

He raised his eyebrows at the challenge. "No. You wished to gain my attention, and now you have it. Hand over the sword before I take it from you."

At his words, she couldn't help but smile. "I'd like to see you try." She shouldn't goad him like this, but having carried this farce thus far, she couldn't seem to stop herself.

He gritted his teeth. "Very well."

In a blur of motion, he twisted the sword from her hand with ease, despite her attempt to evade him, and it clattered to the deck. Somehow, she ended up with her arm pinned behind her back and his arm wrapped around her waist, holding her in place, her back against his front.

His breath tickled her ear as he said, "Well played, Isabella, but this particular game is over, both for your safety and my crew's."

"I assure you, my lord, I am perfectly safe with a blade." *Oh dear.* She liked being this close to him far too much.

"You'll notice that none of my crew practices with steel. If you wish to do sword drills, you must use a wooden sword like the rest of them."

She should demand to be released, but instead she leaned back into him and said, "I'd like a word with you."

"You have my undivided attention. What will you do with it?"

His breath tickled her neck, and her treacherous body went up in flames. She had to fight this. Somehow, she had to get to Yarmouth so that she could save Adelaide. Exhilaration and heat warred with her fear of the consequences of her actions.

"I'll…I'll…" Why was it so hard to think? She found herself shifting against him, craving more contact. This was no good at all.

"You'll what?"

She hardly trusted herself to answer.

"I'm rather enjoying having you at my mercy, you know. If I was feeling wicked, I might nibble on your ear and kiss my way down your neck. Would you stop me?"

"No." *No?* Had she lost her mind?

"Would you welcome it?"

"Yes." Even worse! Her self-control hung by a thread. Or perhaps the thread had already snapped.

His teeth grazed her earlobe, and her breath caught. A hunger unlike any she had ever experienced consumed her, and a tiny whimper escaped her lips.

"Oh, Isabella." He nuzzled her neck, and his lips brushed her skin.

It was unfair the things he made her feel. This was far too dangerous. She couldn't afford to give in, no matter how strong her yearning. "No!"

She pulled away, and he let her go. "I have to go check on Adelaide," she said hastily and fled below decks to the cabin where her sister dozed.

What a disaster! She absolutely couldn't afford to give in to the mad impulses she had around her husband. It would only lead to woe, and the consequences for her and Adelaide would be dire. She couldn't afford any further lapses.

Fanning herself in the dim light, she couldn't help but think that her plan to marry the Earl of Norfolk was getting more difficult by the hour. For a moment there, she'd lost her mind and wondered what would happen if she surrendered to Martin. Would it truly be worse than surrendering to Lord James?

But there was still Adelaide to consider. With difficulty, Isabella hardened her heart once again. She could not surrender, no matter what.

CHAPTER TWELVE

ADELAIDE AWOKE ON their fourth day at sea refreshed and hungry, so Isabella went to the galley and asked for two servings of salted pork and cheese, hurrying in the hopes of avoiding Martin. After their encounter the day before, she couldn't afford any more slips. Fortunately, the man was nowhere to be seen. When she returned, Adelaide was up and dressed, sitting at the little table in the cabin.

"How are things going with Lord Martin?" Adelaide asked as Isabella put down the bowl of pork and cheese.

"I'm not speaking to him." Isabella took a quick bite to avoid saying anything more.

"You'll have to speak to him sometime. He's your husband."

No, she did not. Perhaps it was too much to hope he would stop in Yarmouth, but if she could avoid talking to him for the duration of their journey, perhaps he would finally get the message that his attentions weren't welcome. Not that she entirely believed it herself after yesterday, but she had to keep up the pretense.

"Only in name, and not for long," Isabella said aloud. "How are you feeling?" She desperately wanted to change the subject. If she never spoke of Lord Martin again, it would be too soon. The whole situation was too mortifying.

"Much better. I'd like to go up on deck today and see how the ship works."

Isabella grimaced. If she could have hidden in the cabin all day, she would have, but she couldn't say "no" to Adelaide. "We'll go up after breakfast." It meant seeing Martin, but there was no way around that on the ship. And there were few things she wouldn't do for the sake of her sister.

Lord Martin spotted them the moment they appeared on deck. Isabella's face was aflame as he swaggered over and kissed her hand, looking so irritatingly pleased with himself.

"Good morrow, my ladies. I trust you slept well?"

No, she hadn't. She'd privately relived his kisses along her neck again and again as she tossed and turned. How could a man she held in such low regard make her feel such things? And yet he did. There was no denying it, at least within her own head. To him, she would deny it to the ends of the earth.

Adelaide answered, "Very well, my lord," when Isabella failed to find her tongue.

"You look much better this morning, Lady Adelaide. Has your seasickness abated at last?"

"It has, my lord. I asked Isabella to bring me up to take some air. I'm very curious about your ship."

No! Don't prolong the conversation! But there was nothing Isabella could do, so she stared fixedly at her toes and bit her tongue.

"*The Wind Song* is marvelous, isn't she? What would you like to know about her?"

Gritting her teeth, Isabella looked up to give him a warning glance. Hopefully, he would take her hint and keep it short.

"Is there something you would like to say, Isabella?" His expression was all charm and sweetness.

Quite a number of things, as a matter of fact, but not in present company. "Not at all, my lord. Carry on." She hoped he would see the warning in her expression and back off, but instead his eyes flashed with heated interest.

She didn't know whether she wanted to kiss him or throttle him as her body went up in flames at his appreciative regard.

"How do you know that the ship is headed in the right direction when all you can see is ocean all around?" Adelaide asked, miraculously oblivious to the silent exchange.

He launched into a detailed explanation of navigation and how they used maps, an astrolabe, and the position of the sun to set their course. Adelaide was entranced, much to Isabella's chagrin. It wasn't fair for him to inveigle her sister in his scheming.

"That's all very interesting, but I'm certain you must be ever so busy," Isabella said, smiling her most ferocious smile. "Please feel free to go about your business. We wouldn't want to trouble you."

"No trouble at all," he said with a wink. "In fact, I was just coming to find you. I have a gift for you, Lady Adelaide." He pulled a thin white stick about the length of his hand from the leather pouch attached to his belt, and handed it to Adelaide.

"Oh! A new plectrum! What a thoughtful gift!" Adelaide's eyes shone as she took the odd little stick.

"A what?" Rarely was Isabella at a loss, but this was simply bewildering.

"It's for strumming her lute. I made it myself from whale-bone."

Clever devil. He knew Isabella would never accept anything from him, so he was outmaneuvering her. For a moment, she was tempted to pluck it from Adelaide's hands and throw it overboard, but she couldn't bring herself to do that to her sister.

"Well played, my lord."

Her husband grinned. "I'm playing a long game, dear wife, and I mean to win."

"We shall see, my lord. We shall see."

Fortunately, Ulf called out for him, giving her the perfect excuse to be rid of him. "Don't let me keep you. Clearly you have more important matters to attend to."

He kissed her hand and bowed to Adelaide before turning to attend to business.

She tried to ignore the tingling sensation that shot through her at the touch of his lips. It was with great relief that she watched him walk away.

"Good riddance," she grumbled once he was gone.

"I thought he was very kind and thoughtful," Adelaide said, frowning at her.

Isabella sighed. "Yes. A little too kind and thoughtful for my taste. Don't fall for his act. He's still going to deliver you to Lady Eleanor. The man can't be trusted."

Adelaide opened her mouth to argue, then closed it again upon seeing Isabella's face.

"Let's enjoy the sunshine and sea breeze and forget all about a certain inconvenient baron, shall we?" She intended to do her very best to ignore him for the remainder of their journey, if at all possible.

Isabella and Adelaide spent the morning together, alternating between sitting on deck, watching the crew go about their business, and relaxing in the cabin, Isabella with a bit of embroidery and Adelaide with her lute.

Fortunately, Martin left them alone, at least until early afternoon.

He approached them as they stood by the railing, watching a flock of seagulls drift by.

"Now that you're feeling better," he said, keeping his eyes on Adelaide and ignoring Isabella completely, "perhaps the three of us can dine together this evening, and we can play together after our meal."

"I'd love that!" Adelaide put a hand on Isabella's arm. "May I?"

Isabella nodded after a pause, unable to come up with a reason to refuse.

"Then it's settled. I'll see you at dinner," Martin said, bowing to Adelaide. "And you, Isabella." He bowed to her as well.

She lifted her chin and looked at a cloud formation past his head, and mercifully, he turned to go.

He left them to their own devices for the remainder of the day. On several occasions, Isabella felt Martin's gaze upon her, but he was always looking away when she turned. Apparently, he was still keeping his distance, a tactic she was determined to ignore after her earlier lapse.

It wasn't until the sun sank in the sky in a riot of color that Martin stepped away from his business and approached them once again. "My ladies, will you do me the honor of joining me?"

He offered one arm to Isabella and the other to Adelaide and accompanied them down to the hold he had turned into a pathetic attempt at a sylvan grotto. If he thought to impress her with a few scraggly tree branches, some tent fabric, and a fancy lantern, he had a great deal to learn. She was as impervious to his attempts to create a romantic setting as she was to his wooing. Her heart certainly didn't melt a little at the sight, nor did she allow herself to smile as her sister took in the scene, wide-eyed.

"It's beautiful," Adelaide said, pausing as they entered. "I feel like a fairy princess in here."

"Why thank you, Lady Adelaide," Martin said as he pulled out chairs for each of them in turn. "I'm rather proud of how it all came together. What do you think, Isabella?"

He helped her into her seat as she tried to come up with a cutting response. "Why anyone would want to pretend to eat in the woods is beyond me. What is the attraction? Do you *like* being plagued by mangy woodland creatures trying to steal your food while you eat? For my part, I much prefer the comfort of a great hall, thank you very much. If you hoped to impress me, you have fallen far short of the mark."

Martin crossed his arms and shook his head, smiling. "Liar. You like it. I heard you gasp the first time I brought you in here, and I saw you smile just now when you thought I wasn't looking."

Ugh. Did he have to be so perceptive? "That night, you must have seen me stifling a sneeze, and just now, I was holding back laughter. It truly is ridiculous the lengths you've gone to in your efforts to impress me. Have I not told you I have a heart of stone? You're wasting your time."

Adelaide laughed. "Don't worry, my lord. She likes it. And she does have a heart under all her bluster for all her protestations to the contrary."

"Traitor," Isabella murmured. Didn't Adelaide understand the potential consequences of encouraging the baron? She would need to have a talk with her sister about the dangers of Lord Martin before the night was out. The man wasn't trustworthy. How could Adelaide not see that? "Let's eat quickly and get out of here. I don't wish to endure Lord Martin's company any longer than I must."

"But we were going to play together! You agreed!" Adelaide gestured at her lute.

Curse it, she had. "I'm sorry, sweeting. You're just recovering, and you shouldn't push yourself. And I don't want to spend any more time in his company than I must."

Adelaide sighed heavily and gave Martin an apologetic shrug.

"As my lady wishes," Lord Martin said with a little bow. "I'll have Baldwin bring in the food."

He left the cabin for a moment, and Isabella turned to Adelaide. "I'm trying to save you from being sent off to France. Please don't take his side. It only complicates matters."

"I think you underestimate him. He's been nothing but kind to both of us. I think you'd be far better off with him than some stuffy earl you hardly know. As for me, I'll be fine. I've survived Mother for all these years. Can Lady Eleanor truly be so much worse? I'd rather stay with you, but what hope do any of us have of defying the woman who is poised to become the queen of England any day now?"

Before Isabella had a chance to respond, Martin returned, followed by Baldwin carrying trays with enough food to feed half the crew, and it all smelled heavenly. There was a venison pie with a perfectly flaky golden crust, a bowl of roasted carrots and parsnips, a loaf of fresh bread, a lump of soft cheese, and a pitcher of wine. Her stomach betrayed her by growling as Baldwin arrayed the food on the table.

"Eager for more of Baldwin's cooking, beloved?"

She refused to answer, crossing her arms and staring down at the plate laid before her.

"Thank you, Baldwin. You have outdone yourself. My deepest thanks for your efforts." The man was kind to his crew, not that it mattered. He was still a thorn in her side.

"Yes, thank you, Baldwin," Adelaide called out as the scruffy cook made his exit. "Really, Isabella, you're being terribly rude. Just look at this lovely feast!"

"I will endure this dinner if I must, but don't expect me to enjoy it." And she didn't. Mostly. The food was delicious, and the easy rapport between Martin and Adelaide as they ate made her heart ache. But she had to remain strong. She couldn't give Martin an inch, or all her plans would be for naught.

When the interminable dinner finally ended, Martin insisted on a bit of music, having a sailor bring Adelaide's lute and his citole. Isabella endured it in stony silence, determined not to be charmed by the touching scene. At last, she succeeded in dragging Adelaide away, much to her sister's chagrin.

"I don't understand why you treat him so poorly when he's being such a gracious host," Adelaide said as soon as they were safely back in their cabin with the door closed.

"Because I want a better life for you than I've had. Is it so wrong of me to want to defend you from risking your life by sending you off to serve Lady Eleanor? What if you take ill while you're serving the duchess? Do you think anyone is going to tenderly nurse you back to health?"

Adelaide put her hands on her hips. "I've survived all these years with Mother without your help. How is Lady Eleanor worse?"

Guilt assailed her at her sister's words. "I never would have left you in Mother's clutches for so long if I'd had the means to come to your rescue. I've worried about you every day since you left. Your delicate constitution—"

"Do you think I don't worry about you too? I don't want to see you throw your life away on some awful earl when you've had the good fortune to marry someone kind and thoughtful. You've sacrificed enough already serving Lady Eleanor all those years. And let me worry about my own phlegmatic lungs. I've endured them my whole life. I know how to take care of myself."

Isabella forced herself to take a deep calming breath before responding. "First of all, Lord Martin isn't kind and thoughtful. He's a preening coxcomb who thinks far too much of himself. Can't you see that he's manipulating you? The man drives me mad, and I have no desire to spend the rest of my life with him. Second, I've only just found you again. I'm not ready to let you go. Third and most importantly, I refuse to entrust your health and your life to a woman as volatile and capricious as Her Grace. I love you too much to lose you again."

Adelaide's arms dropped, and her expression softened. "I love you too. Let's stop fighting. If you don't trust Lord Martin, then I'll do my best to follow your lead. Do you truly not like him?"

"I loathe him." She couldn't stand the way he got under her skin and made her feel so hot and restless. There was no way she was going to give in to his campaign of seduction, despite her mad moment of weakness. "You should get some sleep, my sweet. You need rest to keep up your strength."

She folded Adelaide into a hug, praying she could keep her sister by her side for as long as possible. The earl might have to give in to Lady Eleanor in the long run but at least marrying him would buy Isabella time to come up with a plan. As for Lord Martin, distance and silence would hopefully show him that she did not mean to cave. Let him dash himself against her castle walls. Her heart was well-defended.

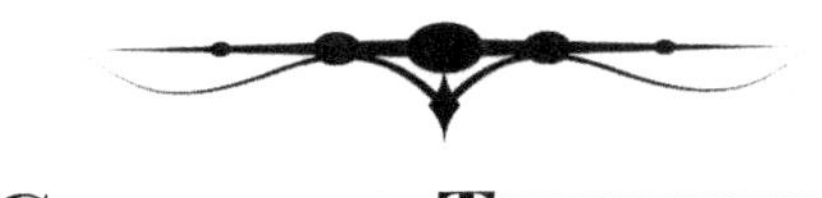

CHAPTER THIRTEEN

FOR TWO MORE days Isabella managed to remain largely silent in Martin's presence, focusing her entire attention on Adelaide. Though Martin and Adelaide were getting closer by the day, bonding over music despite Isabella's warnings, Isabella maintained her distance, refusing to speak a word to her husband if she could help it. All she had to do was keep it up for the entire journey, and she would be free to marry whom she chose.

On their fifth day at sea, Isabella sat on deck, surreptitiously watching Martin manage his ship while her sister rested below. Why was she so affected by the sight of a competent man at work? She never would have expected the teasing coxcomb to be such a good captain. Seeing him shift from mischief and nonsense to brisk efficiency made her insides clench with something she refused to name or acknowledge.

"Halfred, what do you make of that sky?" Martin asked, standing on the raised platform of the aftercastle with a wiry older man with a steel gray beard.

"I don't like the look of those clouds, my lord. There's a storm brewing. Mark my words." The two of them stared up at the gathering darkness ahead, even as the sun brightened the sky behind them.

Isabella couldn't help but follow their gaze. The clouds looked like great tufts of wool smeared with soot. That didn't bode well, but if any captain could weather a storm, she was sure Martin could. The thought made her shake her head. Since when did she put such faith in this bothersome man?

"Think we can avoid it?" Martin asked.

"No, my lord."

"Neither do I. It's moving too fast." Martin stepped to the front rail of the aftercastle. "Clovis, Wymond, trim the sail," he boomed in a clear voice that carried the length of the ship, despite the buffeting wind. "Pascal, Ned, and James, check every corner of this ship and lash down anything that isn't secured. Ulf, steer us east. We need to be in deeper waters to ride out this storm, or we'll risk running aground. Will, come here. I have a special task for you."

Everyone hurried to carry out their assigned tasks with brisk efficiency. It was like watching the inner workings of a windmill, the seeming chaos of wooden cogs moving in concert to achieve the single aim of moving a grindstone. Yet again, Isabella was forced to admire the obvious skill with which Martin led his men, not that she would admit any such thing to him aloud.

A youth of no more than twelve or thirteen with blond curls peeking out of his brown woolen cap practically flew to Martin's side. The boy beamed at having been called upon for a special assignment, his eagerness to please written plainly on his face. Martin said something to the boy in a low murmur that Isabella couldn't hear, and the boy hurried down from the aftercastle, making straight for her.

"My lady," the boy said in a voice that cracked halfway through the words, He cleared his throat and tried again in a lower register. "My name is Will. Lord Martin says I'm to take you below and play chess with you and your sister while we ride out this storm."

Isabella looked up at her husband, who was deep in consultation with Ulf, paying her no attention whatsoever. "Chess?"

"Have you not played it before, my lady? If you haven't, I can teach you." Isabella returned her attention to the boy before her.

He was bouncing on his toes in his eagerness to please. "I'm very good at it. I've even beaten Lord Martin once or twice."

Something about Will reminded her of her brother, even though the two looked nothing alike. Maybe it was the sheer youthful enthusiasm he too had possessed at that age. She couldn't help but smile at him.

"I've played chess many times, and I would be delighted to play with you. Let's head down to the cabin."

She made her way down the hatch and into the dim light belowdecks, past the hammocks where the sailors slept, to the cabin door.

She knocked before entering. "Adelaide, it's me. I'm bringing someone with me."

"Come in," her sister called out.

"Let me, my lady." Will hurried around her to open the door, bowing deeply.

"Adelaide, this is Will." Isabella gestured to the boy, who bowed deeply again. The two of them must have been around the same age.

"There's a storm brewing, and the captain asked me to keep you company. He suggested we play chess. Do you play, my lady?" he asked, addressing Adelaide.

"Not really. I know the rules, but I'm rubbish at it. Maybe I'll play the lute while you play, Isabella."

"As you wish. Lady Isabella, will you join me?"

With a nod, Isabella settled herself on one of the simple wooden chairs next to the small round table in the center of the cabin.

Will opened a cabinet built into the ship's bulkhead and pulled out a cloth bag and a roll of leather before closing it again. He then unrolled the leather on the tabletop, revealing the painted squares of a board. One by one, he pulled beautifully-carved wooden chess pieces from the bag, placed them on the board, and then sat down once the board was set.

"You go first, my lady. I've given you white."

"Very gallant of you," she said, smiling. How very different it was to play chess with this guileless young boy than with Lady Eleanor. With Her Grace, Isabella always felt as if she was being tested. A game was never merely a game. She rather liked playing for entertainment for once. Picking up the king's pawn, she moved it to the center of the board. "Your move."

She was a pawn, she thought, as Will countered. Lady Eleanor had certainly treated her like one, discarding her for a minor strategic advantage when she could have done so much more. It rankled that after everything they had been through together, Her Grace thought so little of her.

"Is everything all right, my lady? You look upset."

With a sigh, she wiped her face clean of expression and put on a smile. "Merely overthinking things," she said, bringing her knight out to threaten his pawn.

"Do you miss your home?"

"Heavens, no," she answered with a bit too much feeling.

Will nodded sagely. "I understand. I don't miss my home either. The best day of my life was the day Lord Martin took me into his service. You're very lucky to have married him. He's such a good man."

A good man? Lord Martin? With all the outrageous things he said? But then she thought about his actions, as well as Adelaide's words when they argued. Martin had no reason to pander to her wishes, and yet he had offered her a way out of this unwanted marriage. He could have taken advantage of her on their wedding night, but instead he'd handed her the poker to defend herself. When he saw her frowning at the storm clouds, he arranged for company and distraction. He was undeniably kind to her sister. And this boy before her clearly revered the man, as did her sister, despite her warnings. Was it possible that she was wrong, and that the baron wasn't all bad?

No. She couldn't afford to entertain such thoughts.

"Do not worry, my lady," Will said as he thwarted her next move by castling. "Lord Martin will bring us through the storm.

He's the best captain there is."

"I'm not worried," she answered, putting on a smile despite the faster beat of her heart. "I'm sure he and the crew know what to do."

"If anyone can get us through the storm, it's Lord Martin. He's as brave as any man I've ever known, and he knows the sea like no one else."

"Oh? What has he done that you think him so brave?" The man was intelligent and obnoxiously witty, and his easy confidence was enviable. But bravery was something else altogether. It required action, not just a general air of brashness.

She moved her queen out. It was time to show this boy how the game was played. "Check," she announced.

Will was forced to block with a knight.

"We were attacked by pirates two years ago," said Will, as she took his knight and threatened his remaining bishop.

"Check," she said, certain that the game was hers in the next two moves.

The boy looked up at her and nodded in respect. "Well played, my lady."

"You were saying you were attacked by pirates?"

Moving his bishop to block, Will continued, "Yes, my lady. They came upon us just after we left Dublin, throwing clay jars of stinging lime onto our deck to blind us. Lord Martin sent Pascal up to the crow's nest with his bow and arrow to pick off who he could, then sent everyone except Halfred belowdecks to arm ourselves, and get ready to plan a counter-attack."

The ship lurched, nearly knocking over a few of the chess pieces, but Will caught them quickly and righted them. Adelaide gave up on playing and secured her lute in a cabinet with a latch.

Unbidden visions of water rushing in from all sides and engulfing her, dragging her under to the fathomless deep, made her heart skip a beat, but she forced herself to take deep breaths and tamp down the burgeoning fear. She was safe. The ship was sound. Martin would not let her drown. Well. Maybe he would, but she doubted her doubt in spite of herself.

"By the time we came back up," Will continued as if nothing was amiss, "he and Halfred had sliced through all but one of the ropes the pirates used to lash our ships together, and my lord was battling three men with swords who had climbed over while Halfred cut the final rope. I've never seen a man move so fast. Before we could come to his rescue, he slit one's throat, kicked the next one overboard, and wounded the sword arm of the third, disarming him."

"My goodness," Adelaide exclaimed.

"Heavens," Isabella said at nearly the same moment. He must have been quite the fighter to prevail under such circumstances.

"And that wasn't all. The pirate he disarmed begged for his life. By all rights, Lord Martin should have dropped him over-board and let the sea take him, but he had mercy."

Isabella's eyebrows shot up. "He had mercy on a *pirate*?" They were the scum of the earth and the scourge of the seas. Surely Martin wouldn't have granted clemency to such a blackguard.

"He did indeed. He gave the man a choice between swearing fealty or being thrown overboard. Cian is part of our crew to this day, and he's proven himself loyal many times over."

"You mean to say there's a pirate aboard this ship right *now*?" Was Lord Martin mad?

The ship lurched again, and this time the game did topple over. Chess pieces went rolling across the floor, and Will dove after them. It was all Isabella could do to stay seated. Adelaide, over on the bed, was starting to look green again. Dear Lord in heaven, they were going to drown. This was the end.

"Perhaps you had best sit on the bed, my lady," Will said as his stool toppled over and started sliding across the floor. Her own threatened to do the same.

She stumbled to the bed next to Adelaide, grasping her sister's hand and bracing herself against the bulkhead. She prayed fervently this wasn't their last day on earth.

Will abandoned the chess pieces and instead pulled off his belt to lash the two stools to the little table, which she now realized was nailed to the floor. "There. That should keep them from rolling around and hitting us." He put the chess set away in its cubbyhole and secured the latch before he staggered over and joined them on the bed. Even he was starting to look alarmed at the violent rocking and creaking groans of the ship.

This was not how Isabella intended to end her days, and she certainly wasn't going to let her sister or this boy see her confidence waiver.

"Take my hands," she said, reaching out to the two youths. "We're going to get through this together. Lord Martin will keep us safe, or I'll have his head."

The wide-eyed boy cracked a smile at that. "I'm sure you will, my lady."

"Does that mean you'll start speaking to him again?" Adelaide teased.

"Hush," Isabella said, rolling her eyes.

She squeezed their hands as the boat juddered in the waves once again. "Tell me more about this madman I've married who lets pirates join his crew. How did you come to be here?"

She might as well learn as much as she could about her enemy while she had the chance. Perhaps the boy would know something that would help her rid herself of her husband once and for all.

The ship bucked and bobbed like the little boats she and her siblings used to make out of leaves and float down the stream when they were little. How long could this vessel last, taking such a beating?

Swallowing hard, Will squeezed her hand. "L-Lord Martin...*whoaaah*..." They all slid into each other as the ship gave a particularly violent jolt.

Isabella wrapped arms around both of them to steady them. She was about to ask Will to continue when someone began pounding on the door.

Will staggered across the room to open it, and in came Martin, soaked to the bone, his clothes clinging to every curve of his muscular form as he carried in the limp form of a tall, thin man with a ghastly gash on his forehead. Perhaps Will's stories of heroism held some truth. He certainly looked like some demigod from ancient legend as he strode in, steady despite the tossing of the ship.

As he met her gaze, his eyes blazed with command and determination. Gone was the teasing twinkle to which she'd grown accustomed. It was like she'd never seen him before. The man before her radiated a strength and power she'd rarely beheld, and her breath hitched as he closed the distance and towered over her.

"Stand aside, ladies. I need the bed," Martin ordered in a voice that brooked no dissent.

Clinging to the bulwark to steady themselves, she and Adelaide vacated the bed as requested. Heat coursed through her at the command in his voice despite the frigid air. She braced herself against the creaking side of the ship, thinking that the sea was not her only danger on this stormy night.

CHAPTER FOURTEEN

MARTIN LAID PASCAL down on the straw pallet as gently as he could manage with the motion of the boat.

"What happened?" Isabella asked, breaking her silence at long last. But there was no time to celebrate his victory as he pulled the wet tunic and shirt off Pascal and covered him in the thick wool blanket. Adelaide huddled in a corner where Will had a protective arm wrapped around her.

"He fell overboard. I had to dive in after him." Martin still felt like shards of ice were flowing through his veins instead of blood. The water had been so cold, his entire body had rebelled. After he jumped in, he could hardly move as the roiling sea pressed the air from his lungs. It was a miracle he'd found Pascal before he himself perished.

"You *what?*" Her voice took on a shrill quality. Could it be that she was reacting out of fear for him? Again, he didn't have time to revel in that idea.

"I jumped in. I couldn't let Pascal die." Memories of childhood games with the baker's son assailed him. They'd used to chase each other around the bailey with wooden sticks for swords, pretending they were knights and brigands. Pascal always seemed to take special pleasure in playing a brigand. No one could plan an ambush like Pascal.

"But *you* could have died!"

Yes. His reluctant lady-wife *was* worried for him. The thought warmed his sea-chilled heart. "I grabbed a rope before I jumped off and tied it around my waist so that my men could pull me back. Besides, I thought you would have been relieved to be rid of me. It would certainly fit conveniently into your plans." Martin rifled through his drawers and found a linen shirt, tearing off a strip and turning it into a bandage for Pascal's head. There was little else he could do for the man after a blow to the head like that except wait and hope he woke up.

The affronted look on his bride's face warmed him even more. She did care, even if she'd never admit it.

"I never wished you dead. I merely wished to be rid of your insufferable company."

From her, that was practically a declaration of love. And she was certainly staring at his chest with inordinate interest. She bit her lower lip as she perused him. If Will and Adelaide hadn't been huddled in the corner looking on, he might have tried his luck at kissing her.

"I'm needed back on deck," Martin said, dragging his gaze away from temptation. By God, she was captivating—as lovely as she was fearsome. If only he could linger, but duty called.

"Stay here with Will. We should come out the other side of this storm soon. Will," he said, turning to the boy, "keep an eye on Pascal, and let me know if he awakens."

"Yes, my lord," Will said from the corner where he was crouched, clutching the bulwark.

"Good boy."

With that, Martin headed back up to the deck. The blast of wind and rain from the storm hit him as soon as his head rose above the hatch. Ulf stood steady at the tiller, keeping the ship turned into the waves. Only the flexing of his muscles spoke to the effort it must have taken to keep the ship under control.

Halfred stood on the forecastle, clutching the railing tightly for balance, and he bellowed, ordering Cian and Wymond below. Martin climbed the ladder to join him.

"Report."

"I think we're through the worst of it, my lord."

Martin liked to think he could read the weather as well as any man, but Halfred seemed to have a sixth sense about it. "I pray it is so. The ship can't take much more of this."

"*The Wind Song* is stronger than you think, my lord. She'll pull through. How's Pascal?"

Martin let out a long slow breath, saying a silent prayer. "Unconscious."

Halfred nodded grimly. "Only time will tell. It was a damned fool thing you did rescuing him, if I may say so, my lord."

"I'd never let any of you die that way. Not if I had the strength to save you."

Halfred chuckled. "You have a lot of your father in you, you know. He never knew when to back down either."

The mention of his father pierced his heart like a dagger. His loss was still too fresh. It had been a year since Lord Gilbert had passed, but not a day went by that Martin didn't mourn his absence. It pained him deeply that the man didn't live to meet Isabella. His father would have liked her. And despite her disdain for barons, she would have liked him because everyone liked his father.

In the distance, Martin caught sight of a patch of stars. Though the wind continued to lash them, and waves crashed against them, the end was in sight. If they could just hold on a little bit longer, they would sail out the other side.

"The storm is breaking up ahead. I see a patch of clear sky." Martin pointed.

Halfred sheltered his eyes with his hand. "So there is, my lord. You'd better speak to Ulf and adjust our course."

Thunder cracked and lightning sizzled as Martin made his way to the other end of the ship. *Too close!* If it got any closer, it would have hit the mast. Hanging onto the slippery railing with an iron grip, he traversed the remaining distance to the tiller as quickly as he dared.

Ulf stood like a statue with eyes glued to the horizon ahead. The only sign of strain was the white knuckled grip of his hand on the enormous spar of wood that steered the ship.

"I saw a patch of clear skies over yonder," Martin said, pointing.

"I saw it too," Ulf said, turning his steely gaze to follow Martin's hand. "But we're far from safe yet. That lightning struck too close for comfort."

"So it did."

As if summoned by their words, thunder boomed, and a sizzling bolt of light spiked down and struck the mast. The entire beam glowed white hot. Then an explosion of splinters went flying as a flaming crow's nest came crashing down to the deck. The top of the mast had split as if cut by an axe, and flames engulfed it. The blaze licked dangerously close to the sail.

Martin stopped breathing as he looked on in horror. If the sail caught fire, they would be dead in the water with no way to reach the shore. And that was if they were lucky, and the fire didn't spread and engulf the entire ship.

Somehow, he had to put out the flames. How could he stop the spread? Here they were surrounded by water, and yet he could not think of a way to get it where it was most needed.

But his bride and her sister were on board this ship. He'd promised Isabella they would be safe with him, and he could not let them perish. Grabbing a length of rope, he ran for the mast and began to climb the rope ladder that barely held as flames licked at the top.

"No, my lord," Halfred yelled, running toward him across the slippery deck.

"I must," he yelled back down. "Fill a bucket with water and tie it to the end of this rope." Martin held out the end of the rope he'd grabbed and gave it a shake, then continued to climb. The ship swayed around him as the ship bobbed in the heavy surf, but he held tightly to the ropes and continued to climb.

There was a snap, and the rope holding one side of the ladder gave way. The fire had burned through it. He didn't have much time before the fire would burn through the rest. Fortunately, he was close to the mast. Easing himself off the ropes, he grasped the wooden beam and lashed himself to it with one end of the rope he carried up, wrapping his legs around it. No sooner had he done so than the other side of the rope ladder gave way. The taut web slackened and fell to the deck.

He had to keep the fire from reaching the ropes that held the spar for the sail in place or they were all done for.

"Bucket," Halfred bellowed from the deck below, pointing to a full bucket of water that was lashed to the other end of his rope. Martin began to pull it up, letting go of the mast so that the rope he'd tied around himself held his weight. Hand over hand, he brought up the precious water he needed to douse the flames. His muscles ached as he reached for it and threw it at the flames above him. The fire retreated a few inches, the charred wood hissing and sizzling in its wake.

"Again," he yelled down, lowering the empty bucket.

Halfred ran to fill it, as Martin rocked with the boat, high above the waves. On the deck below, there was movement. Someone was climbing out of the hatch. *Dear God. No! It couldn't be! How could she risk herself like this?*

"Isabella, no," he cried out. "Go below. It's safer."

Shaking her head vehemently, she made her way to stand in the shelter of the forecastle and stood to watch. She was too far away for him to read the expression on her face. What was she doing out here?

"Bucket," Halfred yelled.

There was no time for him to argue with his wife. He had to save her life and the lives of everyone else on the crew. Yet again, he pulled up the bucket, arms shaking with the strain. Then he splashed the seawater on the flames above, and this time, they retreated by a foot.

"Again," he yelled down to Halfred, lowering the bucket. It was working if his strength would just hold out. But there was no room for failure. Everyone's lives depended on it.

Five times, he hauled up that bucket before the flames were completely doused. By the end, his arms felt like limp eels, no longer capable of supporting his weight, and yet he still had to shimmy down the mast.

Isabella's eyes hadn't left him for a moment as he toiled. Even when he wasn't looking, he could feel her gaze on him like a brush of heat.

Somehow, he had to force his arms to cooperate one last time so that he could get back down the mast. He could almost laugh. How could he have doused the fire that threatened them all and yet be unable to do this last simple task of climbing down?

Hands shaking, he fumbled at the knot he'd tied, loosening the rope and letting it drop to the deck. Then he forced his aching body to climb down the polished, rain-slicked mast, slipping a little each time he moved. Halfred and Cian stood at the base of the mast as if they could catch him if he fell. But he was still too far up, and he knew it.

Every muscle in his body rebelled as he forced it to cling to the enormous beam, lowering himself inch by inch. The deck was close enough now that he could let himself drop and survive the fall. The temptation to let go was almost too much, but he had to make it down on his own power. Isabella was watching.

After what felt like an eternity, Halfred and Cian braced his legs and told him to let go. He could hold on no more and slid down into their waiting arms, earning himself several splinters in his arms and legs along the way.

Finding his feet with difficulty, he turned to his bride and staggered toward her. Fortunately, the storm had calmed somewhat, and the waves were subsiding, or he might have fallen over.

He must have looked a horror, soaked to the bone and covered in soot and ash. He bled from deep scrapes and splinters earned during his descent.

But all he could see were her wild eyes filled with fire and her raven tresses blowing in the wind. After staring him down for a long moment, she stepped forward and reached out a soft hand, cupping his cheek. "You saved us. Thank you."

Her touch set him aflame as surely as lightning. He couldn't move. He could hardly look at her. The temptation to take her in his arms was so great. His gaze dropped to her lips, and he thought he might die of wanting as her tongue flicked out to lick them.

"If you don't move your hand, I'm going to kiss you."

She stepped closer, resting her other hand on his waist. "That would be unwise," she said, but she leaned in closer.

"Very." He placed his hands on her slim waist, unable to stop himself from touching her.

"A truly terrible idea." Her lips parted as she held his gaze.

"Indeed."

Come to me, my vixen. Let me taste your sweet lips.

"And yet…"

She closed the distance, and the soft pressure of her warm lips brushing against his drove every thought from his brain. All his aches and pains disappeared, and the world narrowed to the two of them as he wrapped his arms around her. His fearsome bride melted against him, opening to him exactly the way he'd been dreaming of as he traced the seam of her lips with his tongue.

He deepened their kiss, unable to stop himself from tasting her sweetness and fire. This was everything he'd wanted. The flames he just finished fighting were nothing to the inferno raging within him as their tongues met and entwined. There was a hunger in her kiss that he would never have expected. Was it possible she wanted him as much as he wanted her?

More. He wanted more. And she gave it to him. Their kiss grew desperate, reckless. Her fingers tangled in his hair as he pulled her hips against his own. The friction and heat drove him nearly out of his mind. *Dear God, let this never end. Let this madness never stop. Isabella, I'm yours!*

And then, as suddenly as she'd embraced him, she pulled

away, panting, and he let her go, though it nearly killed him. His whole body screamed to hold her close, but he held himself back. She stood there, and he watched in hungry agony as a war of emotions played across her face. Her eyes narrowed and her lips pursed. She let out a long, shuddering breath and raised her regal head.

"This was a terrible mistake," she said so that only he could hear, then fled to the hatch, climbing down before he could find words.

A shuddering sigh escaped him as he watched her go. He was so close to winning her, but still, she resisted. God, she was glorious, and if it was the last thing he did, he would make her his.

CHAPTER FIFTEEN

WHAT HAD SHE just done? Isabella hurried to the cabin where Pascal still lay unconscious on the pallet. Will and Adelaide still sat in the corner, hugging each other and keeping vigil, but at least no one in here had seen her lose control. If she'd been thinking straight, she wouldn't have left Will and Adelaide alone together. It wasn't proper. But then if she'd been thinking straight, she wouldn't have let terror for her sister propel her up to the deck where the situation was every bit as bad as she had feared, where one man stood between them and certain death, single-handedly battling the flames that could have spelled their doom. One man—her husband.

She licked her lips as she closed the cabin door, trying to ignore how heat churned within her at the taste of him still lingering there. It was beyond intolerable that she had lost her mind and kissed that man. He was the most pompous, irritating, wickedly intelligent, undeniably brave…

Oh no. This couldn't be happening, but it had happened. Somehow her loathing had transformed into consuming passion. He'd climbed that mast like the madman he was and saved all their lives. Watching him risk his life like that was like striking flint next to a barn full of straw. She went up in flames as surely as that mast, and heaven help her, she wanted the man she was married to. *Needed* him. When he'd walked toward her, looking at her like she was his whole world, forces beyond her control had taken over. Before she'd known what she was doing, she'd crashed her lips into his and wrapped her arms around him.

And that kiss! Lord in heaven, that kiss. She would never recover. But he was still the man Lady Eleanor sent and therefore not to be trusted. She had to find a way to undo what she'd just done.

"My lady, are you all right?" Will asked from his corner.

"I'm fine," she said quickly, her voice croaking.

"What happened up there?" Rising from the corner, he took her elbow and led her to the bed where she took a seat on the edge beside Pascal. It was the only place to sit, since the stools were still lashed to the table.

"Go up and see for yourself. I'll keep watch here."

Will nodded and went running out the door.

Grateful for a moment alone with her sister, she put her hand on her belly and took deep, steadying breaths. Adelaide joined her and took her hand, squeezing it.

The kiss changed nothing. Anyone would have been overcome upon seeing such a display. It was the heat of the moment and nothing more. Martin was still untrustworthy, and this marriage was still intended as some sort of punishment for a transgression she never even knew she'd committed. And she still needed to rescue Adelaide.

The cabin door opened, and in walked the man at the center of her turmoil. Immediately, all her best intentions flew out the door.

"Isabella—" he began.

"It was a mistake." Why was her voice so high? She clutched the edge of the bed, desperately trying to ground herself. "A lapse in judgment. It won't happen again."

"Isabella," he took a slow step toward her, palms open. "We have to—"

"Stay back. We aren't going to speak of it. Forget it ever happened."

"What never happened?" Adelaide asked, but Isabella couldn't take her eyes off her husband.

Panic coursed through her at his proximity. If he got much closer, she was in grave danger of losing control and repeating the rash action that had gotten her into this fix in the first place.

He folded his arms and smirked. "Ah, but it did. You. Kissed. Me."

Blood rushed to her face, and her cheeks burned. "It didn't mean a thing," she said as lightly as she could. "I'm still marrying an earl." It sounded weak, even to her.

He looked down at her with an intensity that made her tingle from head to toe. It was so wrong that he could make her feel like this. He took a step toward her. And another step. He was nearly toe to toe with her, looming over her as she sat, but not touching her. Adelaide stood up abruptly and headed for the door, mumbling, "I'll leave you two alone."

Curses! She needed the buffer of her sister to keep herself from doing anything rash.

Martin leaned close. Too close. The urge to close the distance fought with her outrage at her body's utter betrayal.

"Have it your way," he said softly, touching his finger to her chin and tilting her face up. "It didn't happen." He knelt down so that his face was level with hers, lips inches away. "It didn't mean a thing." Leaning in, he stopped just short of a kiss, his breath brushing against her lips. Everything in her tensed. He tilted his head. "You're marrying an earl," he whispered in her ear, letting his mouth brush against it.

She gasped. God in heaven, she was in so much trouble.

"And I," he said, standing and backing away, still with a devilish twinkle in his eye, "need to change into dry clothes. Would you like to stay and watch?"

He began loosening the laces of his tunic. As he pulled it over his head, she bolted, but not before catching a glimpse of his chest, the glorious contours of which were clearly visible beneath the nearly transparent, wet linen shirt that was plastered to him.

Slamming the door behind her, she rested against it for a moment, all too aware of the amused and curious glances she was getting from members of the crew belowdecks.

She cleared her throat and straightened her back. "I think I'll just…" What was she going to do? Where was there to go on a ship that would have easily fit inside her father's great hall? It didn't matter. She had to do something. "I'll go find my sister and get some fresh air."

Up on deck, she found Adelaide in her usual position beneath the forecastle. The storm had abated, and patches of stars shone through the remaining shreds of cloud. Threads of smoke still curled up from the charred top of the mast. It was a miracle they had all survived.

No, it wasn't a miracle. It was her husband—the man she couldn't afford to fall for, the man she had just kissed. In front of the whole crew. Fortunately, they were all studiously ignoring her now. It was embarrassing enough to know they saw without seeing the knowing amusement in their eyes. Her sister, on the other hand, was stifling a grin.

"You kissed Lord Martin," Adelaide said in a singsong. "I knew you'd come around. It was only a matter of time."

"I have not come around, and it won't happen again." It couldn't. She needed to keep her head for Adelaide's sake.

Martin emerged on deck in dry clothes and winked at her, sending sparks all through her. She narrowed her eyes and glared at him, bothered by her body's reaction when she desperately needed to keep her distance.

He cocked his head and shrugged, then turned to Halfred, who rushed to his side the moment he emerged on deck. "We'll have to stop and make repairs. By my estimate, the closest port is Yarmouth. Would you agree?"

Yarmouth. After all that had transpired, she had gotten her way after all. The earl visited Yarmouth regularly, though his seat was inland at Norwich. If she was lucky, she could put her plan to marry the earl in motion while the ship was being repaired.

She did her best to ignore the pang of regret and reluctance that came along with that thought.

"Aye," said Halfred. "That's the nearest port. But is it safe to land there? I've heard there's been unrest."

Martin looked at the mast, then back at Halfred. "We'll have to risk it. We can't sail back to Winchelsea with half our mast missing."

For the next few hours, the ship was a hive of activity as the crew took stock of the damage from the storm and prepared for landing. Isabella couldn't wait to get to shore and away from temptation. It was altogether too dangerous for her to stay on board *The Wind Song* in close quarters with Martin. But her eyes kept straying to the man, admiring his form as he went about his business. Every so often, he glanced her way, and she averted her eyes immediately, hoping he wouldn't notice her gawking. She absolutely could not get off this ship fast enough.

Relief flooded her as the port of Yarmouth came into view with the rectangular stone walls of Burgh Castle on a verdant hill in the distance. The ship she'd taken to Northumberland had stopped here to resupply, and she'd made the acquaintance of Lord Christopher, the local baron, and his wife. They were a friendly couple with a passel of adorable children. If the earl wasn't around, they would certainly pass on a message on her behalf.

The Wind Song docked, and the busy town of Great Yarmouth stretched out before her. Large timber warehouses lined the busy port. Behind them, thatched rooves and half-timbered houses with smoking stone chimneys filled her view. It would be delightful to go indoors and warm herself properly by a fire. It was already warmer here than it was at her father's castle, but it was still winter.

Martin gave orders to his men about repairs and resupply as they lowered the gangplank. He also sent Will for a healer to tend to Pascal. Then he came over to her and put out his arm. She shrank back, clutching Adelaide's arm and not trusting herself to touch him.

"I don't bite, Isabella. Unless you want me to. Or perhaps you want to bite me?" He gave her a long, heated look that made her want to die on the spot. "No? Then perhaps you would allow me to accompany you to Burgh Castle. I'm sure you'll be comfortable there while we make repairs to the ship."

There was no way around it. She and Adelaide could hardly travel to the castle unaccompanied. Reluctantly, she took his arm, keeping as much distance between the two of them as possible. Adelaide took her other arm. God's teeth, this was terribly awkward.

It was a relief to let him go and mount a horse so that they could ride up the hill to the castle, once an ancient Roman fort. Adelaide coughed as she perched herself on the saddle and then coughed again.

"Are you all right?" Isabella asked, studying her sister's features. Adelaide's skin was flushed despite the cold. "You aren't getting sick, are you?"

"It's just the aftereffects of the smoke," Adelaide answered, clearing her throat and straightening her back. "Don't worry about me. I'll be fine."

Isabella didn't believe her for a moment. "When we get to the castle, I'll ask for a healer to see you."

"If you must," Adelaide answered. "But I promise you, I'm fine."

Isabella pursed her lips but said nothing.

"Let's get both of you inside the castle where you can warm yourselves by the fire, shall we?" Martin started forward on his horse, and Isabella and Adelaide followed. Four men from his ship brought up the rear as guards.

Yarmouth was a busy port—not the biggest Isabella had ever seen. It couldn't compare to Calais. But for England, it was impressive. There must have been twenty or more ships docked there. Warehouses lined the docks, and sailors, fishermen, and dock workers scurried back and forth, shouting and hefting cargo in an intricate dance. She ignored the whistles and ribald comments that floated by as she passed, though Martin stared down anyone getting too close with a glare that promised murder.

Soldiers were everywhere, standing guard and watching incoming vessels with a close eye. Even a bustling place like this had been affected by the strife between King Stephen and the Duke of Normandy. Signs of the war were everywhere. As they turned to enter the city, they were forced to pass through a wooden barricade manned by the Earl of Norfolk's men and state their business. Lord Martin talked his way through with ease, and their group passed the spiked, wooden barrier to enter the town.

Vendors with street carts clogged the cobblestone streets, peddling their wares. The smells of civilization wafted in the air, both the good and the bad. The scents of roasted meat and fresh baked bread mixed with the pungent odor of excrement as they wended their way along the broad street that led to the castle.

Fully-armored knights stood guard at the castle gates as they approached. The castle walls bristled with archers. Though there were no signs that battle had passed through here, they were clearly on high alert.

Norfolk supported the Duke of Normandy but had not engaged in open battle with King Stephen. In these uncertain times, however, it was good to know her prospective husband was ready for whatever might come his way.

In the courtyard, they dismounted, and servants led their horses away to the stables. A guard led them into the small keep in the center of the large fortress. Burgh Castle had been built by the Romans as a defensive outpost, not for comfort. There were tight quarters within the keep with few private rooms. Most of Lord Christopher's men slept in the great hall at night. She prayed there would be space for her and Adelaide to have a room to themselves.

The guard passed them off to a servant who led them through the dimly lit entrance hall to the great hall. The long trestle tables and benches were pushed to the sides of the rooms, and petitioners filled the hall, which was brightly lit with torches. It must have been time for Lord Christopher's daily audience with his subjects.

At the far end of the hall was Lord Christopher and sitting beside him was...*What luck!* The Earl of Norfolk was indeed visiting his vassal. Now Isabella could put in motion her plans to leave behind the inconveniently alluring Lord Martin and marry a man she could trust to stand up for her.

If only she could ignore the ache in her heart that told her that she was about to make a terrible mistake.

CHAPTER SIXTEEN

G OD'S WOUNDS! DID the earl have to be here? Martin wanted to punch something when he saw the man Isabella claimed to want to marry seated at the far end of the hall beside Lord Christopher.

He'd met Lord James on several occasions in the past, including twice at tourneys. Both times, the earl had knocked him off his horse far more easily than Martin would have liked. The man had an unfair advantage in bulk. He was a veritable mountain, crowned with sandy curls and a long beard that would not have looked amiss on a Viking. How was a man Martin's size supposed to unseat that behemoth? At least Martin had managed to best him with a sword on one of those occasions. That was rather cold comfort, though, as he watched the earl's lascivious grin at Isabella.

"Lord Martin," Lord Christopher called out, pausing between petitioners. "What brings you to my hall, and how is it that Lady Isabella is traveling with you?"

Now, Lord Christopher was someone Martin liked. He was an affable family man, only a few years older than him, with auburn hair and friendly eyes the color of the sea. When there wasn't a war on, Martin was a frequent visitor to Yarmouth. It was good to see a friendly face.

"Lady Isabella and I were recently married," Martin explained, glancing at the earl to gauge his reaction. He was pleased to see the man's smile sag. "We were headed back to Winchelsea when a storm hit and damaged my ship. I humbly ask that you let us stay with you while I make repairs."

"Of course, old friend. You're always welcome here," Lord Christopher answered. "As you can see, I'm a bit busy at the moment. A servant will show you to your rooms, and you can settle in. We'll catch up after I'm done here." He beckoned over a servant and murmured something in the man's ear.

The servant bowed to Martin, Isabella, and Adelaide, and gestured toward the door.

"Thank you, my lord. I shall see you anon," Martin said with a friendly nod. "And you, Lord James." He bowed, but kept it as shallow as possible, giving only the deference that was required of him.

Isabella and Adelaide curtsied, and they all followed the servant out of the hall. As they traversed the dimly lit, stone corridors, Martin brooded over how to navigate the current situation.

Undoubtedly, Isabella would try to reach out to Lord James. Everything in him wanted to try and stop her, but deep in his heart, he knew that it would be a mistake to try to keep them apart. He needed to *win* Isabella's favor, not trap her into surrender, and that meant he had to risk her honest appraisal of how he stacked up against the earl.

But that didn't mean he had to stand back and let the other man steal her away unchallenged. While they were at Burgh Castle, Martin would need to do everything he could to goad Lord James into showing his true colors so that he himself seemed like the more appealing option in Isabella's eyes.

Most importantly, he needed to win Isabella's trust. He sensed that there was something more holding her back than mere lack of interest. After that kiss, it was clear she was attracted to him. He'd managed to make significant headway with her, but she still wanted to marry Lord James. Why?

She said she wanted all of Norfolk at her feet, but Martin

didn't believe for a moment that was the whole story. There had to be something more to it—something at stake that she couldn't give way on. Somehow, he had to tease it out of her.

The servant tried to put Martin and Isabella together and send Adelaide to a spare bed in the nursery with Lord Christopher's children. Isabella immediately balked.

"Adelaide is unwell. She cannot stay with Lord Christopher's children. She must stay with me so that I can care for her," she said, pulling Adelaide into the room she was supposed to share with Martin.

The servant's brow furrowed. "But, my lady, this is the only room we have for Lord Martin. With the earl and his entourage visiting, we are short on space."

"I will sleep in the great hall with my men," Martin said immediately. There was no question that if Isabella had to choose between him and her sister, she would choose Adelaide every time. And he wasn't entirely certain he could manage to behave if he shared a bed with her. He wanted her to choose him with a clear head and open eyes, not because she succumbed to the undeniable attraction between them. The last thing he wanted was for her to do something she would later regret.

"Are you certain, my lord?"

"Quite certain, thank you. See that Lady Isabella and Adelaide are comfortably settled here and send for a healer to see to Lady Adelaide. She looks feverish." It wasn't a subterfuge from Isabella. Adelaide truly did look unwell, and her cough was worrying. His heart ached to see such a sweet person suffering so.

"Isabella, might I speak with you a moment?" Martin dismissed the servant to go look for a healer and beckoned to his wife, pulling her into the hallway, away from her sister's hearing. "I am truly sorry that Adelaide is suffering. Is there anything I can do to help?"

Closing her eyes, Isabella replied, "She's always struggled with ailments of the lungs. There's nothing you can do. She needs a healer and rest. Everything else is in God's hands."

He nodded slowly. She was right. There was little he could do, much though it galled him. It was up to the healer and the Lord Above now. "And you? What do you need, Isabella?"

"I need—" She paused, biting her lip and looking at him with such sorrow it nearly broke him.

"Yes? Just say the word. I'll do anything." There was something specific she wanted him to say. He was certain of it. But he could not guess what it was.

She shook her head slowly. "Nothing. I need nothing."

He took her hand and squeezed it. "That can't be true."

"It is," she said, pulling away. "I have no heart. The sooner you realize that, the better off we'll both be." Squaring her shoulders and composing her face, she turned away from him. "I need to tend to Adelaide, if you'll excuse me."

"Of course," he said, watching longingly as she returned to the room and closed the door.

Slowly, he made his way back to the great hall, pondering her words. She had a heart, whatever she might think. Her treatment of her sister proved that. If only he could find a way to make her trust him!

He would have to think it over as he decided how to proceed with his rival in residence. What would Isabella want him to do? How could he prove himself to her? Or perhaps, more importantly, how could he convince her to follow the heart she claimed not to have?

The answer coalesced in his mind, and he didn't like it one bit. If he truly wanted to win Isabella, he needed to give her what she was asking for and let her see if she could hook Lord James. He needed to give her the freedom to pursue what she thought she desired and pray that she came to her senses and chose him. She would never trust him if he tried to force her to stay tethered to him.

As he entered the great hall, Lord Christopher was seeing the last of his petitioners. Two farmers were in a heated argument about who a new calf belonged to, as one farmer's bull had impregnated the other farmer's cow when a fence between their properties broke. Both blamed the other for the broken fence and laid claim to the offspring.

Ah, the joys of being a lord.

Martin stepped around Lord Christopher and leaned toward Lord James. "My lord, might you be able to spare me a moment? There is something important I wish to discuss with you."

God's teeth, he did not want to do what he was about to do. *Isabella.* He was doing this for Isabella. If his gamble paid off, and she cared for him, she would be his, and he would be the happiest man in Christendom. But it could all fall apart. She could still choose Lord James.

The earl nodded and murmured a few words to Lord Christopher before following Martin to a quiet corner of the hall.

"Well, my lord, what is it?" Lord James ran his hand through his blond hair and turned his bored brown eyes on Martin.

"I have something important to tell you regarding Lady Isabella." He might as well dive straight in, even if he'd rather go for a swim in the North Sea in February.

"How could anything related to your wife possibly concern me?"

Clenching his hand into a fist, he steeled himself. "Truth be told, she isn't quite my wife yet."

The earl frowned. "What do you mean?"

"We haven't uh… Well, you see we haven't consummated." God's wounds, this was agonizing.

"I do not wish to be privy to your marital troubles," Lord James said, frowning and turning to go.

"Wait. Please. This concerns you."

The earl chuckled quietly. "I can't possibly see how."

"Because she'd rather marry you than me." There, it was done. His heart hung by a thread, but he'd made himself speak.

"Lady Isabella wants to marry *me*." Lord James was staring at him, incredulous.

"Yes. Please don't make me say it again." Martin would rather have cut his own tongue out with his dagger than utter those awful words a second time.

"Why are you telling me this?"

Martin might as well be truthful. "Because Isabella will never truly be mine if I trap her in this marriage. If I'm going to win her heart, I must risk mine. She needs to choose me freely."

The earl's brow furrowed. "Good God, man. Just get her drunk and tup her 'til she's bowlegged. God knows if I had a wife that looked like her, I'd swive her until she thought rainbows came out of my prick."

"And that right there is why she's going to choose me in the end, of her own free will." Because Martin would be damned if he was going to lose Isabella to this man.

"And if I have no interest in pursuing your wife?"

Please, God, let that be true!

But in his heart, Martin knew it wasn't. "You're interested. I saw the look on your face when she came in. And I have no doubt she's concocted some tempting offer to lure you into a match. In the end, if I cannot win her heart, I will go through with an annulment and let her go. You can even have her dowry. You have my word. But I do not plan to let it come to that. Her heart may be better defended than the Tower of London, but I will find a way in."

Lord James narrowed his eyes and scrutinized Martin. "It just so happens I have been thinking about marriage recently, and Isabella was on my list of potential candidates. Her family is powerful, and her father is close to the Duke of Normandy. And, the woman has appeal in her own right. She knows the inner workings of Lady Eleanor's devious mind, and I suspect being on our potential queen's good side will be of immeasurable value, given what I've seen of Lord Henry's court. Beyond that, Isabella is a damned good kisser. I had the pleasure once when I was visiting Falaise. I would have gone a lot further than kissing if she hadn't run away when I reached for her skirts."

God, Martin wanted to punch him in his smug face. "You

touch her without her permission again, and I will run you through with my sword, earl or no."

Lord James chuckled. "I'd like to see you try."

"And I'd like to see you die, but alas, we cannot all have what we want."

Martin rested his hand on the pommel of his sword and grinned at his adversary.

"You think you can take me, Little Baron?" Lord James took a step closer, looming over him.

"I know I can. Because I did. Have you forgotten so soon?"

"Are you calling me out? I could dispatch you today. Then Isabella would be mine for the taking that much sooner."

It was a mistake to let his temper get the better of him. Martin knew that. But at the moment, his loathing for Lord James knew no bounds. The only thing that held him back was the knowledge that Isabella wouldn't want him to do this. He'd started this absurd conversation because he wanted to give her a chance to choose freely, and she could hardly do that if he ran Lord James through with his sword.

Taking a deep breath, he deliberately relaxed his shoulders and forced himself to laugh. "And where would be the fun in that? I'd much rather watch Isabella cut you down to size when she realizes what a disappointing husband you would be."

"If I'm so disappointing, why does she want me for a husband and not you?"

Martin carefully kept his face steady and didn't wince, even if Lord James's words cut deeper than any blade.

"My lord, I have spoken my piece," Martin said, holding the earl's gaze. "I will do everything in my power to win her heart. But if in the end she chooses you without any coercion, she is yours. I will say no more on the matter."

The earl shook his head. "You're a very strange man, Lord Martin. Very strange indeed. You should never have invited me to play a game you've already lost. But if you insist, let the games begin."

"Indeed." With a curt nod, Martin turned to go, heading straight out to the castle's practice yard where he could whack the battered wooden pell to his heart's content with his sword. Perhaps he had just made an enormous mistake, but in the depths of his heart, he knew it was the right thing to do. Now that it was done, he could only pray to God that he won.

CHAPTER SEVENTEEN

ISABELLA RELUCTANTLY LEFT Adelaide asleep to go in search of the Earl of Norfolk. The healer was worried, but the poultice he had applied to Adelaide's chest seemed to have eased her breathing. Her sister was still feverish, despite the potion the healer provided to balance her humors. If Adelaide wasn't improved by morning, the healer was going to bleed her, poor thing. As if her sister didn't already have enough scars on her arm from previous bleedings. But there was nothing more to be done at the moment, so it was time to secure their future.

She found Lord James in the practice yard, battling one of his men with a wooden sword. The earl was positively enormous, and each blow he dealt had such power behind it that the other man was knocked back as he blocked.

Lord James was handsome, she supposed, in a sort of rugged Viking way. She rather liked it when he'd kissed her the year before, even if he had gotten a bit handsy, forcing her to step away. Looking at him now, though, she felt none of the warmth of attraction she used to feel in his presence. Her thoughts shifted to Martin unbidden, to the kiss they had shared, the heat of which far exceeded any kiss in her experience. Her heart yearned for her to turn back, find Martin, and confess everything. But could she trust him?

No, she could not. And while she didn't trust Lord James

either, she was confident that she could manipulate him into doing what she wanted, unlike Lord Martin who had resisted her efforts to manipulate him at every turn. The way he saw through her was uncanny.

She was unaccustomed to having anyone see past her bravado. It felt good to be seen—a little too good. Her heart beat faster at the thought of Lord Martin's all-too-insightful eyes seeing the truth beneath her artifice. But her own heart was immaterial in all of this. She wanted to marry Lord James for Adelaide's sake, not her own.

She caught his eye, and he immediately halted the fight. "If you're looking for your husband, my lady, he's with Lord Charles in the great hall."

This might have been the only opening she got to speak to him alone, so she might as well dive in. "Actually, I was looking for you. I was hoping we might speak privately. I have important news from my father."

The earl's gaze flicked to his man. "Chester, leave us."

The other man departed without a word. *Good.* There would be no one to overhear.

Lord James sauntered over, looking her up and down with a smoldering gaze. Did he suspect what she was about to tell him? But how could he? Perhaps he was merely depraved enough not to care that she was a married woman. The thought sent a shiver up her spine. But she was doing this for Adelaide, and she would see it through.

"So… you have me alone. What did your *father* wish for me to know?" He smirked knowingly, and her stomach churned.

"Actually, it has nothing to do with my father. I wanted to speak with you. I have a proposition for you. How would you like to become the Royal Exchequer when Lord Henry becomes king?"

The earl's eyebrows shot up. She had surprised him. *Good.* She wanted him to see her value as an ally. She had no intention of merely being one of his many conquests.

"What makes you think Henry Fitzempress is going to win this war, and why would he consider me for such a plum position when I've never come out openly in support of him?"

"If King Stephen had the strength to fend off his challenger, he would have done so by now. We both know the Duke of Normandy had more land, more men at arms, and more wealth than our so-called king. He is not bringing the full force of his army to bear because he doesn't wish to destroy the land he hopes to rule, but we both know it is only a matter of time before Lord Henry wins."

He stared at her for a long moment. "It truly is extraordinary how devious your little mind is. One might almost think you a man. Do go on. I'm intrigued."

Isabella forced herself to unclench her fist. He could insult her "little mind" all he liked as long as he took the deal, and she got to keep Adelaide safe. "I know who the duke plans to make exchequer when he takes the throne. I also know a secret about the man that could ruin him utterly with Lord Henry. If you were the one who brought this tidbit to His Grace, you could easily insinuate yourself into the man's position. Think of it. You would have all the wealth of the English crown at your command as soon as Lord Henry wins the war."

The flash of greed in Lord James's eyes was momentary, but it told Isabella everything she needed to know.

"Tell me more of this fairy tale where I'm sitting atop the king's treasury. It amuses me."

Lord James might be trying to act nonchalant, but Isabella could tell she had him hooked, much to her dismay. Success meant sacrificing any chance of future happiness. But if she could save Adelaide, it was all worth it.

"I would, but I'm afraid further details come at a price."

He'd taken the bait, and now it was time to reel him in. It did not escape her notice that she was behaving exactly like the heartless women who made her life so miserable. Was this truly who she was? But what choice did she have but to follow their example with her sister's life at stake?

Steeling herself, she took a deep breath. "I'll tell you everything you need to know if you marry me and allow me to keep my sister with me."

The man didn't blink an eyelash at her demand. How could that be? It was far more shocking than her offer to make him exchequer.

"Tempting. But how could we marry when you are already wedded to another?" He stepped closer and ran his knuckle down her cheek.

It took all her willpower to hold still and not bolt. *Good Lord.* She was going to have to let this man touch her any way he wanted for the rest of her life. The thought made her blood run cold.

"Martin and I have not consummated the marriage. We can still have it annulled," she said, holding very still and wishing he would back away.

"And how can I be sure of that? I have no interest in marrying used goods."

Ugh. This was how he treated a prospective wife? "You'll have to take my word for it."

"No, my lady. I want proof. Come to my bedchamber and show me just how pure you are, and I'll consider your offer."

Shock rippled through her. He wanted her to sleep with him before they were wed to prove her virginity? What was to stop him from taking advantage of her and then refusing to follow through with the wedding?

She took a step back. "Absolutely not. I will not share your bed until we are married. You must take or leave my offer on its merits without such proof."

"And if I refuse?"

"Then I'll find someone who has the vision and ambition to recognize my worth." She really hoped she wouldn't have to. He was by far the most convenient option available to her, and she needed to secure her and Adelaide's futures quickly.

His eyes narrowed. "Why is Lord Martin playing along with your scheme? I could hardly believe it when he came to me and told me of your interest in marrying me. I can't imagine what subtle game you two must be up to. I don't believe for a moment that blather he spewed about how he wants you to choose him of your own free will rather than be trapped in marriage."

Isabella's heart stuttered at Lord James's words. "Martin said what?"

The earl crossed his arms and stared down at her. "He told me that same thing you did—that you hadn't consummated the marriage and that you wished to wed me. One minute he seemed to be encouraging me to steal you away and the next he was threatening my life if I dared to touch you without your leave. And he kept going on about how he had to earn your trust. It was very confusing."

Martin couldn't possibly have meant all that, could he? But what possible reason would he have to tell Lord James? Unless her attempts to convince him that she was a shrew had actually worked. Had she worn him down? But then, why would he have said he wanted to earn her trust?

"I hardly know Lord Martin. I couldn't say what might be going through his mind. But it doesn't matter. He was sent by Lady Eleanor and can't be trusted. I need you to guarantee safety for my sister and me. Marry me, and I will make you one of the most powerful lords in England. That is my offer. What say you?"

He was silent for a long, agonizing moment. "You are asking me to take a significant gamble. What guarantee do I have that you can make good on your lofty promise? And you refuse to come to my bed to provide me with irrefutable proof of your innocence. For all I know, you might have been defiled before your wedding to Lord Martin, and he simply wishes to be rid of you."

How dare he impugn her honor like that! If Isabella were a man, she would have challenged him to combat on the spot. It was only with great difficulty that she refrained from striking out with her bare hands.

"But," Lord James continued, raising a placating hand, "I do like a gamble, and the prospect of being exchequer has undeniable appeal." He stroked his beard. "You are confident you can deliver on your promise?"

"I am, my lord," she said through gritted teeth. She almost had him, and never had she been so reluctant to succeed.

He nodded slowly. "I must consider. You will have my answer within the sennight. In the meantime, I expect you to keep your distance from Lord Martin. For me to even consider this, there must be no doubt as to whether your marriage has been consummated. If there is the slightest appearance that you are anything but chaste, the deal is off."

It wasn't a definitive answer, but she had every reason to believe that he would say yes in the end. For the moment, she had a respite where she might dream of what it would be like if he said no. But within a mere sennight, her fate would be sealed.

"Of course, my lord."

"Very good. Now leave and call my man back. You interrupted my practice, something I would advise against in future."

He was treating her like his servant, and they weren't even married yet. A burst of rage coursed through her, but she forced it down and curtsied. "I won't do it again, my lord."

She hurried from the yard, found the man named Chester, and conveyed the message. Then she found the stairs to the tallest turret in the castle and climbed them. Only when she reached the top did she let the tears she'd been holding back fall. The deed was done. She'd followed through with her plan despite the warning in her heart that she was making a terrible mistake. If she succeeded, her sister would be safe, and her own position of power would be secure.

This was exactly the outcome she wanted, so why did her victory taste like ashes?

Wiping away her tears, she looked out at Yarmouth and the surrounding countryside. All this could belong to her if she could only tolerate being married to a boor. The compensations of putting up with the earl would be immense. And if she succeeded in making him the king's exchequer, she would find herself one of the wealthiest women in England.

While her mother and Lady Eleanor ordered her to marry Lord Martin, they had both spent years instilling a very different lesson. A woman's worth was determined by her husband, and marrying a man of power and position was the most important thing a woman could do.

Sentiment was a luxury that women couldn't afford. It led them to make foolish choices, and men would inevitably disappoint them. Marriage was not about romance. Hadn't Lady Eleanor said as much a thousand times? It was far better to wed a man one knew one disliked than to harbor hopes of something more, which would inevitably be dashed.

The feelings Isabella had for Martin would pass, and what would Isabella be left with then? A lowly position amongst England's gentry. Isolation from everyone she cared about. The guilt of having failed to save Adelaide from finding herself under Lady Eleanor's thumb, and that was if her sister even survived. If Adelaide died alone and neglected by the heartless woman she served, Isabella would never forgive herself.

One way or another, Isabella had to see this through and marry Lord James. She had set the wheels in motion, and now there was nothing she could do to stop them. Her fate was in the hands of God.

Taking deep breaths of crisp, fresh air, she composed herself and reassembled the mask she showed the world of scrupulous indifference and haughtiness.

"I have no heart to lose," she murmured to herself, wishing rather than feeling it to be true. With as much conviction as she could summon, she descended the stairs to seal her own doom.

CHAPTER EIGHTEEN

MARTIN FELT ISABELLA approach before he saw her. In the weeks since they had met, he'd developed a sixth sense that was attuned to her just as a compass needle points north. She entered the great hall, sweeping in with a majesty and hauteur that never failed to take his breath away.

But something was wrong. Very wrong.

Only someone who had studied her at length would see it, but there was strain behind her cool gaze, and a slight, lingering redness around her eyes suggested she'd been crying. If this had something to do with Lord James, he would run the man through with his own lance.

If he hadn't been in the midst of a conversation with Lord Christopher about the progress of repairs to *The Wind Song*, he would have pulled her aside to a private place and gotten to the bottom of what had happened. But he would have to tread carefully in such a public setting. While he would do everything that he could to plead his case, he couldn't do anything that might suggest he was sabotaging her plan. There could be no hint that their marriage was anything but chaste.

Isabella approached and stood beside him at a distance carefully calibrated to avoid any possible contact. Her distance hurt him, but he understood why she maintained it.

"Lady Isabella, what a pleasure it is to see you again," said

Lord Christopher, who was fortunately oblivious to the tension between them. "Welcome to my keep. Please don't hesitate to tell me if there's anything my wife or I can do to make you comfortable during your stay."

"That is most kind of you, Lord Christopher." She smiled and bowed her head. "Where is Lady Diana? I'm looking forward to seeing her again."

"She went to market to purchase provisions. We have quite a full house at the moment, but the more the merrier, as I always say. Isn't that right, Lord Martin? And in these troubling times, it is good to have friends you can rely on. There's safety in numbers, eh?"

"Very true, my lord. Nonetheless, we appreciate your hospitality. Please thank your wife for any trouble she may have gone to on our behalf." Martin had always liked Lord Christopher. He was a pleasant and generous man, if a bit blind to the flaws of his liege lord.

"Congratulations on your nuptials, you two lovebirds! I'm very sorry we didn't have enough rooms to put you together."

Martin stifled a sigh as he forced himself to offer the explanation that would offer Isabella her freedom. "It's probably for the best, my lord. My family is very traditional and wants us to wait to consummate the marriage until we are in Winchelsea." The lie nearly choked him, but he had to do it for her sake.

"Really?" Lord Christopher frowned. "How unfortunate for you. It must be very trying to wait. You have my sympathies."

At that moment, Lord James came striding in. Isabella stiffened beside him. Whatever was upsetting her definitely had something to do with that giant muscular oaf. Martin clenched his fist by his side, even as he forced himself to smile politely.

"Why does Lord Martin have your sympathies?" the big man bellowed.

"His family has insisted that he wait to consummate his marriage until he's back in Winchelsea, poor man." Lord Christopher's expression was all sympathy.

Martin had to bite his tongue to stop himself from complaining that his marital relations shouldn't be a topic for public discussion. After all, he was the one who raised the topic. But it still galled him to no end.

"Poor man indeed." Lord James grinned widely. "If I had a bride like her, I wouldn't wait, no matter what my family said, but not all men have the balls to stand up to their mommies."

This was too much. If the earl didn't shut his ugly mouth, Martin was going to ram his fist into it.

"It is the sign of true chivalry that he is willing to wait and comply with his family's wishes," said Isabella, stepping closer and clasping his clenched fist in her hand.

Martin forced himself to relax and open his fist. She was right to hold him back. He couldn't punch the earl however much he might want to. It would ruin his carefully laid plan to win Isabella's heart and likely make it exceedingly difficult to get out of Yarmouth in one piece. And this small gesture of solidarity warmed his heart beyond all reason.

Lord James's eyes narrowed. "You know, she isn't truly your bride until you consummate. Another man might steal her away."

Isabella stared fixedly at the floor. She must have spoken with him, and as Martin feared, his rival was interested. The mere idea of her surrendering herself to that man filled him with blinding rage.

Martin clenched his fist again, and Isabella glance quickly at him, shaking her head almost imperceptibly. She didn't want him to fight. Of course, she didn't. She'd achieved what she wanted—to marry Lord James. The thought made him want to grab the nearest weapon and carve the earl to pieces, but he held back for her sake.

Wide-eyed, Lord Christopher barked an incredulous laugh. "Surely, no one is going to attempt to steal Lord Martin's bride from him. They've already declared their union before God."

Lord James shrugged. "Perhaps God has other plans for Lady

Isabella, grander plans."

Taking several threatening steps toward Martin, Lord James towered over him. Martin met his gaze and let the man see the full force of his fury.

Lord James blinked and took a step back, then laughed. "It was a jest, my lord. No need to look at me like that. No one is going to steal your wife."

"Ha! Of course! A jest." Lord Christopher's forced guffaw was accompanied by a nervous, darting glance between the two men. "He meant nothing by it, Lord Martin. Have no fear. Your lady is safe beneath my roof."

"Although she could hardly be blamed for keeping her options open, eh?" Lord James clapped Martin on the shoulder and squeezed painfully. "That awful mustache of yours certainly isn't doing you any favors, is it, my lady?" he said, releasing Martin and turning to Isabella.

"I think it suits him."

Pride bloomed in Martin's heart, despite the tension in the room. She liked his mustache! Nobody liked his mustache, not even his own mother. He'd seen a man in Venice wearing one and thought it a very fine fashion indeed. Unfortunately, no one seemed to agree with him. Until his wife.

"Yes, I suppose it distracts from the rest of him, which is, perhaps, for the best."

A weak and uninspired insult if he ever heard one.

"I am as God made me. If you think to prick my pride, you need to work harder. I have been called a boiled-leather cuirass, a goat turd, a lump of putrid cheese, a rampallian, a puke stocking... And that's just by my little sister. I'd tell you what my brother says about me, but I don't wish to offend Lady Isabella's ears."

Isabella turned toward him, eyebrows raised. "Your sister said all that about you?"

Martin shrugged. "In her defense, she was eight, and I'd just dropped her favorite doll in a dung heap playing keep-away with my brother. I deserved every word."

Isabella laughed, and some of the tension left his body. As long as she found him funny and charming, all hope was not lost.

"So, my lord," Martin said, turning to Lord James. "Can you do better than an eight-year-old girl? Sharpen your wit and do your worst."

Lord James narrowed his eyes. "This is absurd. I don't have time to play your childish games."

"A pity. I was rather looking forward to hearing what novel insults you would heap upon my head. But perhaps your wit is not up to the task." Martin ought not to goad the man, but anger still simmered beneath his skin over his rival's inroads with Isabella, not to mention whatever the man had said to make her cry.

"Shut your face, you pathetic fool." The earl took a threatening step toward him.

"Peace, my lords! Peace!" Lord Christopher rose and hurried to stand between them. "This jesting has gone too far. Perhaps we should go our separate ways until supper. I have a lovely garden that Lady Isabella might enjoy. Lord Martin, perhaps you could take your wife for a walk there? Lord James and I have some business to attend to."

Martin forced himself to release the breath he'd been holding and turned his gaze from the loathsome toad trying to steal his wife to Lord Christopher. "That sounds lovely, my lord. Isabella, will you accompany me?"

He held out his arm, and she took it. They left the great hall swiftly, without another word.

The garden was not at its finest, given the season. There was little alive aside from cabbages and conifers, but Martin was hardly going to complain about the surroundings when he finally had a moment of privacy with his wife. He led her to a stone bench and sat beside her.

"Isabella, what happened with Lord James? It looks like you've been crying. Did he threaten you or hurt you?"

She shook her head.

Thank God! But still, something had brought her to tears, and he wanted very badly to know what it was.

Isabella turned her gaze to him before he could form a question. "Is it true that you went to him before I did and told him you would release me if I chose it?"

"Yes." He searched her face for some sign that he'd done the right thing. Her eyes welled with tears that she blinked back. Perhaps he'd gotten it all wrong. "Would you rather that I hadn't?"

She closed her eyes and folded her hands in her lap. "It matters not. I have made my choice and sealed my doom."

His heart sank at the confirmation of his fears.

"Is this not what you want?" Please let her have seen reason! Lord James was no good for her. Or anyone, really. He wouldn't wish that man on any lady who lived, no matter how detestable.

"It is exactly what I want." She twisted the fabric of her skirt in her hands, keeping her eyes closed. "Don't worry about me. I'll be a countess—the envy of all of England."

And yet she looked absolutely miserable about it. This was not the face of triumph or satisfaction, and his heart ached for her. If only she could see that he offered so much more, even though the other man did have more land and more wealth! Money and power didn't lead to happiness, and all Martin wanted was to spend the rest of his days making her smile.

A tear dripped down her cheek, and he couldn't stop himself from reaching up to wipe it from her cheek. "Oh, my love, you don't have to do this if you don't want to."

She stiffened and opened her reddened eyes. "Yes, I do. It's too late. The wheels have been set in motion."

Her words cut him like a blade. It *would* be exceedingly difficult to walk things back. Words spoken could not be unsaid. But he was far from ready to concede defeat.

"It's not too late. We're still married, and he has no power over you. Say the word, and we'll leave Norfolk on the next ship south. Ulf can see to the repair of *The Wind Song*. We needn't stay if we don't want to." *Please, let her say yes!*

"And what of my sister?" She looked at him with imploring eyes. Clearly his answer mattered, but what was she looking for beyond an assurance that they would bring her with them?

"She'd come with us, of course. And then when she was well enough, and we were settled in Winchelsea, I'd send her along to Lady Eleanor as planned."

She stiffened and clenched her fists. What had he said wrong? This had been the plan all along. Far be it from him to interfere with Lady Adelaide's prospects. No doubt, she would have every advantage at court with Lady Eleanor. Clearly, Isabella had benefitted tremendously from her time with Her Grace. Wasn't that what she wanted for her sister?

"What is it, my sweet? What aren't you saying?" Clearly, he was missing something here.

She pursed her lips and shook her head. "I'm going to marry Lord James. You needn't bother yourself about me anymore. I'll be off your hands soon enough."

She stood abruptly and hurried inside the castle without taking her leave.

He'd lost her. God's bones, he had lost his wife. The world turned gray around him, and his blood thundered in his ears.

No. He was not giving up this easily. There had to be some way to win her back. This wasn't over until she said her wedding vows with Lord James. He would respect her wishes, but he would fight for her love. She cared for him. He was certain of it. Something was holding her back, and he needed to find out what it was.

It was somehow related to Adelaide. That was when her expression shifted, and her posture went rigid. But how he had blundered, he couldn't guess. What was he doing except carrying out the orders of the woman Isabella loyally served for years. Was this not what she wanted?

Perhaps a visit to Adelaide's sick room was in order. Filled with renewed determination, he headed back into the castle.

CHAPTER NINETEEN

ISABELLA WAS RIGHT not to trust Martin. He was going to send Adelaide away at the earliest opportunity. He said it himself. The words pierced her heart like a poison dagger. She should have defended herself better. This was what she got for caving into sentimentality. All along, her mother and Lady Eleanor were right. Love was weakness. If she wanted to keep her sister safe, she couldn't afford to be weak.

All those moments when she started to fall for him turned bitter, and a lump of outrage lodged itself in her throat. How could she have allowed him to addle her head like this? She should never have let herself to forget who his puppet mistress was. The thought of the kiss they'd shared made her burn with humiliation. Well, she would teach him that she wasn't so easily swayed.

She needed to find Lord James and convince him to accept her offer before she lost the will to follow through. The man might be loathsome, but at least she knew exactly where she stood with him. There was no danger of her losing her heart to that snake, and she would have no compunctions about manipulating him to her own ends. Adelaide would be safe, and she herself would be a woman of power and position, able to shape her life as she desired.

After a few inquiries, she found Lord James in the stable,

preparing for a ride. She paused before entering, some deep instinct warning her against proceeding with her plan. But it was only her foolish heart, which she had no use for. Isabella de Martillac was made of sterner stuff.

Preparing to enter, she bit her lips and pinched her cheeks to make herself look fresh and rosy. The man had made no secret of his attraction to her. Perhaps she could use that to hasten his decision, much as the thought of him pawing at her made her skin crawl.

As she entered the barn, breathing in the earthy smells of hay and horse manure, it seemed as if even the horses were giving her disapproving stares. *Ridiculous.* She was imagining things. But the alarm bells clanging within her only grew louder.

Lord James was about to mount his horse, a black destrier that was bigger than any she'd ever seen, when she stepped into his view. His brow furrowed, and he paused at the sight of her.

"Lady Isabella, I didn't expect to see you again so soon. Would you care to join me on a ride?"

A ride would the perfect opportunity to get him alone, but would it be safe? The warning in her heart said *no.* "That might not be wise, my lord. I'm certain you would be perfectly chivalrous, but tongues might wag."

"Very well, then. What is it you wish to say?"

This was it. There was no going back. *Think of Lady Eleanor. She would never back down in such a situation.*

"I wondered if you have given my offer further thought, my lord. The arrangement could be highly beneficial to us both."

The words burned her throat as she spoke them, but she was determined to forge ahead.

Lord James looked around and shooed off the stable hands in earshot. "I have, and I confess I am intrigued. One might even say I am interested. But there is one very short and irritating impediment."

She kept her face as blank as she could as he insulted Martin. Though she was furious with her temporary husband, it didn't sit well to hear Lord James insult him behind his back. Something in her face must have betrayed her because he narrowed his eyes, watching her expression a little too closely.

"I see that you dislike him as much as I do."

Fortunately, it appeared he read her wince as agreement rather than outrage on Martin's behalf.

"You have my sympathies, my lady. It must have been a trial to endure his company on the journey here."

"He is irrelevant. I'm here to discuss our potential future together." The words nearly choked her as she spoke them. *Think of Adelaide. She needs you to be strong.*

"And yet you won't give me the proof I requested of your purity."

She fought a shudder. While she might need Lord James to achieve her aims, the very fact that he would demand such a thing proved the depravity of his soul.

"No. Absolutely not." She took a step back to stay out of his reach in case he made a move.

Instead of reaching for her, he laughed. "Such a prude. If I agree to marry you, you had better not put up such a fight."

"Once we are married, I will submit to your attentions, and not a moment before." The thought of sharing his bed made her nauseous, but she knew her wifely duties. He would own her body once they were wed.

"You know, I could bend you over that trough and have you right now. No one here would dare interrupt us." He took a step toward her with a lascivious grin.

God's teeth, the man was a monster! How was she going to get out of here unscathed? "You can't, before the marriage is annulled or the priests will refuse the annulment. And any child that might result would be Lord Martin's by right."

That made him pause. Her heart was nearly pounding out of her chest as she waited to see what he would do next.

"Unfortunately, you are correct. Very well, then. I'll wait." He held up his hands and stepped back. "But I am not a patient man. How quickly can you get rid of your husband?"

"I can tell him today, and we can start the proceedings. The speed of the annulment will depend on the Church." The sooner this ugly business was finished, the better. Though a rebellious part of her hoped the Church refused outright.

Lord James waved his hand dismissively. "Don't bother about them. They'll do my bidding."

While she had no doubt that his influence with the Church was substantial, she didn't believe they would be as compliant as he claimed. The Church had been clashing more and more with local lords who attempted to issue high-handed orders. The pope meant to establish his authority firmly even in such outlying regions as England. Still, she knew better than to argue. "As you say, my lord."

"Then we have an agreement. As soon as you are free of Lord Martin, I will wed you, and in return, you will make me Henry's exchequer."

"Yes." A lump formed in her throat as she spoke. Her heart rebelled, but it was a useless organ, and she was determined to ignore it.

"Excellent. Then you had best go find your husband and deliver the news. I look forward to his impending humiliation. Good day to you, Lady Isabella."

She nodded curtly, turned on her heel, and nearly ran, tears welling and starting to drip down her cheeks as soon as she was out of sight. Desperately, she searched for someplace she could be alone and give in to the tumult of emotions that overwhelmed her after sealing her fate. Her eyes fell upon the dovecote at the far end of the bailey. Surely no one would be in there.

She entered the small, round, stone building with a pointed roof and found herself alone at last, but for the company of warbling birds. Several peered out of their neatly stacked pigeonholes, which checkered the walls all the way to the ceiling, to examine the intruder.

"I mean you no harm. I just need a quiet place to cry," she

said softly, tears flowing unchecked.

Shudders overtook her, and she sobbed aloud. Her future stretched out before her as an unending feast of misery. For the first time in her life, she felt that she truly understood her mother. The woman had sacrificed herself to a miserable marriage with a man she didn't respect for the sake of power and position. As Isabella stood weeping in the dovecote, she could understand all too well how that might warp a woman's soul and make her deeply bitter.

But Isabella had done what was necessary. Despite her tears and deep misgivings, the conversation had been a success. She'd just achieved what she'd been striving for ever since her mother broke the news that she was to marry. Her sister was safe, and her own future position was assured. With Lord James by her side, she would be as safe from her mother and Lady Eleanor as anyone could be. All she had to do was leave a man who had won her heart for a man she detested.

How could she have let herself fall so fast and so hard for Lord Martin? She knew all along he was under Lady Eleanor's thumb. And yet his insidious good humor, cheeky wit, undeniable courage, and dogged courtship had made her let her guard down. She could have been happy with Lord Martin if only it wasn't for his determination to send away Adelaide. Certainly, he would have made a more tolerable husband than Lord James.

But it would be folly to follow her heart. If she balked now, Adelaide would pay the price, and she would far rather sacrifice her own happiness than her sister's. After all, Lord Martin had just confirmed her worst fears in relation to Adelaide. How could she risk everything for a man who would tear her away from the person she loved most in this world?

She had to steel herself against his insidious influence and harden her heart. No one could ever know that she had one or that Lord Martin had very nearly won it. She would follow the example of her mother and Lady Eleanor and marry for position rather than for love.

There had been times with Lady Eleanor when Isabella had suspected the woman had a heart underneath all her cold practicality. After all, didn't Her Grace patronize troubadours who sang of nothing but love all day long? And some of the matches she made between courtiers appeared to be inspired by a desire for their happiness rather than strictly practical considerations. But every time Lady Eleanor seemed to reveal her softer side, she immediately destroyed the illusion by doing something so cold-hearted that no one could doubt her cruel pragmatism and cold calculation.

A pair of doves flew in through an opening in the roof and settled into the cozy nest within a shared pigeonhole. They cooed softly and nestled against each other.

Isabella tried to imagine such simple affection with Lord James and shuddered at the thought. With Martin, on the other hand, she could imagine it easily—curling into his warmth and basking in his devotion. But she couldn't trust Lord Martin, however much she might want to. The time had come to end her wallowing and find Lord Martin to break the news.

But first, she had to check on Adelaide. Wiping her eyes and squaring her shoulders, she strode back into the castle, heading straight for the room she shared with her sister. Never had triumph tasted so bitter. Tears threatened once again as she climbed the stairs, and she blinked them back. This was for the best. She just needed to collect herself and calm down. Hopefully, Adelaide would be asleep. She wasn't sure she was fit company even for her sister in the mood she was in.

As she approached the door, she heard the strains of music coming from within. But how was that possible? Adelaide was too ill to play her lute. And then an all-too-familiar tenor began to sing.

No. She wasn't ready to face Martin yet. She needed a moment to collect herself first. But Lord James wanted her to act swiftly, so perhaps it was for the best that she spoke to him now. It was pointless to delay.

Tentatively, she pushed open the door. The scene before her made her heart ache. Adelaide, wan and feverish as she was, beamed at Martin as he sang to her. The tune was familiar, and when she realized what it was, a lump formed in her throat. Somehow, he'd learned the lullaby their nursemaid used to sing to them in Bordeaux when they were children. His accent was atrocious, but the words were unmistakable. Had Adelaide taught it to him during their journey?

As she closed the door behind her, her husband paused and set aside the citole. His smile dropped as he looked her in the eye. "What happened?" he asked, his voice suddenly gruff.

The words were on the tip of her tongue, but she couldn't force herself to form them. "I—I…"

"Yes?" The hurt in his gaze made her want to run from the room.

Glancing at her sister, Isabella made herself straighten and face him. This was all for Adelaide. With Lord James she would be safe.

"Lord James has offered for my hand. I'd like to request an annulment."

As she spoke the words, everything within her broke. But it was done. Her future was sealed.

Chapter Twenty

MARTIN HAD TO force himself to breathe. Her words ran him through like a lance. This hurt far more than it should have after such a brief acquaintance. And it wasn't as if she hadn't warned him. Time and again, she'd told him in so many words that she planned to marry Lord James. But after their kiss, he thought something had changed, that there was a glimmer of hope. Apparently, he was mistaken.

"You want an annulment? Now? Even after—"

"Don't." She wouldn't meet his eyes. "I don't want to be your wife. You said you would release me if I asked. I'm begging you to keep your side of the bargain."

This was all happening too fast. It wasn't possible that she'd already made up her mind. Or was it? "But you haven't even given me a chance. I thought you would at least wait a few days to get to know the earl and make an informed decision."

"Are you suggesting I don't know my own mind?" She met his gaze at last, eyes blazing. "Do you dare pretend to know what is in my heart better than I know myself?"

There had to be some way to convince her that he was the better option. He wasn't ready to surrender. "I make no such claim. I only thought I had more time, and I thought the man's flaws would speak for themselves."

"He's right, Isabella," Adelaide chimed in. "You hardly know

Lord James. This does seem a rather hasty decision."

"Adelaide, my sweet, please stay out of this," Isabella said softly. Her voice was breaking. "I know what I'm doing. This is for the best. I promise."

"Is it? And why is that?" He really should have bitten his tongue, but he was too desperate to rein in his speech. "How is marrying a man you hardly know but who you do know is guaranteed to make you miserable for the best?"

Isabella whirled around to face him. "I know Lord James well enough to take his measure. May I remind you that I've known him longer than you? I understand the consequences of the choice I am making. You and I made a bargain, Martin. Now let me go. I want an annulment."

He struggled to find words to respond, anything to reverse the horrifying prospect of losing her to that miserable, rotten, philandering, hairy brute. But his silver tongue abandoned him in his moment of need. In the end, the word that came out was, "No."

"No?" Her voice was barely audible. "But you must. You promised!" There was a panicked edge to her voice as she spoke, but he had no intention of backing down. A bargain was a bargain.

"I promised that if I hadn't won you over by Winchelsea, I would release you. Are we in Winchelsea, my lady?"

She blanched. "No, but—"

"We agreed on Winchelsea," he said quietly. He ought to give up. They were in Norfolk, and Lord James held all the power. And there was no reason to believe Isabella would change her mind if he somehow succeeded in bringing her home. But he couldn't let it go. Not now when he was so close to winning her over. "You haven't fulfilled your end of the bargain, and I'm going to hold you to it."

Shaking her head, she backed up and leaned against the door as if she needed support. He expected her to rail, to lash him with her scathing tongue, but instead she simply said, "Please don't.

Please."

That brought him up short. Isabella didn't beg. It wasn't in her nature. Something was off. There was a piece of this puzzle that he was missing.

"Why should I release you from our bargain early?"

She bit her lip and gripped the door. "Because I don't care for you." The words cut him deep, but her voice trembled as she said it. There was something amiss here.

"Why else? What is it you aren't telling me, Isabella?"

A tear dripped down her cheek.

Instantly, all his anger vanished, and all he wanted in the world was to comfort her. He needed to touch her, hold her, assure her that whatever Lord James had promised, he himself would promise her so much more. He might not be able to equal the earl in terms of title or wealth or even rugged good looks, but he would spend every moment of every day for the rest of his life devoted to her happiness. As he watched the tear drop from her chin and land on the front of her dress, something in him broke.

He couldn't stand it any longer. Rising slowly, he crossed the room and raised his hand to cup her cheek, thumbing away the tear. Another tear fell. "Isabella, why are you crying?"

Silence. But she didn't recoil from his touch. On the contrary, she nuzzled against his hand. Her actions in no way matched her words. Isabella still had feelings for him. He would swear it.

Hardly daring to press his luck but unable to resist her allure, he kissed her soft cheek, tasting salt on his lips.

With a shuddering sigh, she fell into his arms, resting her head on his shoulder. He clutched her close as she cried. What her reaction meant, he couldn't say, but tentative hope bloomed within him at her gentle embrace. He didn't dare speak for fear of spoiling the moment.

"Isabella," came a quivery voice from the bed. He'd almost forgotten Adelaide's presence. "Isabella?"

With a sniff, Isabella pulled away to face her sister. He did not want to give her up, but he knew all too well that Adelaide was her priority. "Yes, my sweet?"

A deep, wracking cough shook Adelaide's thin frame, and Isabella rushed to her side, bringing a cup of water to her lips and making her sip.

"We should go to Winchelsea with Lord Martin. You promised."

Isabella shook her head. "It's too late. We must stay. Rest, and don't trouble yourself, dear. All you need to worry about is getting better." She caressed her sister's hair, tucking stray wisps behind her ear. Then she turned to him, eyes full of sorrow. "I'm sorry, Martin, but I cannot remain your wife."

No! She obviously didn't want the future she'd chosen, and he couldn't make sense of any of this.

"Why is it too late?" Clearly, Isabella felt more than she was ready to admit. Something else was holding her back, and he had to know what it was. "What is the real reason for the sudden hurry? Did he threaten you? I'll kill him if he did."

The man was a brute, and it was all too easy to imagine him stooping so low as to threaten a woman so that he could have his way with her. It would explain Isabella's strange behavior and her refusal to relent about the annulment even now. The mere thought made him want to draw and quarter Lord James.

Turning to face him, Isabella said quietly, with tears streaming down her face, "I said I don't care for you, and I meant it. I don't wish to remain your wife. Lord James can protect Adelaide and me in a way you never could. We'll be safe here."

The soft and tender look on her face was at odds with her cruel words. He didn't know what to make of it, and his heart ached with terrible foreboding. Why would she say Lord James could protect them, and he couldn't?

Adelaide gasped and coughed. "Isabella, no. Don't do this. You care for Lord Martin. It's plain as day."

"But he'll send you away. Can't you see?" Isabella said, panic in her eyes. "In the end he'll make you go to Lady Eleanor. We can't trust anyone sent by the duchess. She's a spider, and we're all caught in her web. But Lord James isn't. He can take care of us and let us stay together. That's all that matters, my dear."

Her words hit him like boulders thrown by a siege engine. She didn't *trust* him. She wanted to keep her sister with her. How could he not have seen it sooner?

"I'm not under Lady Eleanor's thumb any more than Lord James is. I will not betray my family for the sake of an alliance. As your sister, Adelaide is family. She would always have the full protection of Winchelsea. If you wanted to keep Adelaide with you, all you had to do was ask. I swear to you, I will defend her with my very life."

"But you said you would send her away."

He did. And she'd immediately fled his company. It was all making sense now. If only he could take those words back!

"I only said it because I didn't know you wished it otherwise. Had you simply told me you didn't want to send her to the duchess, I would have agreed immediately."

He prayed that she would trust him. He believed deep down that she did, but he'd been his own worst enemy, blithely confirming her fears without realizing he was driving her away.

"But Lady Eleanor sent you. How can I trust that you will be true to your word?"

The words twisted in his gut as though he'd been stabbed. Even after everything they had been through, she still didn't trust him. How could he prove himself? What proof could he offer?

"Have I ever given you cause to doubt me? Have I ever deceived you in any way? I have kept every single promise I have ever made to you, Isabella. My heart is true. I swear on my home, on my family, on all that I hold dear that I will do right by you, no matter what it costs me with the duchess. You must trust me on this. My word is my bond."

For a long moment, Isabella stared at him in silence. His future hung on a knife's edge as he waited for her to pronounce his doom.

Then she whispered. "Then I've made a terrible mistake."

He let out a breath he didn't know he was holding.

"What mistake?" Dare he hope?

"If I'd known, I wouldn't have gone to Lord James. And it wouldn't be too late for…" She trailed off.

"For what, Isabella?"

The seconds passed with agonizing slowness. Everything in his world sharpened to a point. The next words that passed her lips could either be his salvation or his eternal damnation.

"For happiness. For us. I could have spent the rest of my life with a man who truly cared—a man who was brave and kind and giving. And instead, I chose a man who sees me as nothing but a tool for his own ambition. How could I have been so blind?"

"Isabella, does this mean you care for me? That you want to be my wife in truth?" He needed to hear her state it plainly. Everything in him longed to go to her and hold her in his arms, but he held back, waiting for proof.

"Yes, Martin. I want to be your wife. You've won your wager. There is no one else I would rather spend the rest of my life with. I don't know what we'll do about Lord James, but I choose you."

For a long moment, he couldn't move, thunderstruck by this final confirmation of her affection. He'd pretended confidence from the very start, but he'd hardly dared believe this day would come. But she'd spoken the words. He'd won his wager. Elation flooded him as he reached out.

She took a step toward him, arms outstretched, tentative hope written in every feature.

It was real. She was truly his, now and forever. He reached for her, desperate to fold her in his arms.

Grasping her hand, he pulled her up and kissed her deep and hard. Isabella was his, whatever might wait for them outside the door. He'd won her heart, and the rest of the world could burn to the ground for all he cared. This was what he'd been dreaming of ever since meeting her—this meeting of equals, igniting of passions.

The sweet taste of her drove him mad, as she crushed her

body against his, hands clutching at his back, and kissed him back with every bit as much fervor as he gave. With every lick of her tongue, he fell harder for her. His heart was hers, utterly hers. He didn't think he could fall more deeply in love than he already had, but each touch tethered him more tightly to her. They were inseparable now. He hardly knew where he ended, and she began. They were so lost in each other that there would be no untangling them.

The kiss began to spiral out of control. The desperate frenzy with which they consumed each other became too much. She was so soft and warm beneath his touch. The herbal scent of her hair drove him made as his fingers caressed her tresses. She tasted of sweetness and spice and boundless possibility. With her by his side, he was so much more. He'd never thought his life was incomplete, but her love filled a hole he never knew he had.

Her luscious body pressed against his and drove him to greater heights. He needed to be closer. Holding her in his arms wasn't nearly enough. He needed her, all of her. Now.

But as he began kissing down her neck, there was a ragged cough from the bed, and they both froze. They had an audience. How could he have forgotten?

Both panting, they stepped away from each other. He thought about diving into the dark and icy sea after Pascal to calm his body and jolt his mind back into working order.

"My apologies, Lady Adelaide," he said as soon as he was capable of speech.

From the bed, Adelaide laughed weakly and coughed again. "I'm happy for the two of you, though I was starting to wonder if I was going to need to dump that water on you both to bring you to your senses," she said, pointing to the pitcher and basin on a small table across the room. "Right now, you two need to figure out how you're going to handle Lord James. He won't be so entertained by your newfound adoration."

All too true, but Martin savored the challenge. He'd won his bride. And no one was ever going to take her away. If Lord James wanted to challenge him, he would fight to the very death for her favor.

"It's too late. I've won. I won't let him take you away from me. Not ever."

But Isabella quailed. Worry creased her forehead, and her hands balled into fists. "I don't think it's going to be that easy."

Perhaps not, but Martin would not countenance any impediment to their union, now that her affection was certain. Let Lord James do his worst. Martin would never surrender his bride.

CHAPTER TWENTY-ONE

"THE EARL IS going to be furious." Isabella closed her eyes and bit her lip. Lord James was not a forgiving man, and he was going to make her pay one way or another for reneging on their deal. Now that she had given in to her feelings for Martin, the perils to them both came crashing in, pushing away the initial elation of her surrender.

"Let's go tell him and get it over with," Martin said, taking Isabella's hand. His confidence almost convinced her. With him by her side, Isabella felt stronger and more capable of standing up to Lord James's wrath. But she still feared for Martin's safety, as well as her own.

"He just went off for a ride. He may not be back for some time." She wasn't sure whether to be distressed or relieved that the confrontation wouldn't be immediate. When the time came, she hoped she wouldn't lose her nerve.

"Then let's find a private place to talk where we won't disturb your sister."

Isabella nodded and turned to Adelaide. "Drink some water and get some more rest. We'll return soon, hopefully with good news."

They left Adelaide to recuperate, and they made their way through the castle halls, looking for a quiet place for a private conversation. But every room they checked seemed to be occupied. There were too many people in this castle for privacy.

"We could go to the dovecote. There was no one but the birds in there earlier."

"Let us go and see."

Hand-in-hand, they headed out into the bailey and across the open yard to the dovecote. As she had hoped, no one was inside the round stone building but a lot of doves and pigeons. Shafts of afternoon light filtered down through the openings in the roof where the birds flew in and out. It was quiet except for the low warbling of the occasional bird.

She turned to face him and found him looking at her with such awe and longing, she could hardly breathe.

"I can hardly believe my good fortune, my love." He raised her hand to his lips and turned it over, pressing a kiss inside her palm and then to the inside of her wrist. "I am humbled that you have chosen me, and I promise to spend every day of my life striving to be worthy of you."

He kissed his way up her arm until he reached her neck. "So beautiful," he murmured, taking her in his arms and turning her into a bonfire of desire.

But now was not the time to lose her head. They were beset by danger. Much as she wanted to give in and surrender herself to the heady mix of sensations and emotions he brought forth with his touch.

"We should plan." Talking about Lord James was the last thing she wanted to do as Martin buried his face in her neck, breathing deeply, but they had to keep their heads until they were safely at sea.

"First, we need to talk." He nipped at her shoulder, and she gasped at the burst of pleasure that obliterated every practical thought in her head.

"This doesn't seem like talking." Wrapping her arms around him, she melted against him, kissing and nipping at his ear. Never mind talking. They had other priorities at the moment.

He groaned as he pulled away and took her face in his hands.

"You shared what was in your heart. Now it's my turn. I need you to know that I am yours. You have utterly undone me. I wanted to win you from the moment we met, but I quickly realized there was no winning with you. I've lost my heart to you and there is no getting it back. I am yours, body, mind, and soul, until the day I die."

Unable to find words to respond, she pressed her lips against his in a desperate kiss to show him all of the love and devotion she'd never allowed herself to feel before. She was drowning in the sensation, letting herself fall, letting herself trust for the first time in her life.

"Say you're mine as I am yours. Let me hear the sweet words from your lips," he murmured, forehead resting against hers.

"I'm yours as you are mine. You've won my heart. I can't fight this any longer. I want to be yours for the rest of our lives and beyond."

He made a guttural noise and pulled her into another bone-melting kiss. She could hardly stand as he walked her backward until her back met the thick wood post at the center of the dovecote. His body pressed against hers as he continued to caress and kiss, and the evidence of his arousal strained against her core, making her tremble and gasp with desire.

"Take me. Make me yours," she murmured in his ear. "I need you."

He shook his head as he rained kisses on her neck and chest, loosening the ties of her dress and reaching into her gown to free her breasts. "I need you too," he said, taking her hand and holding it against his hard length. "Feel how much I need you."

She squeezed, making him moan.

Pulling her hand away, he said, "But much as I need you, I won't take you like this. The first time I make love to you, I want to be somewhere where I can lay you down and strip every scrap of clothing from your body. I want to touch and taste every inch of you, taking my time to pay homage to your beauty as you truly deserve."

"But…" How could she describe the hunger that consumed her? His kisses only made her more ravenous for something she could not put into words.

He licked and nipped at her chest, taking the tip of her breast in his mouth before pausing to murmur, "Have no fear. I know what you need, and I will give it to you. But truly consummating our marriage will have to wait."

Whatever he was doing with lips and tongue to her nipple was absolute heaven, but it sharpened the craving lower down. She squeezed her knees together against the intolerable desire that was driving her mad.

"Do you trust me, Isabella?"

"Yes." A short while ago, the answer would have been a resounding "no," but everything was different now. She trusted him more than anyone else in her life, save her sister. It was terrifying and exhilarating, and she needed what he was offering so badly, even if she wasn't certain what he would do.

"I promised I would never touch you without permission. May I touch you and bring you bliss?"

"Yes, please," she begged, scraping her nails down his back.

Groaning, he rocked his hard length against her, and she gasped.

"Dear God, such sweet torture," he rasped as he pulled away slightly, panting as he began to lift her skirt.

As he grazed his fingers up her inner thigh, she stopped breathing except in little gasps. Her body was an inferno as his fingers slid between her folds to the source of that terrible ache. She sighed deeply as he stroked her.

"You like the way I touch you, Isabella?"

Whatever he was doing, it was making thought and speech impossible.

He nipped at her neck and whispered, "Say it. I need to hear how much you want me, how much you need me."

She needed him with a desperation that was unlike anything she had ever experienced. *Hunger* seemed an inadequate word for the sensations he had awoken within her.

A strangled "yes" was all the response she could manage, but it was enough.

His clever fingers quickened their pace. He played her as skillfully as his citole—strumming and plucking and making her dance to his silent tune. And he strummed with all the tender care and precision that he put into his art. She was his instrument, resonating as he brought her higher and higher.

It was too much. She didn't know whether to clutch him harder or push him away. She couldn't remain silent as he continued his sweet torture, and he kissed her to stifle the noises she was making—wanton noises that made her blush but seemed only to increase his ardor.

Her body was on some precipice, and she clung to Martin, digging in her nails, fighting to remain upright. She couldn't take it anymore.

"Let go, Isabella. I have you. You can trust me."

He slid a finger inside her and curled it to press some hidden place within her that set off a bolt of lightning, and she lost all tether to the world around her. A burst of white light obliterated her vision, and she floated in the heavens. She drifted back down, light as a feather, to find herself still entangled with Martin, both of them panting.

"What did you do to me? I didn't know my body could feel such things." She nuzzled against him, limp and sated, but still craving closeness.

"I told you on our wedding night that I would worship your body and bring you untold pleasure. This is but a taste of what is to come." His voice was strained, and his arousal still pressed against her.

"But what of your pleasure?" She reached for him and brushed her fingers along his rigid length. "Do you wish for me to—?"

"Not today." He pulled her hand away and kissed her fingers. "Today was only for you."

But that flew in the face of everything she had been taught about men and the marriage bed, not that her understanding amounted to much.

"Mother always said men had needs and that they could not restrain themselves when aroused."

He chuckled and kissed her cheek. The hard urgency against her leg lessened. "We can stop. A good man will always listen, no matter how caught up in the moment he may be. Thank you for mentioning your mother, by the way. That seems to have been just what I needed to cool my own ardor."

He stepped back and looked her up and down with such deep love and appreciation that she almost felt the need to turn away. What had she ever done to deserve such devotion?

"You are absolutely glorious just as you are, my love, but sadly, we must put you to rights before someone decides to come check on the birds."

With all the patient attentiveness of a lady's maid, he helped her fix her dress and her mussed hair.

"I love your hair," he said, re-braiding it on one side where her the bun covering one ear had tumbled down. "I was smitten on our wedding night when you let me comb it. It truly is a crown worthy of a queen."

He pinned up her side bun with expert precision. She couldn't have done it better herself.

"Well, you are welcome to comb my hair any time you feel inspired to do so, though I can't imagine why it holds such a fascination for you."

He seemed to revel in playing lady's maid to her, which made no sense. Why would he humiliate himself performing the duties of a servant? But she had to admit that she enjoyed his attentions. No one had ever fussed over her before. She had always been at someone else's service. It was a new experience to be cared for like this.

"Can you not? It cascades down like a river of night. I've never touched anything so soft and silky. And the scent of fresh herbs from your bath oils mingles with the luscious scent of you to send my senses reeling. If you ever wish to seduce me, simply take down your hair, and I'll fall to my knees."

She smiled. "That's good to know, since I wouldn't want you to have an unfair advantage. It seems you are already well versed in how to seduce me."

He grinned and brushed his thumb over her nipple, making her gasp. "I have hardly begun to seduce you, my love. Just you wait."

His words made heat blossom between her thighs. "Promises, promises! I hope you can make good on these extravagant claims."

"Oh, I shall, my love. Believe me, I shall."

A delicious shiver of anticipation ran through her as he wrapped his arms around her and kissed her deeply and thoroughly, leaving her weak in the knees.

At the moment, hooves clattered in the yard, and the sound of Lord James bellowing at the stable hands reached Isabella's ears. "He's back."

The delicious languor that had filled her moments ago drained out of her to be replaced by tension.

"So he is." Martin nuzzled her neck, but his posture stiffened. "Shall we go speak to him together?"

It was so tempting to say yes. She wanted Martin by her side, but she feared what Lord James might do to Martin if they went together.

"No, I think it would be best if I spoke to Lord James alone. I worry that he might do something rash if you accompany me." Truth be told, she was just as worried that Martin might do something rash.

Martin's jaw muscle bulged. "I'd like to see him try."

"I don't doubt your valor or your bravery, but Lord James is twice your size. I don't want to provoke him unnecessarily. I think I might be able to placate him if I can speak to him by myself." She could offer to give him the information he needed to insinuate himself into Lord Henry's good graces, and hopefully he would be satisfied to let her go.

"I don't like the idea of your being alone with him and delivering bad news. What if he loses his temper?"

"Martin, please. I can handle myself. I've been handling myself for many years in far more treacherous waters than these. Please trust me." The period between Lady Eleanor's annulment and her marriage to Lord Henry had been downright terrifying. Not one but *two* prospective bridegrooms tried to hunt them down and force Eleanor to the altar. If Isabella could survive being in the eye of that storm with Her Grace, she could survive anything.

"Very well, but I'll stay in the bailey while you speak to him. If he does anything untoward, just call out my name, and I'll come."

"Agreed." It eased her mind to know that Lord Martin would defend her at a moment's notice if needed. "I must go."

"I know." He pulled her close and pressed a brief, furious kiss to her lips. "I'll see you shortly. Be brave."

"I will."

Holding her head high, she turned to go.

"I love you," Martin called as she was leaving.

Warmth, confidence, and courage flooded through her at his words. Truly, she could do anything with his love to buoy her up.

"I love you too." She back turned and smiled at him before forcing herself to leave the dovecote.

Whatever Lord James might throw her way, she was ready for it.

CHAPTER TWENTY-TWO

I SABELLA'S HEART POUNDED loudly in her ears as she approached Lord James, who was handing off his horse to a stable boy.

"My lady, I didn't expect to see you again so soon! Have you found a way to rid yourself of that little rat you call a husband already?"

"I've spoken with him," she said, evading the question. How should she broach the subject? Should she work up to it, or just tell him bluntly that she no longer wished to proceed with their agreement?

"And?"

Normally, she managed to be cool and collected under pressure, but her mind was still addled by all that had transpired with Martin. Words were not forthcoming for the first time in her life. "Well, he…that is to say I…"

"Get on with it. I have other business to attend to." He frowned at her, and there was a warning in his gaze. This was not going at all as she had hoped.

"I wish to renegotiate our deal. Circumstances have changed, and I don't believe a marriage between us would be wise."

There. She'd said it. Her heart pounded in her ears, but she'd managed to get the words out.

The earl's expression darkened.

"Hmm." Lord James narrowed his eyes. "Walk with me. I

wish to tell you a story."

Reluctantly, she took his offered arm and followed him as he led her to the tower beside the gate, up the winding staircase and onto the battlement. She didn't like being so far from Martin. What if Lord James attempted something? But she could hardly refuse.

From this height, she could see all of Yarmouth spread out before her and the countryside beyond. It was an impressive sight. Not long ago, the thought of being countess of all this would have been her fondest wish, but now it only reminded her how very isolated she was up on this tower with Lord James. Everyone below was simply going about their business. No one bothered to look up. And even if they did, Lord James was their liege lord. He could do practically anything he pleased, and they wouldn't try to stop him.

A shiver crept up her spine. This didn't bode well.

"What is this story you wish to tell me, my lord?" she asked as lightly as possible, trying not to betray her growing worry. It didn't help that she was standing exceptionally close to a very tall ledge. *No.* She wasn't going to think about that. He brought her up here to intimidate her, and she wouldn't let him.

"There was a man who lost a great deal of money to me playing dice. He was a minor noble from one of my domains. His name isn't important. What is important is that he attempted to double-cross me."

Isabella swallowed hard. "Oh?" she said, since he obviously seemed to expect a response.

"I don't like to be double-crossed, Isabella. It makes me very angry." His eyes bored into her. Clearly, he wasn't going to accept her request gracefully.

She should have given him a piece of her mind and run for her life, but he was too close. What if he caught her? "I'm certain it does, my lord. What did the man do?"

"He tried to use weighted dice against me to win his money back. I knew at once that he was trying to cheat me."

"Oh? And how is that?"

"Because I used weighted dice to win in the first place."

Why was he telling her this? It was a rather alarming confession for an earl.

"I don't like to lose, my lady." He stepped closer and loomed over her. Good heavens, he was a large man!

"I…I'm not sure why you're telling me this, my lord."

He gripped her arm painfully hard. "You and I are more alike than you may think."

No, she had nothing in common with this man. He was disgusting through and through. But she bit her tongue.

"We're both devious and like to get our way." He leaned over her, forcing her off balance.

The temptation to call out for Martin grew stronger and stronger. But could he hear her from up here? Would he arrive in time to save her from being thrown over the battlement?

"What happened to the man who double-crossed you?" She hardly dared ask. In truth, she didn't want to know, but some inner voice told her to extend this conversation for as long as she could so that she could find a way out.

"I didn't take my revenge on him. At least not at first."

"No?"

"No. I started with his family. The people he loved. I locked his daughter and his wife in my dungeon and told him they would receive no food until he paid me. I knew he didn't have the money, but I enjoyed watching him squirm. Every day, I made him visit as they grew thinner and thinner, hungrier and hungrier. He sold everything he had and gave me the money, but it only covered half of his debt. So I gave him a choice. He could have his wife back or his daughter. Since he'd only paid half of his debt, he only got half of his prisoners back."

Generally, Isabella thought that gamblers got what they deserved when they were punished for their profligacy, but punishing the man's family was too cruel for words. "What happened then?"

"He chose his daughter, and he fled, thinking his debt was paid. But I had one of my men dispatch him before he left Norfolk. The mother and daughter now work in my kitchens where they will serve me until the day they die. They're both rather pretty, and it seemed a waste to let them perish of hunger. They've both borne me several children since joining my household."

Bile rose in Isabella's throat. He was a monster. If only she were a man and had the strength to throw him off the battlement herself!

"I hardly know what to say." The thought of those poor women being forced to submit to his attentions after what he'd done to their family made her furious. She balled her fists at her sides. If only she were a man, she would challenge him to a duel for his dishonorable behavior.

"Listen closely, then," he said, grasping her arms roughly and pushing her back against the battlement. "You will rid yourself of your husband and make me exchequer and do it swiftly, or I'll take matters into my own hands."

"What do you mean?" She struggled in his grasp, desperate to escape. "Let me go!"

"I mean," he said, looming over her so that she was bent backwards over the battlement, "that I will dispatch your irritating husband if you don't get rid of him quickly enough. And your sister is not welcome to leave until you comply. Do I make myself clear?"

He was a disgusting, horrible, dangerous man! How had she ever considered him a palatable husband? Her heart thundered as she tried to tamp down her panic at being at his mercy at such a height. The only way she could get out of this unscathed was to acquiesce. That much was clear. But then what? Could she and Martin sneak away? Perhaps they could find a way, but there was Adelaide to think of. What would Lord James do to her sister if Isabella reneged on her deal? And even Lord Christopher, kind and cordial as he was, could not take action against his liege lord.

"Very clear, my lord. But would you consider releasing me from our bargain if I gave you the information you needed to become exchequer without marrying you? I would gladly aid you in return for safe passage for us to leave Norfolk." She had to try. If it was wealth and position that he sought, perhaps she could give him what he wanted without sacrificing her own happiness.

"The problem with that, Isabella, is that I don't trust you. What would prevent you from double-crossing me and sending me to my doom rather than making my fortune? No. I need you under my thumb, or I suspect you will stab me in the back. Our deal stands, and you will abide by it or your weaselly little husband will pay the consequences." He shook her, and several of her hairpins fell out, dropping to the ground several stories below.

There was no way out. She had to agree, at least for the moment, or she might follow them over the long drop.

"I will do as you say." There was no other way to get down from this battlement and away from his presence.

"I'm glad to hear it. Now go find that worm of a husband and be quick about it. I expect to hear you've convinced him by nightfall." He pulled her away from the battlement and set her on her feet. "Don't fail, or you know the consequences."

Her knees shook, but she forced herself to stay upright. "Yes, my lord," she said without looking at him, and she fled before he could make any further threats.

As she flew down the stone steps in the dark tower, her mind reeled at the tangle she had made of things. It was all her fault that Lord James had taken notice of her. She had planted the seed of a potential marriage, and now she was entangled in the twisted vines of her own plot. Martin's life was at stake, and her sister wasn't much safer. She had no doubt that Lord James would try to use Adelaide against her before this was all through.

Martin, at least, could defend himself, even if the two men were unevenly matched to all outward appearances. Her husband was brave and capable, and he did say he had bested Lord James in a tournament. But Adelaide was ill and completely at the earl's mercy.

Her heart quailed at the thought, but she couldn't let herself weaken. Her loved ones were threatened. She had to find a way out of this. It was all her fault that they were in this situation in the first place.

She made her way across the yard, and Martin took her by surprise, rushing to her side. "You didn't stay in the dovecote?"

"I didn't trust him, so I came out to the yard and pretended to practice sword drills, hoping to keep an eye on you. But the two of you disappeared into the tower beside the gate. I almost came after you. I was worried for your safety, alone with him like that."

"And with good reason. The man is a snake." She should have held back. They were still in the middle of the yard where anyone might overhear. She looked around quickly to see if anyone had. Fortunately, everyone was still going about their business.

Martin stopped in his tracks, taking her elbow and turning her to face him. "What did he do to you?"

Was it wrong that it sent a little thrill down her spine to see his fury on her behalf? No one had ever been willing to fight for her before. But she had to put an end to his questioning until they were somewhere more private. "I am unharmed. Let us return to my chamber before we say anything more. There is much I need to discuss with both you and Adelaide."

"Then let us make haste." Together, they hurried into the castle as quickly as they could without arousing suspicion. Too many of Lord James's men roamed the halls and crowded the bailey.

She needed time to think. If only she had long hours sitting peacefully aboard *The Wind Song* to puzzle through it. It was so much easier to clear her mind when they were at sea. In this castle there were too many dangers and distractions, and her guilt over her misguided actions bore down on her, making it difficult to form a coherent thought.

But Martin's reassuring presence beside her steadied her. She had a good husband who loved her. There must be some hope as long as he was by her side.

When they reached the room, Adelaide was awake but lying in the bed. She sat up in alarm as they rushed in and bolted the heavy wooden door behind them.

Isabella looked back and forth between the two most precious people in her life and wondered how she was going to find the words to tell them of their peril. It was no use hiding. She had to get on with it. "I'm afraid we're in great danger, and it's all my fault."

As she recounted her conversation with Lord James, Martin's expression grew thunderous.

"How dare he threaten you!" Martin began pacing, his hand on his sword. "That no-good, cheating, bull's pizzle. He isn't fit to lick your shoe, earl or no."

Isabella hurried to his side and put a placating hand on his arm. "Please, Martin, don't do anything foolish. He'd be all too happy to dispatch you. Then not only would I lose the man I love, but Adelaide and I would be completely at his mercy." The story Lord James told about the wife and daughter of the man who owed him money sent a chill down her spine.

She couldn't lose Martin, not right after she had found him. And Adelaide had to be protected from Lord James at all costs. They needed cool heads to find their way out of this, and unfortunately, it appeared that her words had the exact opposite effect.

CHAPTER TWENTY-THREE

T HAT BASTARD. MARTIN'S hand flew to the pommel of his sword. "I'd like to see him try to take me down."

"Don't, Martin. He'll crush you like a fly."

He knew she was only saying it because she loved him and didn't want to lose him, but it hurt a bit that she had so little faith in his fighting skill. Lord James was a big, lumbering bear, and Martin knew how to get beneath his guard. He'd done it before.

"No, he won't. He may be bigger and stronger than me, but I'm twice as cunning. I'll make him pay for this." He strode to the door.

Isabella caught his arm. "Please don't. Stay. We'll find another way out of this. You don't have to confront him."

Except that he did. He had to prove to the woman he loved that she hadn't married a coward. And he had to put that stinking midden heap of a man in his place.

"What of Adelaide and me? Do we mean nothing to you? Will you risk our futures on your thirst for revenge?" Her eyes were wide, and her voice shook as she said it. It was so easy to think her fearless as she faced down challenges that would make a grown man blanch, but this had brought her low. He couldn't storm out and leave her fearing for her and Adelaide's futures.

"What do you have in mind?" He planned to separate the man's head from his neck at the earliest opportunity, but he needed to at least hear her out.

"He's a gambler."

He narrowed his eyes. "A cheating gambler."

"What of a wager? We offer to comply and annul our marriage if he wins, and if he loses, he leaves us in peace and lets us leave freely."

Did he dare gamble on their future? The urge to seal the other man's fate by running him through was almost overwhelming.

Though, he supposed, he could always do that after trying Isabella's plan.

"And what form of wager would you propose? We know he cheats at dice. I wouldn't trust him at cards."

"Then we pick something he can't cheat at. Something where you have the advantage."

The first thing that came to mind was combat. It was what everything in him desired at that moment, but she clearly wanted a more peaceful option. "What do you propose?"

"An archery contest, a game of chess, a mast climbing competition… Anything but combat. Please. I'm begging you."

A game of chess. That could work. Martin was certain he could outsmart that oversized cretin.

"Very well. I'll propose chess. There's no cheating in chess. It's just his skill against my own. I'd crush him like a fly. But he'll probably refuse. He knows he's no match for me."

He didn't want her to get her hopes up for a peaceful resolution. Frankly, he hoped Lord James would turn down the chess game. Fury still simmered beneath the surface, though for the moment, Martin was keeping it in check for Isabella's sake. He longed to unleash it on the object of his ire.

"Stay here. I want to know you're safe in case this plan of yours fails. I'll be back as soon as it's over," he said, kissing Isabella swiftly before striding out of the room.

All his life, people had underestimated him, especially in comparison to his not-so-little brother. Lord James was no different. He would show that prick the error of his ways if it was the last thing he did.

Storming into the great hall, he found Lord James deep in conversation with Lord Christopher. At his arrival, both men looked up, Lord Christopher with surprise and Lord James with a smug smile, the bastard.

"Lord James, I have a wager for you."

There was no point in prevaricating. He wanted to finish this and return to Isabella as quickly as possible.

"A wager?" Lord James raised an eyebrow. "Why would I gamble with you? You have nothing that I want."

"Ah, but I do, and we both know it." Martin held the earl's hostile gaze for a long moment. "Don't bother to deny it. I have a proposal to settle this once and for all."

Lord Christopher looked back and forth between the two of them. "What is going on here? I don't understand."

"What do you propose?" Lord James leaned forward, ignoring his vassal. "I do like a good wager, and the thought of humiliating you is too tempting to pass up."

"I propose a game of chess." Now to see if the earl would take the bait.

Lord James laughed. "I'm not playing chess with you, you little piglet. Go squeal somewhere else. I have business with Lord Christopher."

He turned away and started talking of tax collection. It was a clear dismissal. The man couldn't even be bothered to engage.

Blood thundered in Martin's ears. He'd tried a peaceful route. Isabella couldn't say he didn't try. Now it was time to take matters into his own hands.

"Very well, then. If you won't play chess, then you leave me no choice. I challenge you to single combat."

"Good God, man, what are you thinking?" Lord Christopher asked, rushing to stand between him and Lord James.

All remaining patience drained out of Martin as he watched the earl rise slowly, grinning from ear to ear.

"He's trying to steal my wife from me, and he's threatened my life. I demand satisfaction." Fury roiled within Martin as he looked at the man he detested. That blackguard wouldn't get away with it. Martin was going to bring the earl down or die trying.

"There must be some mistake," Lord Christopher said, placatingly. "Why would Lord James try to steal your wife?"

"I can't help it that she prefers me to you," Lord James said, rising and casting a long shadow in the torchlight. By God, the man was tall. He was like a walking castle turret. But Martin refused to be cowed. Isabella loved him, and nothing else mattered. He would face Goliath himself for her sake.

Lord Christopher blanched. "Don't tell me it's true. Lord James, why would you—?"

"I appreciate your concern, Christopher, but this is none of your affair." The earl swept his vassal aside and drew his sword. It glinted in a shaft of daylight pouring in through one of the slender windows at the side of the hall.

"At least have the decency to take this outside, my lords," Lord Christopher pleaded.

The earl stared down at Martin with utter disdain, and Martin's sword hand twitched with the urge to teach the smug coxcomb a lesson he would never forget.

After a long moment, Lord James jerked his head toward the door, and Martin nodded.

Following his nemesis, they headed outdoors.

Together they stalked onto the pounded dirt, Lord James dispersing a few soldiers that had gathered to practice with a mere look.

"Wait! Stop!" Isabella ran out into the yard between them.

No! She shouldn't be here. It was too dangerous. And the last thing Martin wanted was to have her be forced to watch them butcher each other. "Go back inside, Isabella. Please. This is going to get ugly."

"You think I'm going to stand by and let my fate be decided

by you two fools as you try to tear out each other's throats like dogs in a pit?"

Before Martin could prevent it, the earl grabbed Isabella by the shoulder and dragged her out of the ring, shoving her toward the castle. "Listen to your husband, my lady. This is men's business. I'll call for you when I've dispatched him and it's time for us to wed. Expect me within the hour."

Blood pounded in Martin's ears as he launched himself at Lord James in a blind rage. "Don't you *ever* touch my wife again. I will tear you to pieces like a wild boar."

Steel clashed as the earl blocked Martin's blow as if he were swatting a fly. "You won't be her husband much longer. It's a shame you never went through with the wedding night. I assure you I don't plan to deprive myself of the pleasure."

No. That rutting beast could never be allowed near her. The mere thought of him—

Martin blundered toward his nemesis again, this time to be met with a bone-shattering counterblow that he just barely deflected, though he felt it all the way up his arm.

"Does that bother you? The thought of me tupping your wife? I promise to make her scream my name over and over as I take her hard and fast. I can hardly wait to make her bleed for me."

Thank God Martin's body remembered what to do because his mind was lost in a haze of pulsing red. A bitter taste filled his mouth as he struck again and again, only to be blocked at every turn.

"Don't let him goad you," a voice cried out that made his heart clench. Isabella was still here, watching this, hearing this. "Please, Martin, keep your wits about you. If you keep fighting like this, we'll all lose."

She was right. He was reacting on instinct alone, letting Lord James get the better of him and goad him into rage. He wished she would go back inside. She shouldn't be subjected to this. But there was no arguing with her advice. He would surely lose if he didn't clear his head, and there was far too much at stake for him to allow that.

Drawing in a deep breath, Martin steadied himself and studied his enemy as he circled. He'd beaten this man once before, and he could do it again. All he needed to do was use his head.

The dust of the yard filled his nostrils as his feet scuffed the ground and he tried to remember how he had won victory against Lord James the last time they fought. But all he could see was the image seared in his brain of the earl manhandling Isabella and shoving her toward the castle. If he didn't clear his head soon, he was going to be in serious trouble.

CHAPTER TWENTY-FOUR

I SABELLA'S HEART WAS in her throat as Martin squared off with Lord James. The two looked so unevenly matched. She couldn't imagine how Martin had defeated Lord James in tournament, but she prayed he could do it again. His life depended on it, as did her and her sister's futures.

Men from around the bailey were starting to gather to watch the fight. She couldn't blame them. It was riveting. No matter how much she wished she could turn away from the awful scene before her, she couldn't do it. They had all come to watch her husband die. A low murmur arose as they began placing bets, not around who would win but around how long Martin would last before Lord James demolished him.

There was no way Martin could win trying to match Lord James in terms of brute force. Fortunately, her husband seemed to have heeded her warning. Something in his stance changed after she cried out, and he took a few steps back, no longer hacking at the earl in a blind fury. For a moment, she could almost swear she saw a twinkle in his eye like the one he wore when he traded barbs with her on the day they first met.

Yes, you can do this, Martin. You've done it before. Just keep your wits about you.

Lord James advanced on Martin and swung with all his might, aiming to separate Martin's head from his body. Isabella closed her eyes, unable to watch. The crowd gasped. Then, she heard the clang of metal and dared to open them again. Martin was still alive, still fighting. Hope and pride surged through her each second that her husband fought back.

Martin was quicker than the earl, and he was using it to his advantage, making Lord James lumber about like a bear on its hind legs. And then Lord James roared like one as he swept down in a strike that aimed to cleave Martin in two.

Isabella shrank away, wanting to hide but unable to tear her gaze away from the awful scene before her.

"Missed again," Martin quipped as he stepped aside, just out of reach. "Your aim is truly disgraceful."

Oh, thank God he's still in one piece! Isabella clutched at her chest as if she could slow the terrible pounding of her heart.

But what was Martin doing, goading the man? The last thing he needed was to make the earl angrier. But her husband just smiled as he circled.

"Shut up and fight, you miserable little gadfly." Lord James attacked again with all his might.

"I like to talk while I fight," Martin said lightly as he dodged and deflected a blow that should have sliced through his belly. "You don't mind a bit of civilized conversation while we try to disembowel each other, do you?"

Isabella's mouth dropped open. The man she had married had lost his mind.

Lord James's only response was a low grumble and another forceful strike that missed at the last second, thank God!

"Is that all you have to say?" Her husband parried the earl's heavy blows one after another. "I see. Well, I suppose I'll just have to carry the conversation myself."

Martin ducked beneath the earl's next blow and slashed out with his blade, missing flesh but slashing a hole in the earl's sleeve.

Isabella clenched her fists and gasped. A hit! Did she dare hope? Did Martin stand a chance against Lord James after all?

"I'm sorry to ruin such a fine garment. It looks like it was quite costly. Is that real gold embroidery on the sleeve or just straw?" Martin buzzed around the big man like a wasp looking for an opening to sting.

The earl roared as he struck back with a low, sweeping slash aimed at Martin's knees. Her husband had to jump to avoid losing half his leg. Isabella stopped breathing. For a moment, he was unsteady as he landed, but he recovered quickly and stepped back. Relief flooded her at his narrow escape.

"Straw embroidery is nothing to be ashamed of, you know. I've seen some truly stunning garments embroidered with straw to look like gold. It glints in the sunlight so beautifully."

"God's wounds, do you never shut up?" Lord James yelled as he slashed again, this time slicing at Martin's arm.

Isabella covered her mouth as a line of blood bloomed in the fine linen of her husband's shirt sleeve. Too close! And the earl had drawn first blood. That didn't bode well. Isabella felt the sting as if the sword had cut her own flesh.

Martin hissed through his teeth as he dodged another blow aimed at his neck. "Nice try, my lord, but I've had worse pinpricks from my tailor."

A few of the men watching chuckled, and Isabella put her hand over her mouth to hold back a horrified guffaw.

"I'm going to carve out your tongue, you imbecile." Lord James was not amused, and he glared at his subjects, defying them to laugh again.

"Ah, but to do that, you'd have to catch me."

Isabella's heart was ready to pound out of her chest as Lord James feinted and slashed down Martin's chest, leaving a long, shallow wound.

"No," she cried out as blood darkened the green of her husband's cotte to black.

This couldn't happen. There had to be some way to stop this madness before Lord James chopped Martin into pieces. She'd only just found the joy of love, and she had no intention of losing it so soon.

"You see? It's me she cries out for," Martin said, chancing a moment's glance at her before returning to his adversary. In that moment of connection, she tried to convey all the feeling she'd failed to express—all the tenderness and affection that she'd hardly dared to speak of. "She's chosen me. I've won her heart."

At his words, Isabella's heart swelled. He had won her heart indeed. Now, if only he could survive!

Martin suddenly began to attack with such swift blows, Lord James could hardly keep up and was forced to stagger back.

"Enough," Lord James bellowed as he countered and advanced on Martin with renewed fury. "I don't care about her heart. I only care whether she delivers on her bargain. And I intend to hold her to it."

As if she needed further confirmation of the man's callous, selfish nature.

"Over my dead body." Martin struck out and nearly caught the earl in the side.

"That is the general idea." Lord James snarled as he lashed out again, cutting into Martin's left shoulder before he could get away.

Guilt assailed her at the thought that she had brought him into this mortal peril. If only she hadn't tried to make a bargain with Lord James, none of this would be happening. Her own fear and selfishness had brought them to this pass. And now the husband she loved—who loved her in a way that no one had ever loved her—would pay the price for her folly.

"I won't lie. That smarts." Martin gritted his teeth as he dodged another killing blow.

Oh no. He couldn't even come up with a witty quip. He must have been hurt badly.

It wasn't right that she had only just found love and now she was in danger of losing it. But how could she help? The earl wanted Martin dead, and there was nothing she could do about it.

Or was there? *Think, Isabella. Think! What would Lady Eleanor do?*

No, that was no help. Lady Eleanor would let them fight it out and celebrate whoever survived as the stronger man. The weak deserved what they got, according to her. Trying to think like the deposed queen had gotten her into this mess. She had to find her own way out of this, leading with her heart instead of hiding it behind high walls built by her own ambition.

A clang of metal brought her back from her thoughts. Martin danced around the earl like a court jester, wearing him down bit by bit. If she wasn't mistaken, the earl was starting to slow, the lag between Martin's jabs and his ripostes growing by the minute. Still, Lord James struck with a force that made her quiver each time metal hit metal.

Martin circled. "There once was a man from Calais," he sang in a teasing voice. "Who thought all his enemies to slay."

Lord in heaven, what was her husband doing?

Lord James snarled and swung his blade at Martin's head.

In just the nick of time, Martin ducked beneath the blade, his full lips curving in a teasing smile and his eyes twinkling. She couldn't help but admire his brashness in the face of danger.

"He fought a court fool, who cut off his tool. Now he sings falsetto all day."

Ducking low, Martin stabbed Lord James in the upper thigh, quick as a flash. The earl bellowed in wordless rage. Isabella threw up her arms and cheered. There was hope! Her husband was a mad man, but his ridiculous swagger was undeniably effective at throwing his enemy off balance.

Martin ducked just out of the earl's reach as his blade came crashing down on where he'd been a split second earlier. "Missed me," he chided.

"I. Will. End. You," Lord James said, punctuating each word with a murderous slash of his sword.

And he very nearly did. Isabella could hardly breathe as she watched. She tasted iron as she bit the inside of her cheek. Every muscle in her body tensed as she gripped the rough timber of the fence enclosing the yard.

A hairsbreadth away from those deadly blows, Martin danced out of the way and spun around the earl's flank as if this was all a game. He was behind the earl now.

Get him, Martin! End this. Don't let him get away!

"Can't find me?" Martin taunted as the earl spun in circles trying to catch him. "But I'm right here." On the final word, Martin jabbed his sword into the earl's buttock, making him howl and nearly drop his sword.

Huzzah!

Isabella's heart swelled at the sight. Surely, he had won now. How could the earl recover when Martin had dealt him such an injury? And what a fitting revenge for Lord James's threats and browbeating!

"Take him down, Martin! Finish this," she called out. "You can do it!"

Taking advantage of Lord James's momentary lapse, Martin jabbed again, this time at the back of the earl's knee. The giant man stumbled as his knee gave way, and he fell on all fours.

"Yes! Huzzah!" Isabella cheered and waved her fists in the air. He'd done it! Her husband had bested the earl! She never had to fear Lord James again!

Martin stepped on the earl's sword and levelled his blade at his opponent's throat.

"Yield." All teasing was gone from her husband's voice. It was cold and deadly as the North Sea. In that moment, he seemed to be as tall as the mast of *The Wind Song*. "Let us go, and I will spare your life. We'll buy passage on a ship and be gone within the hour."

A gruff laugh escaped Lord James's lips. "You little prick. You think you're leaving Yarmouth alive?"

The earl moved too quickly to see, and Martin let out a bloodcurdling scream, falling over. For a moment, Isabella couldn't tell what had happened, and then she saw it. The hilt of a dagger protruded from her husband's foot.

Lord James threw himself on top of Martin, tearing his sword from his hand and throwing it away. The earl's sword was still pinned under her husband, and he didn't bother trying to retrieve it. With a wicked laugh, Lord James wrapped his hands around Martin's throat and squeezed.

No. Please no. Don't let this be how it ends.

No matter how her husband thrashed and twisted beneath the other man's grip, he could not escape. Martin's face turned purple and then began to take on a blue tinge. Before her very eyes, Lord James was squeezing the life out of the man she loved. The crowd around them went silent, and several turned away with looks of disgust. But no one dared intervene and challenge their liege lord.

She had to act. She couldn't lose Martin now, not when they were so close to escaping this place to live a happy life she had hardly dared imagine. There had to be something she could do to save her husband. As long as Martin lived, there was hope.

And then it came to her. She knew what she had to do, even if the thought sickened her.

"Stop," Isabella cried out. "I'll give you what you want. Just spare him."

The earl squeezed harder. "Once I end him, there's nothing to stop me from taking what I want."

No. This can't be happening. I won't let it. "If you kill him, I'll never tell you what you want to know. I'll take my secrets to the grave."

Lord James laughed. "I have ways of making you talk."

She was sure he did, but nothing he could threaten her with compared to the abject terror of watching the breath squeezed out of the man who had won her heart.

"Maybe so," she said. "But you'd never know if I was lying. What if I feed you a secret that makes The Duke of Normandy kill you on the spot?"

A long moment passed as she and the earl stared each other down, a collision of steel wills. Martin's movement was slowing. He was going to lose consciousness if this didn't end. This had to work. She could not face a world without Martin in it, even if it meant sacrificing herself.

At last, the earl loosened his grip, and Martin gasped in deep, ragged breaths.

"You had better keep your word, my lady. You will both remain here until the annulment goes through. I'm not taking any chances. Guards," he said to his men, "Take Lord Martin away and lock him in the dungeon."

"Isabella, no," Martin wheezed. "Don't do this."

Tears filled her eyes as she watched Lord James's men take her husband away, red marks clearly visible on his neck. The look of betrayal and horror on Martin's face nearly undid her, but she had to be strong for his sake. If he died, she would never recover, especially not if she was forced to marry his murderer.

She stood frozen until Martin was out of sight. Then she turned to the loathsome man to whom she had just promised her life.

A slow grin spread across Lord James's face. "Now, you're mine," he said, grasping her arm with fearsome strength.

That, I will never be, she thought to herself as he hauled her inside. She would find a way out of Yarmouth with Martin and Adelaide if it was the last thing she did.

CHAPTER TWENTY-FIVE

T HIS WASN'T BAD…FOR a dungeon. At least that was what Martin tried to tell himself, sitting in near-total darkness with his back against the stone wall, gingerly touching his fingers to the bruises on his neck. A meager shaft of light came through the bars from a tiny window in the hall—just enough to make out the shadows of things but not enough to truly see.

At least the dirt floor was dry, and Martin hadn't heard any scurrying. *Yet.* It was like sitting in a harmless cave in the forest. With excruciating, throbbing pain in his left foot. And a very sore throat. And with his wife in danger.

Isabella wouldn't really go through with the annulment, would she? What if he didn't consent? He had sworn to let her be free if she didn't want to be with him, but he had never said he would let her go under duress. And wouldn't the Church require him to consent to dissolve the marriage? There was nothing that Lord James could threaten him with that would convince him to cooperate as long as Isabella still cared for him.

Martin tried shifting to a more comfortable position but hissed as pain from his foot spiked through him. The guard had been none too gentle when he had yanked the dagger out. Would they send him a healer? If the wound wasn't cleaned and dressed, there was a high risk of infection. Maybe that was what Lord James was hoping for, that cheating bastard.

The earl had lost that fight. Martin's sword had been at the man's throat. Maybe he should have taken the earl's head off and not given him a chance to yield. It certainly would have been satisfying. But instead, he'd been honorable and chivalrous about it, and the blackguard had taken full advantage.

It wouldn't do any good to rehash what had gone wrong. He had to figure out a way out of this. Somehow, he had to escape this dungeon, rescue Isabella and Adelaide, and get them all on a ship to Winchelsea, whether *The Wind Song* was ready or not.

But to do any of that, he had to stand and walk. Using his hands to brace himself, he tried to pull himself up. His ruined foot dragged along the floor, and he yelped. It was too much! But he forced himself to breathe. He had to walk, or he'd be completely helpless. Digging deep, he kept going, every movement excruciating. After what felt like an eternity, he was standing.

Sweat poured down his neck, despite the chill of the dungeon as he attempted to catch his breath. That wasn't so bad, was it? He grimaced and ground his teeth, trying to ignore the shooting pain that seemed to engulf his entire leg. Now all he had to do was walk. Easy, right? Just one foot in front of another. He'd been doing it his whole life.

Ever so slowly, he lifted his left leg and lowered it until his injured foot rested on the floor ahead of him, and he shifted his weight with torturous care onto the heel. Lightning struck out from his wound at the slight pressure, and next thing he knew, he was sprawled on the floor.

Footsteps sounded in the hallway beyond, and Martin struggled to sit, failing miserably.

A loathsome chuckle set his teeth on edge as torchlight flickered into the cell. Lord James stood before him in clean clothes, no doubt bandaged up neatly beneath his garb. It was satisfying to see that the man limped as he walked. That jab in the posterior couldn't have been comfortable, Martin thought with grim satisfaction. He hoped it got infected no matter how skilled Lord Christopher's healer was, and that Lord James would never sit comfortably on his unsufferable ass again.

"How sad, you miserable little rat," Lord James said, eyes glinting with malice while a guard unlocked the cell. "How does it feel to lie there helpless while I steal your wife?"

Forcing himself into a sitting position at last, Martin answered, "Go to hell." His voice rasped from the damage Lord James had done to his windpipe. It wasn't the wittiest retort, but it was all he could manage at the moment.

A tall thin man draped in black stepped into the cell beside the earl, a heavy cross hanging from a chain around his neck. "This is the husband you spoke of?" the priest said, looking Martin over warily.

"It is," Lord James said, narrowing his eyes at Martin. "He wishes for an annulment. Don't you, Lord Martin?"

"I said, 'go to hell,' and I meant it." Lord James could threaten all he wanted, but he would not give in.

The earl smiled. "*Tsk tsk*, my lord. So uninspired. Your wit must be failing you."

The priest stepped forward and looked down at Martin, furrowing his brow. "Is it true that you have not consummated the marriage?"

Martin's shoulders sagged. How could he deny it when he had already said so in so many words to Lord James? "It's true."

"And do you wish to dissolve the marriage?"

"I do not." He held Lord James's gaze defiantly.

Lord James's gaze sharpened. "Wrong answer, my lord. Give me what I want, and I'll send in a healer to see to your foot, put you on a ship, and send you home. Refuse, and I'll let you rot down here until infection takes you."

A shiver ran down Martin's spine. It would be all too easy for Lord James to let nature take its course. And where would Isabella be then?

"My lord," the priest said tentatively, "the Church tribunal will never grant an annulment where the husband is unwilling. Perhaps you should—"

"Perhaps you should consider whose largesse you live on," the earl interrupted.

"But, my lord, it isn't up to me," the priest pleaded, wringing his hands. "You'll have to convince—"

"Lord Martin will change his mind. He just needs some time to himself to think things through." Lord James towered over Martin and gave him a mean little kick in the foot. "Don't you, my lord?"

Martin grunted in pain. Could he steal the earl's sword? He was almost close enough. A fat lot of good it would do him, though, if he couldn't get off the floor.

Lord James stepped out of Martin's reach, as if he could see his thoughts.

"The only way I will ever agree to an annulment is if Isabella tells me of her own free will that she wants to leave this marriage. As long as you are threatening her, or threatening me to get to her, I will never yield."

A slow smile spread across Lord James's face. "*Hmm.* Perhaps that can be arranged."

"What?" This couldn't be good.

"Let us go." The earl turned toward the door, beckoning for the priest to follow. As soon as they were out, a lock clicked into place, and the torchlight disappeared.

Martin sagged against the wall, his thoughts frantically turning, trying to find a way out of this predicament. There was no way the earl could change Isabella's mind now, could he? After all that had transpired earlier, there was no doubt of Isabella's feelings, and she had let them be known publicly during the fight by cheering him on. Some twenty men must have seen her take his side over the earl. What would that cave troll do to her to get her to agree?

Whatever it was, Martin needed to get out of here to foil the plan. If only he could get a message to his men… But how would they be able to get him out of the castle without Lord James and his men noticing? They were far too few to fight their way in, let alone out again. And stealth was too risky for them. No, he would have to think his way out of this rather than relying on the strength of his men.

He couldn't wait too long to see a healer, though. He could hardly save Isabella from Lord James if he was dead. Should he pretend to go along with the earl's plan for the sake of having his wound tended to and then renege before the Church tribunal? The idea of pretending to accept filled his stomach with bile. What would Isabella think? But did he have any other choice?

There had to be another way. Perhaps he could prevail on Lord Christopher, if he could get the man alone. They'd always had friendly relations. It wasn't the man's fault his liege lord was a monster. Given the opportunity, Lord Christopher might very well do the decent thing and give him the aid he needed—at the very least, have his wounds tended to, though that would be in opposition to Lord James's wishes. But how could Martin get him alone, and how would he convince him to go against his liege?

Hours passed, and the pain in his foot grew as he stewed in the cell, watching the meager light wane in the window in the hall. Every idea he had came up short, and worse, his mind was growing hazy from pain and exhaustion. As the light of day winked out completely, he was left in total darkness, with no options left to him but to wait for someone to return.

He wasn't sure how much time had passed when he jerked awake to the sound of footsteps. He didn't remember dozing off, but Lord only knew what hour of the night it might be.

Torchlight flickered, casting ominous shadows, as Lord James opened the door, and the priest walked in behind him, followed by Isabella.

His heart leapt at the sight of her but then quailed at the look in her eyes—cold, resolute. No, the earl couldn't have convinced her. It wasn't possible.

"Go ahead. Say what you have to say, my lady," Lord James prompted, his voice oozing with triumph.

Squaring her shoulders, Isabella turned her impassive gaze on

Martin. "I don't care for you. I've never cared for you. I do not wish to remain married to you. Please agree to an annulment so that I can marry Lord James. Our arrangement is finished."

Each word pierced his heart like a dirk, and he could hardly breathe by the time she was finished. This couldn't be. Lord James must have done or said something terrible to convince her. The Isabella whom he'd held in his arms this very afternoon would never allow this man to win.

"What have you said to her to make her agree?" Martin's voice was still rough and ragged from being strangled, but he did his best to infuse every word with ice.

"Not a thing," said Lord James with a smug smile. "I have neither threatened her nor have I threatened you to get her to agree. Have I, my dear?" he said, turning to her, pinning her with a steely gaze.

Isabella gave the earl a resigned look then turned back to Martin, her gaze cold and distant. "He has not threatened you or me." For a moment, her expression shifted, as if there was something specific she wanted him to know. But what?

"I merely wish to be free of you," she continued in a chilly monotone. "All this time I've been toying with you to goad Lord James into making a better offer. There is nothing between us and there never was. I was always meant to be an earl's wife, and now I shall be."

Martin stared at his bride in horrified silence. He could read no lie in her eyes, no secret message that this was all a ruse. Still...he couldn't believe her words. There had to be more to this.

"Whatever he's done to you, I swear I'll make him pay." As soon as he was able, he would tear the earl limb from limb.

"He's done nothing to me. This is *my* choice. I wish to marry him, and you promised you would release me if I asked. So, I am asking. Will you release me, or are you going back on your promise?"

For a moment, a spark of fire glimmered in her eye, and then it was gone, masked behind layers and layers of cold will.

Oh, Isabella, what did he say to you?

But she did not relent as she stood there in stony silence, staring him down. Whatever Lord James had done, it was bad enough that she needed him to at least appear to give in. "I am a man of my word, my lady. If you wish to be free of me, I won't stand in the way," he said at last, each word leaving a bitter taste in his mouth.

Lord James grinned and clapped. "Now, was that so hard? Father Michael, you heard the man. Are you satisfied now?"

The priest nodded slowly. "Yes, I believe that gives us enough to work with, as long as he doesn't change his mind before the tribunal."

"The only reason I would change my mind is if Isabella changes hers," Martin said. Whatever game was afoot here, Isabella needed him to make this look convincing. "Since she wishes to be rid of me, I will do as she asks."

Lord James nodded and turned to the door. "Eadric, take Lord Martin to the room we've prepared for him, and have the healer tend to his wounds. We need him well enough to stand before the tribunal."

Martin narrowed his eyes. "Why bother healing me and going through with the annulment? You could just kill me."

"Isabella has convinced me that it would be unwise to anger Lady Eleanor by killing an ally when I'm trying to ingratiate myself to her husband."

Selfish bastard. At least it meant Martin would live to see another day, and as long as he drew breath, he could fight this. Isabella would never wed Lord James. Martin would see to that.

Lord James turned to go, taking Isabella and the priest with him.

"Yes, my lord."

Two guards entered and pulled him up, none too gently. He put an arm over each of their shoulders and did his best to hop along as they manhandled him out of the dungeon.

This was not the end, Martin swore to himself as he winced and grunted. He would save Isabella from that beast, whatever it took.

CHAPTER TWENTY-SIX

As soon as the door shut behind her, Isabella ran to her sister's side and sobbed.

"What is it?" Adelaide said weakly, her voice little more than a croak.

"I'm marrying Lord James," Isabella confessed, hating every word. "Martin agreed to an annulment."

"But why?" Adelaide took her hand. Her sister's skin was burning with fever.

"Lord James said he would take his vengeance on you if I didn't convince Martin to let me go." He'd said Martin wouldn't agree if he thought she was asking because either of them was threatened. So he'd threatened her sister instead, the cold-hearted snake.

"I had to go through with it. I had to go down to the dungeon and put on the show of a lifetime, convincing Martin that I never cared for him and that it was all a ruse to goad Lord James into making a better offer. And God forgive me, it worked."

"No," Adelaide whispered, squeezing her hand.

"Yes. He said the words, and he meant them." She'd done her very best to look cold and aloof. Did he know her heart was breaking beneath it all? Did he understand the pain each word had caused her?

"Then find a way to fix it." Her sister's earnest gaze broke

Isabella's heart all over again. The choices before her were impossible. Even Adelaide should be able to see that.

"If only I could." More tears dripped down Isabella's cheeks.

"You can," Adelaide said, barely audible. "You're my sister. You're too strong and smart to let this happen. You'll find a way. I know you will. You *must*."

"Rest, my sweet. Don't worry yourself about me. You just focus on getting better, all right?" Her sister's blind faith in her abilities was almost as painful as Martin's words in the dungeon. She'd let everyone down, and she couldn't see a way out.

Adelaide nodded against the pillow and closed her eyes. Isabella smoothed her hair back and watched her breathing slow to a deep and regular cadence.

Exhaustion weighed Isabella down as the events of the day played over and over in her mind, but she knew there would be no sleep for her tonight. The horror of it all was too much, and she couldn't let go of the tiny sliver of hope that maybe her sister was right. Maybe she could find a way out of this if she could only clear her mind enough to think.

Perhaps she didn't need to come up with the entire plan on her own. If she could find a way to see Martin, they could think together. Surely between the two of them, they were clever enough to come up with a plan.

She got up and went over to her chest of clothing, pulling out her plainest woolen gown and an unadorned brown wool cloak with a deep hood. Quickly, she put them on, before she could reconsider this rash plan.

Slipping out the door, she snuck out into the hallway. Which door was Martin's? He had to be here somewhere, but she couldn't risk waking the wrong person. Then she spotted the room at the end with the dozing guard by the door. That had to be it.

Tiptoeing, she made her way down the hall. The guard was snoring and smelled of alcohol. She prayed he stayed unconscious. Reaching up, she began to unlatch the door, but the scrape of metal against metal made just enough sound that the guard was startled awake.

"Who are you?" the guard grumbled.

Isabella's heart nearly stopped. "The healer sent me. I'm supposed to change Lord Martin's bandages."

The guard blinked at her. For a long moment, Isabella hardly dared breathe. If she was caught sneaking into Martin's chamber, heaven only knows what Lord James would do.

At last, he said, "All right. Go in." Leaning his head back, he closed his eyes.

She eased into the room as quietly as she could manage. And closed the door behind her.

"Who is it?" Lord Martin asked from across the pitch-black room. She heard the rustling of bedclothes and the rasp of a flint, and then the light of a candle filled the room with soft, flickering light. Martin was sitting up in bed, bare from the waist up, eyes wide and wary. Suddenly, she was far too warm, despite the chill of the night.

She threw back her hood, and he gasped. "What are you doing here?" he asked in a barely audible whisper.

Rushing to his side, she sat on the bed and lowered her lips to his ear. "Lord James made me say what I did by threatening Adelaide. I didn't have any choice, I swear."

"I believe you, my love," he whispered back, caressing her cheek and kissing her ever so softly on the lips. The slow sweetness robbed her of any coherent thought. She felt the loss keenly when he pulled away. "I knew he had to be manipulating you somehow."

He was so warm and close, and he smelled of the sea and sunshine. He must have washed himself because all traces of the dust, blood, and sweat from the fight earlier were gone. She wanted to drown herself in the comfort of his arms, but there was no time.

"I don't know what to do. With Adelaide so ill and now in danger from Lord James, I can hardly think straight. I was hoping if we worked together, we might come up with a plan to escape this awful mess."

"You mean to tell me you haven't figured it all out with that magnificent mind of yours?" There was a playful look in his eye that reminded her of their first meeting. How could he tease at a time like this?

"Not yet," she said, narrowing her eyes and pursing her lips.

A wicked half-smile curled his lips. "Then we'll have to figure it out together because I cannot wait to escape this place and spend weeks on end worshipping you. You were very brave today. I can't tell you what it meant that you stayed for the fight and cheered me on, even though you were surrounded by Lord James's men. I'm starting to think you like me."

He drew his finger down her cheek and let it trace down her neck and chest, brushing over her hardened nipple.

Desperate hunger flooded her body, and she arched into his touch, even as she knew she couldn't afford this at the moment. *Soon, but not now.*

Reluctantly, she pulled back. "Keep your hands to yourself until you propose something," she murmured. "We have little time and can't afford to get distracted. Do you have any ideas?"

"So many. Most of them very wicked, but if you're asking me how to win our freedom…"

"You know I am, you tempting devil."

"Then we need leverage over Lord James. What would bring him to his knees? What would make all his dreams turn to ash? You know him better than I do. What does he fear most?"

She turned it over in her mind. What would make Lord James quiver in his boots? "He fears losing his position. He's stayed neutral in this war for fear of choosing wrongly and ending up with nothing."

Martin grinned. "Then we'll have to make sure he loses if he doesn't let us go. He wants to be Henry's exchequer, does he not? Let's draft a letter to the duke saying Lord James is plotting against him with King Stephen."

Interesting idea. How could she build on it? "Let's also draft a letter to King Stephen saying he's plotting with the Duke of Normandy. That way he loses everything and has no one to run to."

Martin's gaze glinted with appreciation. "Have I told you I love how your mind works?"

Heavens, what she wouldn't do to have him look at her like that forever. But she had to stay on task. "How does it help us, though? It's not as if he'd ever let us send such missives."

"True, but…" He paused, thinking. "How would he know if these letters exist? All we must do is tell him we've smuggled them out and that the letters will go out if he doesn't release us by sundown."

That could work. But… "What if he calls our bluff?"

"Hmm." He placed a distracting hand on her thigh, which she plucked off immediately as though burned. But it was too late. Flames licked up her leg to her core, even at that light touch.

"Not until we're done planning," she murmured through gritted teeth.

He gave her an innocent look, as if he didn't know exactly what he was doing to her. "Does he know Lady Eleanor wants Adelaide to take your place as her lady-in-waiting?"

She sat up and studied his face. "I didn't think it would be a good idea to disclose that part until after we were wed. He knows I want to keep Adelaide with me but nothing more. Why?"

"Can you fake Lady Eleanor's hand?"

"Yes, but why?" She'd drafted enough correspondence on Her Grace's behalf that she could duplicate her handwriting well enough to fool any but the most discerning observers.

"Do you think you could draw up a letter from Lady Eleanor demanding that I deliver Adelaide to her personally? Let's put a deadline on it too. Something soon. Easter, perhaps? He'd have no choice but to let her go, not if he wants to avoid angering Her Grace. We'll offer to have my men take her, and once she's safely out of the castle, we'll tell him about the letters."

She frowned. Could that work? Would the earl let Adelaide go on the basis of a letter from Lady Eleanor? It would certainly put him in a bind. He could hardly ingratiate himself to her if he was directly defying her wishes. But still…

"I'm not sure the letters by themselves would be enough for him to let her go, but perhaps the letters in combination with an offer from me to tell him everything he wants to know to become exchequer if he lets her go would convince him? It's risky, but I don't see that we have a choice."

"Then it's a plan," he said, eyes darkening. "And now I can touch you."

"Wait," she ordered as his hand traced up her leg. "I have letters to write first."

She pulled away and went over the desk in the corner of the room, which, fortunately, was stocked with parchment, quills, and ink.

Doing her best to ignore Martin's heated gaze, she wrote the letters they'd discussed, including the one she forged in Lady Eleanor's handwriting. "There. Finished. Have a servant deliver the letter from Lady Eleanor to me first thing tomorrow, and I'll take it down to him, distraught at the thought of saying goodbye to my sister. And I'll find a way to sneak the other two to your men. I want Adelaide safely out of this castle before we tell him of the letters to the king and the duke."

"Come here," he said, beckoning.

She rose and went to his side, wondering what he was up to now.

He reached out and caught her hand. Kissing the inside of her wrist, he reached beneath her cloak with his other hand and grazed down the side of her breast, his thumb brushing against her sensitive nipple.

Holy Mother of God, she was going to go up in flames!

"This is the first time we've been alone together in a fully private place since our wedding night. It would be such a shame to waste the opportunity." His thumb kept making slow circles around her nipple, and she thought she might die. "I can tell by the way you're looking at me you that you're as hungry for me as I am for you."

"No, I'm not," she answered, hearing the lie in her own voice.

He pulled her down into a kiss, and she surrendered all too easily, letting him addle her wits with lips and tongue until she no longer knew which way was up. "I have ways of making you confess," he murmured against her lips before claiming them again.

"Oh? Are you going to put me on the rack?" she asked when he relented at last.

"Far worse than that. Come lie beside me. I need you closer."

To her consternation, she found herself obeying, slipping off her shoes, and climbing onto the bed to lie beside him. "This is dangerous. What if the guard comes in?"

"You'll just have to stay very, very quiet while I torture you. Do you think you can do that, Isabella?"

He was kissing down her neck, and she never wanted him to stop. Reaching down, he pulled her dress just high enough to draw slow, lazy circles on her calf. Desire rippled through her. She wanted more, though precisely what she wanted more of, she couldn't say.

"I'm stronger than you think. You're a fool if you believe you can break me." She squirmed beneath his ministrations, restless with the heat coursing through her.

His hand moved higher on her leg, still making slow circles. He brushed the sensitive skin behind her knee, and she gasped. She wanted to feel him everywhere. With wild abandon, she explored his bare chest and back. How could a man be so hard and soft at the same time? Muscles rippled beneath delicious expanses of smooth skin, and she wanted to caress every inch.

"*Mmm*," he murmured into her neck. "Keep that up, and I'll sentence you to twenty lashes with my tongue."

"And where would you whip me, you scoundrel?"

He grinned and ran his hand up her thigh and she opened

herself to his touch, craving so much more. The buzzing heat between her legs was growing almost intolerable. "Make it forty lashes for asking impudent questions. I'll whip you where you are most sensitive, where the mere touch of my tongue will shatter your resolve into a thousand pieces." Fingers grazed against damp curls between her legs. Where had all the moisture come from? She could feel it on the insides of her thighs. It was rather embarrassing.

She tried to scoot away, but he pulled her back.

"Do you trust me?" he said, suddenly serious.

"Completely," she answered without hesitation. It was incredible how quickly he had gained her trust, given how they had started, but after everything that had befallen them, after he had sworn to keep her sister safe and then fought for her against Lord James, her faith in this man was absolute.

His finger slid between her folds, just as they had in the dovecote, and brushed over the nub of flesh that sent an explosion of sparks through every part of her body. Unable to help herself, she moaned, and he sealed his lips to hers to swallow the noise, as if he knew she would be unable to hold back.

"And now," he whispered against her lips, "let the torture begin."

CHAPTER TWENTY-SEVEN

MARTIN WAS PLAYING a dangerous game, and he knew it. But he couldn't stop himself from touching her, caressing her, wanting her. She was within his reach, and he was finally certain of her affection. This was not the time or place to make her fully his, but he needed to make her come apart in his arms—radiant, passionate, and ferocious. He would take a little taste, whet her appetite for things to come, and send her on her way.

As he stroked and teased her, he reveled in the way her body trembled in response—her little gasps, the slick warmth where he was touching her. And she trusted him enough to allow this. It was a miracle, given how they had started. Their courtship had begun as a game he aimed to win, but she had utterly ensorcelled him. There was no thought of winning now, only of cherishing her affection and worshipping her as she deserved.

But her tiny reactions were playing havoc with him, threatening his self-control. She was every bit as magnificent as he had dreamed with her heavily lidded eyes and parted, kiss-stung lips, squirming at his touch. Her nipples pebbled beneath the fabric of her dress as he teased them lightly, making her shiver in delight. The way she was touching him, the naïve exploration of his chest, made him ache with need. But he needed to hold back. He was injured and their privacy was far from assured with a guard right outside the door. His turn would come in time. For the present, he needed to be patient.

"Are you ready for your punishment, temptress?" Without waiting for her response, he flicked his tongue against her earlobe. "One," he whispered.

Her breath hitched so beautifully as he nuzzled her neck and licked again. "Two."

"Wha—what are you doing?" she murmured as her whole body shivered against him. He flicked his finger over the bundle of nerves below, and she convulsed. If she could still ask questions, he had work to do.

"I promised you forty lashes, remember?" He traced his tongue delicately down her neck, then blew on it. The whimper it drew forth went straight to his cock. "That makes three," he whispered, his own breathing wildly uneven and she moved against him, pulling him closer, her fingernails digging into his back. *Oh Christ.*

He rolled on top of her, allowing himself the momentary relief and torture of pressing his length against her hips. She lifted her legs to welcome him, though layers of fabric lay between them. But even so, it was almost too much to bear.

Claiming her mouth, he delved deep, caressing her tentative tongue with desperate urgency, which she then answered with a fury of her own. She learned quickly, his magnificent queen, and he rocked against her barely able to believe she was his at last. If this kept up, he was going to lose control and embarrass himself. Pulling back, he whispered, "four."

"Five, six, seven," he said, drawing back and kissing and licking his way down from her collarbone to the cleft between her ample breasts, so enticing in the soft candlelight. He'd dreamed of her surrender, but the reality far surpassed his imagination. It was like sipping mead, honey and intoxication drowning out all thought of anything but drinking her in.

"Eight." He nipped at her bare shoulder.

"Nine." The divot at the base of her throat called to him, and he explored it thoroughly, delighted by the little whimpers she made.

"You're driving me mad," she murmured, making him grin.

"Oh, I know," he said, nibbling on her neck. "And I'm thoroughly enjoying it."

He couldn't resist kissing her lips once more, exploring her reactions as their tongues entwined. As they kissed, she ran her fingers through his hair with one hand and pulled him flush against her with the other. How he longed to lose himself in her embrace! But it was too soon. He could bide his time a little while more, knowing he could take her properly as soon as they escaped this mess.

Pulling back, he tugged on her lower lip with his teeth, then soothed it with his tongue. "Ten. Have I told you how much I love the way you taste? Like mint and fresh herbs... I want to savor you for hours on end."

He kissed her again just because he could, and they rocked together in a slow rhythm sending shivers of desire down his spine despite the aching throb of his foot. If he didn't pull back, he was going to give in to his need. Holding her close like this was too much. Just a little bit of cloth separated him from total bliss. So he turned on his side and kissed his way down her neck.

"Eleven." He traced her neckline with the tip of his tongue, raising goosebumps on her decolletage. But it wasn't enough. He needed more, and so did she from the way she arched beneath him. He wanted to treasure every inch of new flesh exposed to him. Every gasp and sigh was worth more than gold and jewels as he drew them forth.

With fumbling fingers, he loosened her laces as he continued his slow, relentless stroking between her legs, reveling in her reactions. He loved the way she trembled with each touch, squirming beneath him. Soon he freed her breasts, nudging them above the neckline of her dress. God in heaven, what a sight! Somehow, she was even lovelier than he'd imagined, and Lord knew he'd imagined it in great detail.

"I am speechless, my lady. Your beauty robs me of words."

She grinned and preened. "Is this all it takes? I should have tried it sooner."

"Siren." For truly, she was a temptress sent to destroy his resolve.

"Beware, lest I drag you down to the depths with me." She dragged her nails lightly down his back, and he gasped. Tendrils of sensation spread far beyond the light scratching on his back. He found himself panting, unable to draw a full breath as he struggled to keep his head.

"If this is my reward," he murmured, "I'll follow you to my doom and be glad of it."

Needing to distract her, and himself, he drew a taut nipple into his mouth, licking and sucking, as she pressed into his hand beneath her skirts. As she started to moan, he was forced to put a hand over her mouth. Grazing her nipple lightly with his teeth, he pulled back and looked at her glorious dishevelment. "Twelve."

"More," she whimpered against his hand.

Yes, Isabella. That's what I want to hear. Beg for my tongue against your silken flesh.

"Are you so eager for punishment? I shall have to lash you harder." He drew her other nipple into his mouth and sucked hard, flicking it with his tongue in fast, repeated strokes. At the same moment, he pressed a finger inside her as he continued to stimulate her bud. She convulsed, the telltale pulsation within her building and building.

His own need was almost intolerable. Watching her bliss only made him hunger for her all the more. Her pleasure became his sole purpose in life. There was nothing he desired more than to see her tremble and shake beneath his hand. Or his tongue. She had no idea what he had in store for her.

Just as she was about to reach her peak, he pulled away, leaving her wild-eyed and desperate. "I believe we're up to twenty-three. Do you surrender, my lady? Are you ready to confess your secrets?"

"Wha—?"

Good. Speechless. That was right where he wanted her. Granted, he wasn't in much better of a state. All he could think about was what it would be like to unlace himself and slide inside of her. The spicy scent of her arousal was playing havoc with his willpower. But he wouldn't. Not tonight. Not until she was ready for a true wedding night. He would have to wait until they were safely away from Yarmouth to make love to her as she deserved. He refused to make her his while still on Lord James's land.

Ignoring the painful throbbing of his cock as it strained against his braies, he sat up on his knees, gingerly to avoid further pain in his injured foot, and took a deep breath. The picture before him was almost more than he could endure. Her legs bracketed him, and her skirt was rucked up to her waist, revealing her lovely sex. Her breasts heaved with her panting as she tried to press herself against his leg, seeking friction to finish what he had started. The sight made him ache with mixed need and wonder. This woman was his wife. How had he ever gotten so fortunate?

"Put the pillow over your mouth," he whispered. "What I'm about to do will make you cry out, and I don't want to wake the guard. I promised to lash you where you were the most sensitive, and now it's time to take your punishment."

She smiled and obeyed, and he positioned himself between her legs, nibbling and licking his way up her thigh until she was sobbing into the pillow.

He blew on her sex, and her whole body shook in response. "I believe we're up to thirty-three now. Just seven more lashes to go, my love. Are you ready?"

He brushed her bud with his thumb as he eased a finger back inside her.

Clutching the pillow to her face, she let out a long, low moan as she arched and squirmed. That was all the answer he needed.

"Good. Very good."

With no further ado, he sucked her bud into his mouth, and the glorious salty tang of her burst upon him. Unable to help himself, he squeezed himself beneath his braies. It was too much to take.

She yelped into the pillow as her legs clamped around him, and he sucked harder. He could feel the pulsation building within her once again as he gently thrust his finger in and out, curving it just a bit when it was fully seated to intensify the sensation for her. Her reaction was the most perfect thing he'd ever experienced. She was the wild and untamed creature that he had suspected lived beneath her skin from their very first meeting. All that fire, all that passion was at his command, and he was humbled to bear witness to it.

"Thirty-four," he murmured, pulling away for a moment to look up at her.

Her fingers twisted in his hair. "More. Now," she commanded in a hoarse whisper.

"Are you sure you can take it?"

An inarticulate groan resonated through her as she pulled on his hair, the pain sending little shocks of pleasure straight to his poor, straining cock. He squeezed himself again, desperate for some relief.

"Now," she ordered again.

"As you wish."

He sucked her into his mouth again and licked around her bud, continuing to pleasure her with his finger, until she was frantic beneath him. Christ, it was too much! He was losing his ability to concentrate. This had to be good for her. With difficulty he reined himself in and focused on serving his beautiful queen as she deserved.

Carefully, he kept her on the edge, teasing her as he counted. "Thirty-five... Thirty-six... Thirty-seven... Thirty-eight... Thirty-nine..."

So close. So very close. She moaned into the pillow and pulled on his hair, pressing herself against him. God's bones! How he loved this wild woman! If this was what she was like now, just imagine how she would react to being filled by him.

"Final one," he murmured against her swollen flesh.

Sucking her bud into his mouth one last time, he flicked her fast and hard, over and over with his tongue, pumping in and out of her with his finger until she fell apart completely beneath him, crying out into the pillow with an uncontrolled wail.

The sight before him was holy, as she was transported in ecstasy. It was too much. Too beautiful. Too awe inspiring.

Grasping himself helplessly, he burst, unable to contain himself any longer. He came so hard it hurt, everything in him pouring out as his vision went momentarily black. *Holy Jesus.* If it felt like that when she hadn't even touched him…

As the world around him came back into focus, he wiped off his mess in the sheets and climbed back up to lie beside her, pushing aside the pillow so that he could see her face.

She looked as dazed and addled as he felt, utterly boneless in his arms. He kissed her tenderly, and she didn't balk as she tasted herself on his lips.

They lay together in companionable silence for a long moment, as he gently stroked her back. There was no doubt that Isabella owned him heart and soul. He was as far gone as any man could be. Any further, and he would surely lose his mind entirely. But they were far from safe in this chamber, and he needed to keep his head.

"You should get back to your room before we are found out," he said, reluctantly. Someday soon, he would be able to keep her with him and cherish her all night long, but they were still in danger, still under Lord James's thumb. Loath though he was to let her go, he knew he must.

He tried not to wince at the look of disappointment that crossed her features. "I wish you could stay, and soon enough we'll have all the time together we could dream of. But tonight, you must go."

"You're right, of course," she said, sitting up slowly and fixing her dress. "That was…" She trailed off as if unable to find the right words. He couldn't wait until the day when she found them. He looked forward to her putting her wicked tongue to use for something other than roasting him over a spit.

"It was," he agreed. "Go to bed, Isabella, and dream of me. Tomorrow, we rescue Adelaide and then leave this place forever. You need your sleep."

She kissed him on the forehead and took the letters to King Stephen and Lord Henry, leaving the false letter from Eleanor behind. "Don't forget to send a servant to me with the letter from Her Grace first thing tomorrow. It needs to look as if you're taking my sister to punish me for disloyalty."

"I will," he whispered. "Sleep well, my love. Tomorrow, we escape."

"Goodnight." The warmth in her candlelit smile completely undid him. If he'd been able to walk, he would have pulled her back into bed at once. Danger be damned.

But before he could so much as move, she pulled the hood of her cloak over her head, opened the door, and tiptoed past the sleeping guard. When the door snicked shut behind her, he finally let out his breath. This had been a night to remember. What the morrow would bring, none could say, but he would do everything in his power to ensure they all escaped so that he could spend the rest of his life showing Isabella how grateful he was for her trust and affection. Perhaps someday, she might even grow to love him. He hardly dared hope.

It was no good thinking that far ahead when they still had to escape Lord James. He prayed their plan would work and that before the sun set again, they would be on their way to Winchelsea once more.

CHAPTER TWENTY-EIGHT

ISABELLA AWOKE TO her sister's coughing just after dawn. The deep rasp of it washed away every shred of the delicious languor her dream had inspired. A dream of Martin and his wicked tongue. Had the events of last night been real, or had they been a dream as well?

Adelaide coughed again, and Isabella sprang out of bed and poured her a cup of water. Propping herself up, her sister took a sip. Isabella pressed a hand to Adelaide's forehead, and her heart sank. It was still hot.

After finishing the water, Adelaide set the cup aside. "Where did you sneak off to last night?" Her shredded voice made Isabella wince.

"Don't strain yourself by speaking, love," Isabella brushed a strand of sweat-dampened hair from her sister's face.

"Where?" Adelaide demanded, struggling to sit up straight. "Please tell me it wasn't to Lord James."

The very idea sent a sickening chill down Isabella's spine. "*Shh.* Sweetling, I needed a word with Martin, if you must know."

Adelaide relaxed and managed a wan smile. "Good," she croaked.

"We hatched a plan to escape." Isabella explained what they were going to do. "Are you strong enough to travel? We're aiming to get you out of here by nightfall, and by noon tomorrow, we should all be on our way to Winchelsea."

"I'll be fine," Adelaide whispered, placing her hand on Isabella's.

It never ceased to amaze Isabella how strong her sister was despite the frailty of her body. Somehow, she'd survived years alone in their parents' household unscathed, and her bravery here and now, when everything hung in the balance, made Isabella's heart swell with love and pride.

"I swear to you, this nightmare will soon be over, and I'll get you the best care in Christendom. We'll be a proper family together, and live long, happy lives." Before Martin, she'd never let herself believe in the possibility of such a fairytale ending, but the wicked, silver-tongued baron from Winchelsea had changed everything.

A silver tongue… Forty lashes…

Shaking herself, Isabella forced her mind back to the present. There was too much to do to start daydreaming about the unspeakable things her husband had done in the night.

Adelaide started coughing again as she tried to reply.

"Don't speak. Just rest. You'll need your strength for the journey." Isabella handed her the cup of water again.

Adelaide nodded and settled back down in the bed after taking a sip of water. Isabella hated to move her under such circumstances, but they had to escape. There was no choice. She was relieved to see Adelaide close her eyes and drift off to sleep once again.

With brisk efficiency, Isabella began preparing for the day. She put on a woad-blue wool gown with delicate white embroidered trim and bell sleeves that dripped to her knees. It was one of her favorite dresses—practical, but fine enough for a future countess. And that was the part she must play today. Lord James couldn't suspect that she and Martin had been conspiring, or he would never let Adelaide go. To all outward appearances, she needed to have surrendered.

There was a knock on the door, and a servant handed her a scroll, saying it was from Lord Martin. *Good. Things are proceeding as planned.*

Now, she had to prepare for her performance. Lord James needed to think that the contents of the letter had driven her to tears. It didn't take much. One look at Adelaide, lying feverish in bed, her breathing ragged as she dozed, and the tears began to flow.

She'd failed her sister so many times and in so many ways. How could she ever deserve happiness if she couldn't even defend her little sister from harm? Years of guilt made the tears fall fast and hot. She should have found a way to get Adelaide away from her parents sooner. And now, she'd put Adelaide in danger again, all because of her own wrongheadedness. If only she had trusted Martin instead of speaking to Lord James, they wouldn't be in this terrible mess.

Isabella rubbed her eyes to make them look as red and raw as she felt. The only way to make her mistakes right was to convince Lord James to let them go. If she failed, then she deserved whatever befell her. But she would not fail Adelaide or Martin. She couldn't. They were too precious to her.

Standing and sniffing, she picked up the scroll written in Eleanor's hand and hurried down to the great hall before she could lose her nerve. She found Lord James at the high table, eating a hunk of bread and washing it down with ale. His eyes sparked with lascivious intent upon seeing her until he took in her red, teary face.

"Good morrow, my lord," she said with a curtsy.

"Good morrow to you too, my lady," he answered, studying her coldly. "Come sit next to me. We have things to discuss. The tribunal will convene before the week is out to hear your case. I sent riders out to gather them here yesterday. We'll wed before Easter."

She squeezed her eyes shut, and an unfeigned tear dripped down her cheek. Thank God he couldn't see inside her heart and know how deeply it pained her that she had ever contemplated marrying him.

"Compose yourself, woman," he grumbled. "Need I remind you that this was all your idea in the first place?"

"My distress has nothing to do with you, my lord. I'm upset about this letter from Lady Eleanor." She held up the scroll, praying that this ruse would work.

"Give it to me now." He yanked it from her and read, his expression growing more thunderous by the moment as he took in its message. "Where did this come from?" he growled.

"Lord Martin had it. He had a servant bring it to me this morning. He hid this from me until this morning, no doubt trying to worm his way into my affections. But now he intends to carry out Lady Eleanor's orders and take my sister from me. Please stop him. If you have any kindness in your heart, please let Adelaide stay with me."

She prayed she was right, that the harder she begged to keep Adelaide, the more inclined he would be to send her off.

"If he thinks he'll escape staying for the annulment tribunal—"

"He's proposing to have his men take her today while he stays here. I'm terrified of what might happen to her on the voyage. She's so ill already. But I hardly dare to defy Lady Eleanor. She doesn't take it kindly when someone crosses her. If I don't send Adelaide, I don't know what she'll do to us."

She was laying it on thick. Would he see through her ruse?

"I have no desire to anger Her Grace," he said, studying the letter. "Adelaide leaves today, but not with Lord Martin or his men. I'll send her myself with my own trusted men and a healer to see to it that she survives the journey."

Oh no! That would never do. If Adelaide went with Lord James's men, the plan unraveled completely. "But she can't," Isabella said, attempting to improvise as quickly as she could manage. She lowered her voice to a murmur only Lord James could hear. "Lord Martin is carrying secret messages to Her Grace regarding King Stephen's allies, their strength at arms, and where they are mustering. If his men don't come bearing those messages along with my sister, the duke and duchess will both be furious."

Lord James shrugged. "Then I'll make him hand over the messages to me."

"He and his men would die before telling you where to find them."

"I have ways of making men talk," he grumbled. "Have no fear. I'll soon possess all of their secrets."

This wasn't going at all how she had hoped. "But you won't possess them in time. The letters are in a hidden compartment on the ship. Only Lord Martin knows how to find it and open it, and he'll never give you what you want."

"That pathetic wretch? I'll have him singing my tune before the midday meal. Hezekiah," he bellowed, and one of his men hurried over. "Prepare Lady Adelaide to depart on *The Falcon* for Normandy before the day is out. Find a healer to accompany her. And get Lord Martin out of bed and dressed. We're all going to take a little trip down to the docks. Prepare the carriage."

He turned to Isabella as Hezekiah rushed off. "Go say your goodbyes to your sister. We leave for the docks within the hour."

Isabella hurried back to her room to make sure all of Adelaide's things got packed. Fortunately, she arrived before any of Lord James's servants.

Adelaide blinked her eyes open as the door closed behind Isabella. "What is it? What's gone wrong?"

Isabella wished she could shield her sister from everything that was happening, but under the circumstances, it wasn't possible. She was going to have to trust in her sister's inner strength. "Lord James is going to try to send you to Normandy on his own ship with his own men. I made up a story about secret documents on *The Wind Song* that Lady Eleanor required and that only Martin could find. He's going to bring all three of us to the dock. At least it gets us out of the castle, but I have no idea how we'll escape from there."

"I'm sure you and Lord Martin will find a way," Adelaide

croaked. "I'll help any way I can."

Rummaging through Adelaide's chest, Isabella pulled out a thick wool gown to keep her sister warm despite the wintry weather. "Let's get you dressed and packed. We need to get you out of here, no matter what. I can't let him use your health as leverage over me ever again. If anything bad happens to you because of that coxcomb, I'll strangle him myself."

There was a knock at the door. "Come in," Isabella called out.

A young woman dressed in servant's clothes entered along with an older woman with snowy hair who Isabella recognized as the healer. "I'll just get Lady Adelaide packed up while you examine her," said the servant.

"I don't like that they are moving you," said the healer, as she took Adelaide's pulse. "Your humors are still badly out of balance. I should bleed you, but I fear it would weaken you too much for the journey ahead. My apprentice, Lizbeth, will accompany you on your journey. She will meet you at the docks. The earl has arranged everything. Drink this," she said, handing Adelaide a flask of some pungent concoction of herbs and spirits. The scent of it filled the room.

Adelaide choked and sputtered as she drank it down.

"You're all packed, my lady," said the servant, closing Adelaide's trunk with a thunk. "The carriage is waiting below. Can you walk, Lady Adelaide, or do you need someone to carry you?"

Adelaide slowly, agonizingly, pushed herself to standing, letting Isabella wrap an arm around her to steady her. "I think I can make it to the carriage with my sister's help."

Together, their small party made their way down the stairs and out to the courtyard where an enormous carriage that looked like a house on wheels stood. Isabella helped Adelaide climb in and settle on a leather-covered seat while the servant lashed her trunk to the back. Moments after they settled on the bench, Martin came hobbling in with a cane to help him walk.

As soon as Martin was seated, Isabella whispered, "He's going to try to send Adelaide away on his own ship instead of with yours. I told him there was a box of secret messages aboard *The Wind Song* that Lady Eleanor is expecting and that only you knew where to find. We have to find a way to make contact with your men and enlist their assistance to help us escape."

"I will—" Martin closed his lips abruptly as Lord James peered into the carriage.

"The healer will travel with you to the docks to keep an eye on Adelaide," Lord James announced, making way for the flustered-looking older woman.

With the healer there, they wouldn't be able to talk freely. At least Isabella had been able to explain her deception to Martin in time.

"How is your foot, Lord Martin?" the healer asked, taking a seat beside him. "I hope you're staying off it."

"I couldn't step on it if I tried, good woman," he said with a grimace. Clearly, he had tried and failed. *Poor Martin!* They all had to get away from this place before anything worse happened.

They rode in silence to the dock, as Isabella racked her brain for some plan for how to get them away from Lord James. From Martin's furrowed brow, she could tell he was doing the same. Adelaide slumped against her as the carriage thumped and bumped over the stone-paved road.

As the carriage door opened, the cacophony and smells of the dock washed over them. All Isabella could do was pray that they found a way to end this nightmare before her sister was torn away.

CHAPTER TWENTY-NINE

I T WAS ALL a matter of timing, Martin thought to himself as he led Lord James along the dock toward *The Wind Song*. After a tearful goodbye with Isabella, Adelaide had boarded Lord James's ship, which was scheduled to depart when the church bell rang for afternoon prayers. He needed to absorb enough of Lord James's attention to give Isabella a plausible chance to have a private word with someone from his crew. Then he could raise the threat of the letters and hopefully, they could all leave. But Lord James had to be made to believe the letters went out, which meant he had to distract the man as long as possible. But not so long that the ship Adelaide was on set sail.

Each step was torture, even though he only placed the lightest pressure on his injured foot as he hobbled along the quay with a gnarled branch that currently served as his walking stick. Halfred and the men were hard at work putting up new rigging to attach to the new mast they had installed, but work ground to a halt as he limped his way up the gangplank, followed by Lord James, Isabella, and three of Lord James's men.

"God's bones, my lord! What happened to your foot? And why are there bruises around your neck?" Halfred demanded after bowing in greeting to each of them.

"Don't worry yourself. Lord James and I had a little disagreement, but we sorted it out. Did we not, my lord?" He gave the earl his iciest smile. While Lord James had three men with him, there were far more Winchelsea men on board *The Wind Song* at the moment. If the blackguard tried anything, he would be severely outnumbered. At that thought, Martin's smile grew. The man's hubris would be his downfall. "Will, get Timothy and accompany Lady Isabella to the cabin. She wishes to retrieve some things for a longer stay here in Yarmouth."

Will blinked and stared for a long moment. There was no Timothy on their crew.

Martin winked discreetly at him, and Will's eyes widened in comprehension.

"Of course, my lord," the youth said, hurrying to Isabella's side and offering an arm. "Timothy is working on repairs belowdecks. I'll take Lady Isabella to the cabin and go fetch him. Come with me, my lady."

Isabella caught his eye for just a moment. For a split second, her gaze was raw and unguarded, and his heart stuttered seeing all the concern and affection there. But she looked away quickly, squaring her shoulders and striding forward with purpose. "Take me below, boy, and be quick about it," she snapped, her haughty mask back in place.

To his relief, Lord James didn't bother to send anyone to follow her. Now for his part of the ruse. "Halfred, I need the key I told you to hide—the one to the secret chest." God bless Halfred because he didn't even blink at the lie. "And be quick about it. None of your absent-minded dilly-dallying," Martin said, as if Halfred had ever dilly-dallied in his life. "Lord James needs the papers I keep hidden in that chest. Do not, I repeat, do *not* keep us waiting. Time is of the essence. The repercussions of any delay would be most unfortunate."

Martin could only pray that Halfred got the message that he was to draw this out.

"Understood, my lord," Halfred answered with a careful nod. "Let me go below and look for it. I will return with it as soon as I find it. I've hidden it well. It may take me some time to retrieve it."

Good. He understood.

"Then hurry, man. We can't wait all day," Lord James grumbled.

"You don't mind if I sit, do you?" Martin made his way gingerly over to a crate and sat down. "Halfred is a good man, but he's sometimes forgetful. It may be some time before he brings up that key."

What a blessed relief it was to take his weight off his injured foot. He wasn't sure he could remain standing much longer.

"Ned," Martin called out, and the man came running. "Bring up some wine for our guests. We might as well refresh ourselves while we wait. And while you're down there, check on the contents of the chest next to the door of the hold on the starboard side." Martin—and Ned, and the other men—knew was full of weapons. "And get the other men working below to help you. There are thieves and brigands about." He flicked his gaze to Lord James. "We wouldn't want anything to happen to our cargo. Would you care for a game of chess, my lord, to pass the time?" he asked, turning to Lord James.

"Never liked chess," Lord James grumbled.

"No, I suppose not. You don't seem like the intellectual type. Dice then, perhaps?"

Lord James's only answer was a low rumbling noise in his throat.

At that moment, Isabella climbed back up on the deck, trailed by six men carrying crates and trunks. "I have my things," she announced airily. "Just a few necessities, since we'll be staying a very long time."

The men proceeded to the gangplank and instead of descending, they piled everything up to block the exit from the boat.

"What are you doing, you lazy dogs? Take them to the castle," Lord James bellowed, rising and storming over to the offending men, who all drew swords as he approached. "What's this? What do you think you're doing?" The man turned bright red, his fury boiling over as he realized he was trapped.

As if on cue, Halfred led a dozen armed men up onto the deck from below, and they swiftly surrounded the earl and his men, who had all drawn their swords, ready to fight.

"Entertaining as it would be to watch you get torn to shreds, my lord," Isabella said as she approached the earl with a triumphant smile, "I need you to bring my sister back. The game is up. You cannot win. Send Adelaide to me, and let us all depart, or I let my husband take his revenge for all you've done. I assure you he'll make it slow and painful."

Lord James laughed. "This is my land. Yarmouth is filled with my people. If I call out to say their lord is in danger, men will come swarming to my rescue."

"I think you overestimate your popularity," Isabella said dryly. "But we have taken other precautions. Would you like to tell him, Martin, or should I? It was your idea. I think you should do the honors." Isabella walked at a leisurely pace over to Martin and put an arm through his, then kissed him on the cheek.

A rush of pride flowed through him, knowing that this glorious woman was his. "We sent two letters with Timothy just now—one to King Stephen and one to Henry, Duke of Normandy—accusing you of betraying their trust. He's awaiting our signal about whether to proceed with delivering them. If you let us leave Yarmouth with Adelaide today, he will destroy the letters. If you try to prevent our departure, the letters will go out, and you'll lose everything."

The earl scowled. "You think I can't find a measly messenger in Yarmouth?"

Martin shrugged. "You can try, but Timothy knows how to disappear and avoid even the most determined pursuers. Did you even notice him leaving this ship right under your very nose?"

Of course, he couldn't have since Timothy didn't exist.

Meanwhile, Lord James's face grew thunderous as his neck and face turned puce. It was far too much fun taunting the earl.

"That's what I thought." Martin's grin couldn't be wider. His cheeks were starting to ache with it. "Drop your sword and tell your men to do the same."

With a low, rumbling growl, the earl obeyed and signaled his men.

"There. Was that so hard?" Martin asked, lowering his sword. "Halfred, how long before *The Wind Song* is seaworthy again?"

"At least a week, my lord," the old sailor answered.

That's what he'd thought. Unfortunately, returning home aboard his beloved vessel was not an option. "Lady Isabella, Lady Adelaide, and I need to depart today, and we need to bring a healer with us. Go book us passage on a friendly ship. I think I see the *Lady Mary* and the *Angelus* in port. Either of them would do nicely. Or find us another, if they can't take us. Just make sure it isn't one of his." Martin gestured with his chin at the earl.

"Aye, my lord. Right away," Halfred said. The men cleared a path to allow him to depart.

"As for you, Lord James, I'm going to let you go retrieve Lady Adelaide in a moment. But I need your solemn oath that you will not interfere with the repairs to *The Wind Song* or with any of my crew. If you make trouble, we'll signal Timothy, and he'll go running with those letters. Do I have your promise?"

Lord James looked daggers at Martin, but the man had no choice. "I swear on all that is holy that *The Wind Song* will depart in its own good time and that your men will not be bothered."

Isabella squeezed Martin's arm affectionately and whispered, "We won."

"Yes, we did," Martin murmured and planted a kiss on her forehead.

Lord James made a noise of disgust.

"I expect Lady Adelaide and her healer to join us here within the hour." Martin lowered his blade and signaled with his hand for his men to do the same. "You may go."

Martin could hardly contain his glee as Lord James and his men trudged down the gangplank, defeated.

As soon as they were gone, Martin pulled his wife close. "You were brilliant, my love."

"So were you." He reached up and pulled her in for a kiss. She tasted of sweetness and triumph and everything that he held dear as she opened to him, her tongue tantalizing his own. He lost himself in the taste of her, the feel of her, so soft beneath his hands and yet so full of passion and strength. *His Isabella. Forever.*

Unfortunately, they were not alone. His men hooted and hollered at the sight, forcing him to break the kiss with a laugh. "Leave us alone. Can't you see I'm busy?" he called out, and his crew roared with laughter.

"There's a cabin below, my lord, if you and your wife need some privacy," one of them called out.

Several others made obscene suggestions and gestures that left even Isabella blushing. "If it wasn't for Adelaide, I would take you below for a true wedding night right this minute," she murmured, eyes full of promise.

Martin sighed. Alas, his wedding night had to wait until they had time and privacy, though resisting temptation required a degree of physical restraint that he could barely manage. "Chess," he said, desperately casting his mind about for something they could do for distraction until Adelaide returned to them.

"Chess?" Isabella asked, an incredulous look on her face.

"Would you care to play? It would pass the time while we wait."

She nodded, looking as flustered and flushed as he felt. "I'm sure I'll play horribly under the circumstances, but I accept your challenge."

Martin called out to one of his men who brought up the board and pieces. They set themselves up to play sitting on crates with a barrel between them. They were only three moves into their game when Lord James reappeared with Adelaide and her healer.

"Here. Take her. I've fulfilled my end of the bargain. Now call off Timothy," Lord James said, in a voice dripping with vitriol, before he turned to go.

"Not yet," Martin called back, making the earl pause. "Not

until *The Wind Song* leaves in peace."

Lord James turned slowly to face Martin, staring him down with violent promise. But all he said was, "Fine." Again, he turned to go.

Martin prayed that was the last they ever saw of him.

Isabella ran to her sister, helping the healer settle her on some sacks of grain, leaning her back against the forecastle, until Halfred returned.

Fortunately, Halfred came back swiftly. "The *Angelus* can take you to Winchelsea, my lord. I've booked you two cabins. It departs within the hour."

Arrangements made, they wended their way along the docks to his friend's ship. Halfred carried Lady Adelaide in his arms because she was too faint and feverish to walk.

Martin greeted the captain as the ladies got settled belowdecks.

"I hear congratulations are in order, my lord," said Captain Samuel, a man close to his own age with sandy hair that he tied back beneath a striped cloth. The captain made frequent stops at Winchelsea, and they'd known each other for years.

"Indeed. I'm a married man, if you can believe it."

"Best wishes to you and your new wife," Captain Samuel said with a little bow. "We'll get you home safe and sound. From what Halfred told me, you've had quite an eventful journey so far."

"I'll tell you all about it over a tankard of ale once we're underway, but first, I must see to my wife."

"As you wish. My ship is yours."

Martin made his way belowdecks just as Isabella closed the door of her sister's cabin behind her.

"How is she?" Martin asked, seeing the distraught look on Isabella's face.

"Still feverish, but she's sleeping now. The healer is with her."

"Does that mean that you and I can have a private moment to ourselves in our cabin?"

Isabella crossed her arms and shook her head. "Wicked man." But she was smiling, and Martin could see her blush even in the meager lanternlight that bathed everything around them in gold.

"I was merely inviting you to finish our game of chess. What did you think I had in mind?" he asked, all innocence.

She grabbed his arm and hauled him into their empty cabin, right beside Adelaide's. As soon as the door shut behind them, she pulled him into an embrace. "If you attempt to play chess with me, husband, I'll devise such tortures that you'll spend the rest of eternity begging for mercy. It is time to finish what you started last night."

"Oh? You want to write more letters?"

"Don't toy with me. You know what I need, even if I'm not sure I do."

Her fingernails raked down his back, and his whole body came to attention. "Are you sure, Isabella? We could always wait until Winchelsea."

"I want a true wedding night, and I want it now. Here. With you. I want you as my husband in truth, to have and to hold until death do us part. Is that plain enough for you?"

It most certainly was. Heady pleasure and need flooded through him as he locked the latch on the door. Oh, how he'd dreamed of this! From the moment he'd met her, he'd been smitten, and now she was truly going to be his in every sense. And now it was time at last.

Chapter Thirty

I SABELLA TRIED TO calm the rapid beating of her heart as she stepped into the simple, lantern-lit cabin she would share with Martin for the remainder of their journey to Winchelsea. She wasn't entirely sure she understood what was about to happen, despite Martin's description of the act on their wedding night. But after their encounters the previous day, she was aching for his touch. And not just because she craved the pleasure that he could give her.

After all that had transpired, she needed to be close to him in every way she could. He filled her mind and her heart, and she could hardly think of anything else. He was her partner, her equal. Together, they could overcome anything. She loved the way they played off each other, attuned to each other's thoughts even in the direst of circumstances. He had set out to woo her, to win her, but this had long since ceased to be a game for either of them.

He pulled her gently into his embrace, and she whispered in his ear, "Don't let it go to your head, you pompous coxcomb, but I think I might be madly in love with you."

He froze, not even breathing, and for a moment, she wondered if she'd gone too far, said too much. Maybe she'd gotten everything wrong, and now she'd ruined everything by confessing her feelings.

But a moment later, he crushed her to him so hard she could barely draw breath. "Thank you," he whispered against her shoulder. "I swear I will love and cherish you for the rest of my days."

His lips brushed tenderly against her cheek, and she melted. All her worries, all her defenses disappeared. It was terrifying to feel like this, but there was no denying the raw power of what she felt for this man who was cradling her closely as if she was the most precious thing under the firmament.

"As will I," she murmured into his hair. And she meant it with all her heart. He had rescued her first from her family, then from a storm, and lastly from Lord James. Her husband had proven himself time and again, despite every hurdle and barrier she could throw at him. There was no more running. Her heart had a home for the first time in her life. Never before had she allowed someone so close. Even her siblings she'd kept at arm's length, always taking care of them and never letting them in. But with Martin, she didn't have to be strong. She could simply be herself.

And miraculously, he loved her for it.

His lips brushed against hers in the tenderest of kisses, and joy and light welled up within her. She opened to him, letting all that was in her heart shine through as they tasted each other. The press of his body against hers made her tremble, as his kiss grew hungrier and deeper. His tongue glided against hers, and it was as if the sparkling threads of their souls were being woven together into a single tapestry. She no longer knew where she started and he ended as they savored the bright intensity of their embrace.

Isabella lost track of time, or her surroundings, of everything as one of his hands caressed down her back to her buttock, pressing her against his hard length, while the other grazed the side of her breast. She moaned into his mouth as their kiss grew wilder still. Somehow, he had backed her against the cabin door, and he pressed again, groaning with her as he ran his hand down her thigh, pulling her closer still as she wrapped her leg around him.

He pulled away and began kissing along her jaw and neck. "Oh, Isabella," he murmured against her skin.

She leaned her head back, arching for him, aching for each touch of lips and tongue as he set her alight. Bowing his head, he grazed the peak of one taut nipple with his teeth through the fabric of her dress, and she thought she might die.

"Please," she begged, though for what she couldn't say. She only knew that every inch of her cried out for more, more, more.

"Oh God," he swore as she wrapped her other leg around him, pinned between him and the rigid wood of the door. His eyes grew wild. He ground against her, feral and desperate, kneading her breast, and she loved it—loved that she could make him lose control like that. She wanted to see him undone, beyond words.

A moment later, he turned them around and walked her backwards across the cabin to the bed. By the time he reached it, he seemed to have recovered a modicum of control. She gasped at the loss of contact as he laid her down gently, then backed away.

But he didn't give her time to object before he pulled her legs to the edge of the bed, kneeling between them. He skimmed his fingers up the backs of her calves to her thighs, pushing up her dress until her lower half was bare to him. She shivered in anticipation, knowing what was to come.

He sat back on his heels and stared at for a long moment with hungry reverence. "You are a goddess, my love. I don't know what I've done to deserve you, but as long as I draw breath, I swear I will worship you."

Slipping off her shoes and letting them drop to the floor, he hooked her bare legs over his shoulders. The awed look he gave her made her feel like she might indeed be some supreme being, ready to receive his devotion. But she wasn't. She was all too flawed. And so she couldn't stop herself from shifting the mood with a smirk. "Heathen."

In a flash, his gaze turned from worshiping to wicked as he grinned. "I am certainly no saint."

Before she could reply, he pressed his hands to her knees to spread her thighs as wide as they could go before he bent and licked her. Everything in the world contracted to a single point. Nothing existed but the sensation of his tongue against her flesh and the lightning bolt that it sent to every part of her body. Her vision went white. She could barely hear herself crying out. She could only feel as everything within her pulled taut.

A moment later he slid a finger into her molten core, and she bucked off the mattress.

"Exquisite," he murmured against her tender flesh before licking her again and pumping his finger into her.

Her whole body shuddered with the shock of sensation. She pulsed and sparked like the heart of a bonfire as he drove her beyond what she could bear, beyond words and thought, beyond the bounds of her very existence into a place of pure bliss. Everything she was burned to cinders in the heat of her need as he kept up his relentless rhythm until everything turned white and her body convulsed.

"Martin," she cried out as he slowed his pace, and she floated down from the celestial sphere where he'd transported her.

While his pace ebbed, he didn't stop. Adding a second finger, he filled her, stretched her. "Again," he said in a hoarse voice. His eyes met hers. "And this time I want to watch."

His calloused thumb brushed over the secret spot, so sensitive after his attentions. "Yes, Isabella. Come apart for me. Let go, my love."

And she did. Again.

She was completely boneless when he relented after the final tremors. It would be a wonder if she could ever move again. But she knew there was more to come. They had not yet consummated the marriage, she didn't think, and she yearned for the completion he'd described to her—to be fully united body and soul with this man she loved.

"I want to see all of you," he said in a rough voice as he untied the laces of her dress and pulled it and her shift over her head. She was as useless as a rag doll and immediately collapsed back on the bed.

He looked at her, fully revealed for the first time, and the expression on his face was almost pained. "God have mercy," he murmured. "You rob me of words."

She couldn't help but grin at that. "At last! I've rendered you speechless. I've silenced that wicked tongue of yours."

"My tongue is good for more than talking. Need I show you again?"

He pulled off his cotte and shirt, throwing them to the side without breaking his gaze. "Because I will."

"You wouldn't." She didn't think she could take another round of tongue lashing without losing her mind entirely.

"I most certainly would," he said, pulling off his boots and tossing them away, then doing the same with his hose.

By God, he was gorgeous. Every plane of his muscles seemed to gleam in the lantern light as she unabashedly trailed her gaze down his naked body until it rested on his engorged cock. A pearl of liquid had formed at the tip. She was tempted to reach out to touch it but didn't quite dare.

"But I would rather make you mine at last."

And just like that, the bonfire within her stirred once more.

"Do you want me, Isabella? Would you like to feel me inside you? Shall we end our little game and consummate our marriage at last?"

He stepped toward her, leaned over her ever so slowly, and settled between her legs, the hard length of him grazing against her bud, so sensitive after all his ministrations.

"Yes, now. Please." She wasn't above begging. There was nothing she wanted more in the world, even as a little frisson of nerves ran through her.

"Are you certain?" He took one of her breasts in his mouth and lazily laved it with his clever tongue.

She gasped, wriggling beneath him, not quite sure what she was supposed to do but knowing she needed him closer.

"This is the part with the blood?" she asked, unable to stop herself.

He switched to the other breast and grazed the nipple with his teeth.

Dear Lord in heaven, she might die if he didn't take her right now. Who cared about blood or a little bit of pain? "Not that it matters."

"Yes, my love. This part may hurt a bit, and there may be blood, but I swear I will do everything in my power to make up for it. And it will only be that way the first time. After that…" He grinned at her. "Are you ready?"

She was so enraptured, she couldn't answer fast enough for him. He nipped at her nipple again, and she moaned, wrapping her legs around him and moving against his hot, hardened flesh.

"Christ," he swore as his eyes squeezed shut and a shudder shook him from head to toe.

"I'm ready. I want you inside me. I want to be your true bride. I want to spend the rest of my life with you. Please make me yours."

"Yes," he hissed through gritted teeth.

Reaching between them, he stroked her as he nudged at her entrance. He slid in an inch, then another inch, giving her body time to adjust. She was not accustomed to such fullness, but she hungered for more. With a gentle rocking motion, he pulled out, then pressed a bit farther. It was unlike anything she'd ever felt. He continued to stroke her, coating himself in her dew so that he slid in and out easily, progressing a bit farther each time until…

She sucked in a breath as he their hips met, and he was fully sheathed. There had been a momentary twinge she hardly noticed, but theirs was now a marriage in truth. They were husband and wife for as long as they both shall live. The thought made her clench and tremble.

"We're married," she whispered, awestruck.

"We're married," he said, panting and straining to hold still. "Did I hurt you?"

"No."

"May I move now?"

"Yes." No sooner was the word out of her mouth than he pulled out slightly and thrust, making her see stars. And he did it again. She hadn't thought her body could take anymore, but he was proving her wrong as the slow, steady rhythm of his strokes made pleasure build once again.

But she didn't want him to be slow and steady. She wanted to undo him just as he undid her. So she began rocking her hips to meet each thrust. The sensation was so much deeper, shaking her to her core. It was as if she was a bell, reverberating with each stroke.

"God's bones, Isabella." His lips found hers, and their tongues entwined in a rhythm echoing their coupling.

She moaned into his mouth, and his movements quickened. Each beat brought her closer to fruition. Each thrust seemed to bring him closer to the brink beyond which he would lose control. She wanted to see that, wanted to feel him wild and reckless within her, around her.

Scratching her fingernails down his back did the trick. At that little twinge of pain, he unleashed himself upon her, and she responded in kind. They scratched and nipped as their frenzied movement grew faster and faster.

It was too much. She was tipping over the edge. And then she was floating once again as he let out a yell in her ear, and she was barely aware as his whole body tensed and jerked above her. Hot liquid spilled out of her and dripped down her leg, and he collapsed on top of her, beathing heavily.

As awareness of the world around her returned, he pulled out slowly and rolled to the side, folding her into his arms so that her head rested on his heaving chest.

For several minutes, all they could do was lie there and breathe. Then he kissed the top of her head and stroked her hair tenderly. "How do you feel? Did I hurt you?"

She assessed the state of her body. Lethargy had spread to every limb. She wasn't sure she could lift a single finger at the moment. There was a modest, throbbing ache between her legs but no pain to speak of. "I feel as if I never want to move again, but otherwise I feel fine. Wonderful, actually."

She kissed his chest and traced the curves of his muscular arm.

"I'm glad. I lost control a bit at the end. I meant to be gentle the first time."

Tracing along his chest, she flicked his nipple, and he gasped. So she did it again. "I wanted you to lose control. I liked it when you were wild."

He put his hand over hers, staying her motion. "Keep doing that, and I'm going to pounce on you again."

She looked down at his cock, slightly smeared with blood and even more sticky liquid, and sure enough it stirred. "I wouldn't mind that at all."

"*Mmm.*" He turned toward her, his legs tangling with hers. "Much as I would like that, I should leave you in peace for at least a day. I don't want to make you sore."

"And after a day?" she asked, resting her forehead against his.

"I am at your disposal to give you unspeakable bliss as often as you'll have me."

She kissed him lazily, nipping at his lower lip.

"Temptress," he chided, pulling away.

"Tease."

"Tigress."

"Troublemaker."

"T—" He was interrupted by a knock at the door. "Who is it?"

"It's Elsa," answered a timid voice. "Adelaide's healer."

Fear gripped Isabella's chest as she sat up. "What is it?" she called out. "Tell me now."

"I wanted to let you know that Adelaide's fever has broken.

She's through the worst of it and should recover quickly with proper care. I'm sorry if I interrupted anything, but I thought you would want to know."

Relief flooded Isabella, and she wrapped her arms around Martin. "She's safe," she whispered, gripping him tight.

He stroked her hair and kissed her forehead. "I'm so glad."

Wrapping a blanket around her, she got out of the bed and went to the door and opened it a crack. "Thank you so much for telling us. I'll come by Adelaide's room shortly to check in on her. Just give me a moment."

"Yes, my lady." The healer didn't look at her as she gave a curtsy and hurried away.

She dressed swiftly, hardly daring to look at Martin for fear she would climb back into bed with him. When she was ready, she turned to him. He was beaming at her with a look of complete adoration. Unable to help herself, she stepped over and kissed him, and just like that heat flared up between them again. Pulling away reluctantly, she said, "I won't be gone long. Don't go anywhere."

"I can't. Not with this foot. Go see your sister. I'll just be lying here, thinking of you," he said, pushing her playfully toward the door. "Naked," he added just as she was about to leave.

She rushed out the door and closed it rather forcefully behind her, leaning against it for a moment to compose herself. *Coxcomb.* He knew exactly how much his parting word would fluster her.

Taking a deep breath, she straightened her spine and thought of her mother's icy bedchamber. That put an immediate damper on her ardor. She grinned at the thought that she never had to see that awful place again. It was hard to believe, but her fortunes had turned at last. For the first time since she was a child, she was filled with hope, and the future was full of promise. She could hardly wait to get to Winchelsea to start her new life.

CHAPTER THIRTY-ONE

MARTIN'S HEART OVERFLOWED with pride as the outline of Saint Mary's Abbey appeared on the horizon, marking the entrance to the harbor. He rested his knee on a strategically placed barrel and leaned on the railing for support, as his foot was still healing. Isabella stood beside him, holding his hand, his partner and equal in all things. The sun was shining, and a brisk breeze blew that was invigorating rather than icy. It was good to be back in the south.

"Are you ready to see your new home, love?"

She squeezed his hand. "With you, I have to be ready for anything."

"I could say the same of you."

"Me?" She placed her free hand on her chest. "What have I ever done?" As she batted her eyelashes, her teasing gaze belied her protestation of innocence.

"You're lucky I love you so very much." He kissed her on the cheek. "And it's a good thing you made amends with the crew. After what you put them through on the way to Yarmouth, I wasn't sure you could win them back."

"Nonsense. No one can resist me when I'm determined to win them over."

It was true. She was a force of nature. "Then it's a good thing I won *you* over."

Her smile made his heart swell with joy. "A very good thing indeed." She squeezed his hand, and he reveled in the warmth and awareness that crackled between them whenever they touched.

Though they had spent the better part of their days on the journey from Yarmouth in bed, exploring each other at length, he still craved more. He quite looked forward to the delights of a featherbed and a bedchamber where she could make as much noise as she wished without being heard through the thick stone walls.

"I should go get my sister. She's been looking forward to seeing her new home." Isabella pecked him on the cheek and left his side.

He sighed as he watched her walk away, hips swinging in a mesmerizing rhythm.

Ulf broke away from the group of sailors he was speaking to and came over. "You are quite besotted, my lord, if you don't mind my saying so."

Martin laughed. "I have been from the first day we met. She's magnificent, isn't she?"

Chuckling, Ulf shook his head. "You never could resist a challenge. Are you ready to introduce her to the family?"

"I can hardly wait. Mama and Eglantine will love her." Isabella was very much from the same mold—strong, intelligent, and full of an unquenchable inner fire. He very much looked forward to seeing the three of them get acquainted.

"What about Lance? Are you worried about him?"

"Not a bit." Not since Yarmouth, at any rate. Isabella was his, heart and soul. He had no fear that his tall and handsome brother might draw her eye. "If anything, I look forward to making him jealous."

Ulf guffawed at that. "Don't rub it in too much. I know you two have never gotten along, but he looks up to you, believe it or not. You set an example that he has difficulty living up to. And you were always your father's favorite."

It wasn't the first time Ulf had said such things. And Martin couldn't deny that bringing Isabella home put an end to any hopes Lance might have had of someday becoming baron.

"I promise to keep my gloating to a minimum." At least, his outward gloating. Inside, he was doing a victory dance.

Isabella reappeared through the hatch with Adelaide by her side.

"I'll leave you be," Ulf said with a wink. "Don't worry about a thing. I'll take care of bringing us into port."

His wife and his sister-in-law joined him at the railing as they passed the abbey, the entrance to Rye Harbor. He wrapped an arm around Isabella's waist, enjoying the way she melted against him. The two of them were a perfect fit. "You arrived just in time to get your first view of Winchelsea."

He pointed across the water to the familiar silhouette of the church and the castle. The port teemed with ships of all shapes and sizes.

"It's bigger than I thought," Isabella said, shielding her eyes from the sun.

He grinned and murmured in her ear, "That's what every man wants to hear." Then he nipped at her earlobe. He couldn't help himself.

She elbowed him in the side. "You're incorrigible."

"You bring it out in me. Every time you're near, my thoughts turn wicked."

"Well, try to drag your mind out of the bedchamber for a bit. I'm nervous enough about meeting your family without you distracting me with your nonsense."

"You? Nervous? I don't believe it for a moment." Her poise was unbreakable.

"What are you two whispering about?" Adelaide asked, interrupting their little *tête-à-tête*.

"Your sister was just telling me she's nervous about meeting my family."

Adelaide raised her eyebrows. "Isabella? Nervous? She faces

every challenge like an army general."

"You see, my love? You can't convince either of us."

Isabella folded her arms. "Just because I don't show it doesn't mean I don't feel it."

There was a moment of vulnerability in her expression that made him wrap his arm around her and kiss her forehead. "They will adore you. I know they will."

"I can't wait to meet them," said Adelaide, looking out over the water as they made their approach. "Did your sister Eglantine really win an archery competition against your men when she was my age?"

It was nothing short of a miracle what a change the last week had wrought on Adelaide. Her color was back. She hardly coughed. The young lady looked healthier than he'd ever seen her. And she seemed delighted by every outlandish tale he'd told about Eglantine. He looked forward to seeing the two of them together.

"She did indeed. She's an expert falconer as well. I'm certain she'll introduce you to her goshawk, Horus, before the day is out. I swear she spends more time with that bird than with her own family. She even lets him sleep in her room, much to Mother's annoyance."

Adelaide's eyes widened. "Heavens! I've never heard of such a thing."

"It's true! But you'll see for yourself soon enough."

As the ship made its final approach to the dock, the familiar sights and sounds of his hometown washed over him as he saw them fresh through Isabella's and Adelaide's eyes. The port bustled with endless commotion. It was the heart and soul of the town, a center of commerce and raucous activity. The stench of fish and sea salt mixed with the enticing smells of meat roasting and bread baking at local taverns and inns. All paths led to Castle Street, the main thoroughfare leading up to his home. He was deeply proud of Winchelsea, and he hoped Isabella and her sister would come to love it as much as he did.

Horses awaited them when they disembarked, along with several carts for transporting their belongings up to Winchelsea Castle. He was glad they wouldn't be cooped up in a carriage. He wanted to show Isabella and her sister all the town had to offer as they progressed up the street. It would also provide him with an opportunity to show off his new wife, now Baroness of Winchelsea, so that the people could get their first view of her.

In fact, quite a crowd gathered around their ship as they disembarked. He paused on the gangplank, leaning on a wooden crutch with Isabella beside him, and waved to the onlookers.

"Welcome back, my lord," one of them called out. "What happened to your leg?"

"It's a long and thrilling tale, and I promise to come down to the docks and tell it. But at present, I must convey my wife and her sister up to the castle. May I present Lady Isabella, Baroness of Winchelsea, and her sister, Lady Adelaide?"

The two ladies in question waved and smiled as applause, huzzahs, and whistles sounded all around them.

"Welcome to Winchelsea, my ladies," someone shouted above the din.

"I promise you will all have plenty of time to get to know them in the days to come, but at present, we must go to the castle to greet my mother. If you will all excuse us."

With many calls of congratulations and felicitations, they mounted their horses and started up the cobblestones of Castle Street.

They made something of a parade as they rode toward the castle at a leisurely pace. The crowd from the dock followed them, and people came out of their stone and half-timbered shops, inns, taverns, and houses to gawk at the new lady of Winchelsea. He had intended to point things out along the way, but they were too busy smiling and waving for him to give a guided tour. That would have to wait for another day.

As they rode through the castle gates, the boisterous crowd fell away. "That was quite a greeting you just received. The people of Winchelsea seem very excited to meet their new lady," he told them.

Isabella smiled as she dismounted. "It's heartening to see how beloved you are by your people. They wouldn't be half as excited about me if they didn't think the world of you."

He handed a stable boy his crutch, then dismounted gingerly, being careful not to put any weight on his injured foot.

His brother Lance came striding out into the courtyard just as he found his footing, looking as tall, dark, and handsome as ever. "What in heaven's name happened to you? No, don't tell me. On your wedding night, your wife fended you off with a hot poker."

Martin couldn't help but laugh at how close that was to the truth. And for once, Lance's jibe didn't bother him. With Isabella by his side, his brother's jests slid off him as if he was wearing invisible armor. "I had a run-in with the Earl of Norfolk, if you must know. It's a long and tangled tale. Let's go inside, and I'll tell you all about it."

"Aren't you going to make introductions first? Who is this vision in green? Don't tell me she's your wife. She's far too pretty for you." Lance bowed over Isabella's hand, raising it to his lips.

Martin narrowed his eyes and tamped down the urge to order his brother to step back. "Did you think I was going to marry a cave troll?"

Rising, Lance shrugged. "More or less."

Taking a deep breath, Martin swallowed a sharp retort. "Lance, I'd like you to meet my wife, Lady Isabella, and her sister, Lady Adelaide. I'd appreciate it if you could at least make some attempt to be civil in their presence."

Martin's brother bowed over Adelaide's hand before saying, "It is my great pleasure to make your acquaintance, ladies. I hope you don't mind Martin and me. I love my brother, but he's always been so lucky in everything that I have to deflate his big head from time to time."

Isabella walked to Martin's side and wound her hand around his waist. "He is insufferable, isn't he?" She pressed a kiss to his forehead. "It's a good thing I love you, big head and all."

Despite the audience, he couldn't help but nuzzle her. "And I love you too, you glorious vixen."

"*Ugh*. You two are disgustingly adorable," said Lance, stepping back and grimacing. Then he smiled down at Adelaide, and offered his arm to escort her. "Lady Adelaide, may I accompany you inside? I don't think I can stand to watch another moment of their marital bliss."

Adelaide smirked in a very un-Adelaide-like way. They began walking.

Martin followed his brother and sister-in-law into the castle with Isabella on his arm. As she looked around, assessing, a knot formed in his chest. What if she didn't like it? What if she truly did find it cramped and provincial? She'd spent years in the company of royalty. How would Winchelsea Castle measure up?

"Do you like what you see, my love?" he asked, hoping his anxiousness didn't come through too clearly in his voice as they paused just inside, taking in the familiar entry hall with its tapestries and statues, wide stone steps leading up to the living spaces on the second floor.

"I love it. I've had enough of enormous, drafty castles full of conniving people. This is exactly right for me."

She gave his arm a reassuring squeeze, and they followed Lance and Adelaide into the great hall. He saw the hall as if for the first time, imagining how it might look to his bride. Braziers were scattered around the long trestle tables to take the chill off the winter's day. A merry fire burned in the hearth at one end. It had a lintel carved with mythical beasts. Colorful tapestries showing nobles frolicking in flower gardens covered the walls, adding a promise of spring in the midst of winter. All in all, it was a far less-forbidding space than the icy great hall at Bamburgh.

He glanced as Isabella, but she wasn't focused on the surroundings. All of her attention went to the two ladies who rose to greet them—his mother, on Eglantine's arm. Despite her lack of vision, his mother moved with stately confidence, trusting her daughter not to lead her astray. His sister's eyes sparkled with amusement and delight at the sight of him with his new bride.

"Welcome to Winchelsea, Lady Isabella," her mother said with a curtsy. Her head was streaked with more gray than it had been when he left. She always worried for him when he took to sea, no matter how many times he had come back safely. "It is my pleasure to welcome a new baroness to take my place. I've been at this too long and am more than happy to pass the mantle. If there is anything I can do to make you at home here, don't hesitate to mention it."

Relief washed through Martin at having finally fulfilled his duty to his mother by relieving her of the heavy burden of being the lady of the castle. She had done all she could to support him after Father passed, but her grief and loss of sight weighed heavily on her. He was glad she was free of her obligations now so that she could relax and slow down.

"Indeed, welcome," Eglantine echoed as she also curtsied, her chestnut curls cascading over her shoulder. Her eyes twinkled with undisguised curiosity. "We are so excited to meet you. And who is this lovely young lady you've brought with you?"

Isabella bowed her head, acknowledging each of them in turn. "It is a pleasure to meet you both. Martin has told me so much about you on our journey that I feel like I practically know you already. Please allow me to introduce my sister, Lady Adelaide."

"I'm delighted to meet you both." Adelaide curtsied. "Thank you for the warm welcome to Winchelsea."

"Lady Adelaide plays the lute most beautifully," Martin said, knowing his sister would be delighted at the news.

As expected, she responded with enthusiasm. "Do you indeed? Why, that's wonderful! I play the lyre. As you know, Martin plays the citole, and on occasion, we've been successful wheedling Lance into playing the drum. What music we shall make together!"

Isabella laughed beside him, and his heart warmed at the

sound. "Perhaps I shall take up the flute so that I may join you."

As the conversation meandered across every possible topic, Martin kept unusually quiet, not quite trusting himself to speak. The sight of his newly expanded family getting along so well moved him deeply. He never thought he lacked for anything growing up, but with Isabella by his side and his family surrounding him, he felt complete and contented as never before. The future unfurled before him, full of possibility, despite the war. For the rest of his life, Isabella would be his partner and companion in all things. Whatever life held for them, he knew it would never be dull.

EPILOGUE

Five years later

ISABELLA SAT ON a cushioned bench in a wide field with her daughter, Alais, asleep on her shoulder. A passel of flower-crowned children capered in and around a circle of dancers from the village. The scents of new flowers and fresh grass wafted over the field, making Isabella's heart sing. Bright afternoon sun warmed the spring-crisp air as the sounds of music and revelry filled her with a sense that all was right with the world.

Her beloved brother, Crispin, sat beside her, decked out in finery befitting the new Earl of Bamburgh. It was so strange to see him in such formal attire and was completely at odds with his unruly chestnut hair and warm brown eyes. But even as her thoughts were with her brother, her eyes were on her rambunctious children.

"Charles, no pulling your sister's hair," she called out, interrupting her son as he chased little Carenza at high speed between dancers, cackling with glee.

Carenza, gripping her flower crown in one hand, darted in and out of the circle of dancing children with all the speed her four-year-old feet could summon to escape her brother.

Martin grinned and winked at her from where he sat on a raised dais with a group of musicians from the town, playing merry tunes with a galloping beat that seemed to egg the children on to even greater heights of wild revelry. She smiled back and blew him a kiss. The smoldering look he gave her in return made her squeeze her knees together, even though she was round with their fourth child.

"It's good to see you so happy," Crispin said beside her. "I don't think I've seen you this content and relaxed since we were children in Bordeaux."

She chuckled ruefully. "Even in Bordeaux we still had to deal with Mother. Are you sure she's dead? I was convinced she would live to be as old as Methuselah just to spite us."

"She's gone. I buried her myself a month and a half ago. After Father passed, she seemed to make it her life's sole purpose to make me miserable. But then she was done in by her own horse. You know how she treated all of God's creatures. I suppose the poor palfrey decided she'd been whipped one too many times and took revenge."

Isabella took a deep breath, or as deep a breath as she could take with the infant in her womb dancing a jig on her ribs. News of her mother's death, when she had received Crispin's letter earlier in the month, had brought up a complicated mix of emotions. Living a happy life in Winchelsea, far from her mother's poisonous influence, Isabella could almost pity the woman. What must her mother have gone through to have such a twisted and vindictive soul? In the end, all she could concede was that Mother didn't live a happy life.

Alais stirred against her, and she rocked her sweet baby back into a doze. Isabella intended to be a very different kind of mother to her daughters. She couldn't entirely shake off the influence of how she was raised, but she would do her very best. "I won't speak ill of the dead. May she rest in peace and leave us alone is all I'll say. I was so sorry to hear about you and Eilidh."

Crispin hung his head. "She's married to someone else now and far beyond my reach. But I don't want to spend such a glorious day speaking of such depressing subjects. Tell me about Adelaide."

Isabella smiled at the thought of her sister. After all she had been through in her youth, she'd somehow managed to grow into a healthy and strong young woman with a mind and will entirely her own.

"She's in London right now, visiting my sister-in-law at court. To say she's thriving would be an understatement. She's blossomed into a beautiful, talented young lady. Her health improved dramatically when we came to Winchelsea. The milder weather and freedom from our parents did wonders for her. You'd hardly recognize her if you saw her."

Crispin's eyebrows rose. "You let her go to court? After all you went through trying to keep her away?"

She certainly had her misgivings, but Adelaide was her own person now. She could make up her mind about these things. "I could hardly keep her away from Eglantine, and I've long since forgiven the queen for marrying me off to Martin. I've visited with her a few times since my marriage."

And fortunately, those visits had gone far better than she expected.

"Have you now?" Crispin shifted to look her in the eyes.

"I never would have suspected it, but I do believe she has a soft spot underneath all her prickliness. The first time I met with her after my marriage, I was prepared to do battle on Adelaide's behalf, but the queen said she only asked for Adelaide for my sake. She never liked my mother and thought Adelaide would be better off away from her. And she truly did marry me to Martin because she thought we would make a good match. Much as I resisted, I can hardly argue with her wisdom now."

It had surprised her greatly how much she had misjudged the queen. Well, not entirely misjudged. The queen took diabolical pleasure in the execution of Lord James after he was found to be plotting with the King of France to unseat Henry. And it all happened without her and Martin's plotting. Isabella was there for the beheading, and the queen's smile was filled with cruel malice as the axe fell. Much as Isabella loathed Lord James, she couldn't bring herself to revel in his demise the way the queen did. But relief washed over her when his head rolled. To think she had almost married a traitor! If she had, she very well might have shared his fate. For so many reasons, she was glad that her husband had prevailed in the end.

She glanced again at Martin, who was thoroughly in his element, making music with the townspeople he loved. Her heart swelled with adoration at the sight of him in all his mustachioed glory. He was such a kind and loving soul. In every way, he was the opposite of Lord James. How she had ever found the earl more attractive was beyond her. She had eyes only for her husband now. There was no more handsome man in all of England, at least to her.

"You two can't keep your eyes off each other, can you?"

Her cheeks heated at being caught out. "We like each other well enough," she said lightly. The truth was that they were now so deeply entwined in each other's lives and hearts that she could hardly remember what it was like before he came along.

Crispin laughed. "This is no marriage of convenience, however it may have started. You two are utterly besotted with each other. I can only hope that I find such marital bliss someday."

Isabella put her hand on her brother's and squeezed. "Don't worry. You will. As soon as your heart heals from losing Eilidh, I'm certain the right woman will cross your path."

Her brother sighed. "That could be a very long time."

She squeezed his hand again. "We shall see."

The musicians came to the end of a song and launched into another. Carenza came running over, crying like her favorite pony had died.

"Mama, Charles took my flowers."

Sure enough, Charles was scampering around waving his sister's flower crown above his head.

"Charles," she called out in the sternest voice she could muster.

Her son's eyes went wide, and his shoulders slumped as he trudged over to face the consequences of his actions.

Isabella pursed her lips and shook her head, doing her best not to laugh at her two children, who were now jabbing at each other with grubby, sticky fingers. Exactly how many honey cakes had they eaten today?

"Charles, did you steal your sister's flower crown?" she asked carefully, keeping her mirth at bay.

"Yes, but she stole my wooden horsey." He pointed an accusing finger at his little sister.

"Carenza, is this true?"

Her four-year-old daughter crossed her arms and glared at her brother.

"Tell the truth now, sweeting." As she looked down on her strong-willed daughter she thought, Heaven above only knew what she'd be like when she was grown. "Carenza, I'm waiting."

Carenza dropped her arms and dug into the tiny pouch she wore on her belt. "Here," she said, thrusting it at her brother. "Now give me my flowers." She made a grab at the crown, and Charles yanked it out of her reach, cackling with mischief.

"Charles," Isabella warned.

Her son sighed, dropped the crown on the ground, and kicked it to his sister.

"Now, Charles. That wasn't very chivalrous of you. What would a good knight do?"

At present, her son was mad for all things related to knighthood. She could get him to do just about anything by saying it was what a knight would do.

With a groan and an eyeroll, Charles knelt down and picked up the flower crown. He dusted it off roughly, then placed it on Carenza's head. "My apologies, Lady Carenza."

He bowed, and Carenza curtsied.

"Thank you, good Sir Charles," Carenza said with all the ruffled dignity of a queen.

Crispin burst into laughter beside her, and Isabella couldn't help but follow suit. The children were too adorable for words. Her heart squeezed at their antics.

"Will you play sword fighting with me, my lady?" Charles asked. It wasn't exactly a fit game for a young lady, but Carenza was only four. And despite their frequent fights, she idolized her older brother. Everything he did, she wanted to do too. There would be time enough to turn her into a young lady. And after all, she too had enjoyed engaging in a good sword fight when she was younger.

"Can I, Mama?" Carenza asked, her face aglow.

"Go on and have fun, sweeting."

The two of them ran off to find sticks, and soon they were recreating the Battle of Hastings beneath the budding trees.

Her gaze turned once again to her husband, who caught her eye. He excused himself as the musicians started up the next tune. He came and sat on her other side, taking Alais gently from her tired arms. The baby hardly noticed, nuzzling against Martin's neck with a contented coo as she melted against him. His way with the children was almost magical. The man had infinite patience and a gentle hand in all things. It made her heart ache with love to look at him holding their baby.

"What mischief are our children up to now?" he asked once the baby was settled.

"Oh, the usual," she said, gesturing toward the pitched battle taking place under a nearby oak tree. Several other children had now joined the fight, and it was a regular melee.

"Have you danced yet, my dear? It is May Day after all."

When she shook her head, he laughed. "Watch out, or Jack-in-the-Green may come over and make you dance."

Isabella pursed her lips. "If Master Hammond attempts to accost me with my giant belly and force me to dance, I cannot be answerable for the consequences."

Martin pressed his hand on her lower back and dug in his fingers just where her muscles ached the most. "Have no fear, my dear. I don't think even Master Hammond would dare try his luck when faced with such a scowl."

She couldn't help but let out a soft moan as his fingers found a particularly tender spot.

"Should I leave you two alone?" Crispin asked, smirking. "I think I might try my luck at winning a dance with the Queen of the May. Something about her smile reminds me of Eilidh."

"Go on then." She waved her hand in dismissal. "Abandon me. Never mind the fact that this is the first time I've seen you in seven years."

Crispin rolled his eyes. "I've been here for a week already. I think you can spare me for a dance or two."

"Of course she can," said Martin. "Can't you, love?"

Her husband's fingers continued their delicious work, making her breath catch. "Very well then. Off with you."

She shooed her brother away and watched him dive into the revelry with an abandon that belied his melancholy mood. Perhaps there was hope for him after all.

Martin placed Alais gently into the wicker bassinet, lined with lambswool, beside him. Fortunately, she was deeply asleep and oblivious to the raucous noise around her.

"Turn." Her husband guided her with his hand to turn her back. Now both hands were at work turning her into a puddle.

"*Nph*," she muttered, leaning back into him. "Your hands truly are magical."

"*Mm.* That's what I like to hear." His lips brushed her ear, then he nipped at her earlobe. "What about my tongue?" He traced the edge of her ear with it, sending warmth rushing to unmentionable places. It was astonishing what he could still make her feel even when she was round as a gourd.

"Wicked as always." She reached behind her to smack his knee playfully. "I married a very naughty man."

His laugh was full of sinful promise. "Do you remember our first May Day here?"

How could she forget? They'd snuck away from the festivities to a private grotto amongst the trees where he'd knelt before her and proceeded to drive her out of her mind with that wicked tongue of his. The mere thought made her cheeks heat.

"I'm glad to see you remember it as fondly as I do." He shifted to sit astride the bench so that she was embraced by his thighs on either side of hers, practically in his lap.

"I hardly recall it at all," she fibbed, smiling at the memory.

"Liar, you stopped breathing, and your pulse jumped in your neck." He kissed the spot in question, making her heart beat all the faster.

"Too bad I'm too large and ungainly for such things at the moment." It was hard to be passionate when everything was swollen and aching all the time. Although at that moment, his fingers were almost making her forget.

"You are more beautiful than ever, round with the child I planted in your belly, your marvelous breasts heavy with milk. You are a miracle, my love. My adoration for you grows every day. And as for my desire… Lean back, and you'll see for yourself."

Against her better judgment, she did. "Mercy! Perhaps we should retire to the castle early."

"As my lady wishes." He nipped at her earlobe again. "Let's go celebrate May Day properly."

With a word to the nursemaid and her brother, they made their excuses and headed back to the castle, leaving Charles and Carenza behind with their Uncle Crispin to enjoy the festival. As they rode in a carriage the short distance back to the castle in the waning afternoon sun, she couldn't help thinking that life was full of promise, and she could hardly wait to see what the years ahead with Martin would bring.

About the Author

Leslie Vollard has a longstanding passion for the Middle Ages. Her obsession with all things medieval dates back to college when she dug through archives at the Bibliothèque Nationale in Paris to study the 12th century troubadour, Arnaut Daniel. In her work, she brings courtly love, chivalry, and the troubadour tradition to life. Romance reigns supreme in her steamy novels about how love conquers all.

Leslie lives in Long Island with her delightfully nerdy husband and two cats. She loves gardening, baking, and reading love poems in dead languages.

www.ingramcontent.com/pod-product-compliance
Lightning Source LLC
Chambersburg PA
CBHW072105300726
48975CB00003B/705